To Roxanne, my forever cheer bestie. Go Bears!

Welcome to the Coffee Loft!

#TheCoffeeLoftSeries

Welcome back to The Coffee Loft, where a new round of stories has been brewed especially for you!

Those of you stopping by to visit again: We've missed you! The feeling of home is the same that you loved before. If it's your first time, prepare to be swept off your feet.

While our menu hasn't changed, we think you'll be pleased with the fall favorites we've added. Fans of pumpkin spiced lattes, peppermint mochas, and rich, chocolaty cocoas will not be disappointed. This multi-author collection of stand-alone sweet rom-coms is filled to the brim with the swoons you love and adore.

From sweet kisses to grand gestures and matchmaking surprises, each mug and story will be filled with everything you crave. So come on in and let us serve you with the happily-ever-afters you've come to expect!

A Note from the Author

Welcome to Palmer City!

I'm so glad you've come to visit this charming old Western town, where residents have been following their dreams for more than a century! In 1888, the Palmer and the Brewer families settled the land, dividing what would become a prosperous mining town into two equal parts. The details were decided by card games, and when the chips settled, the Brewers owned the land west of Snowpack Creek, and the Palmers had control of everything east to the Colorado Springs border, as well as naming rights.

Over the years, the Palmer family began to dwindle, and in the '90s—the 1990s—Quinn Brewer and his wife, Angie, opened a sports bar and grill across from the new arena and mall—on the Palmer side of Snowpack Creek. Quinn's mother was a Palmer, and, well, the sale of that land is a story for another time!

With the addition of the arena, an all-in-one-stop sport-splex popped up on the west side, providing a place for professional athletes and townies alike to learn and play.

Featuring pro hockey players to Olympic figure skaters to world-class all-star cheerleaders, the Plex rivals the Creek Walk on a Saturday night for the busiest place in town.

Local businesses along the creek are owned by the kindest and quirkiest residents this side of the Colorado River. Rock on a swinging creekside bench or stroll along Restaurant Row to the town park, a magical place to find love and solace in all the seasons. Everything is light and peaceful here in Palmer City ... mostly. With several new businesses popping up, including Quinn and Angie's daughter Brenna's wedding barn venue and a German-Italian fusion restaurant that'll be in direct competition with Brewski's, the laid-back residents of Palmer City are in for some unexpected drama.

Find a cozy corner, settle in, and enjoy your visit to Palmer City!

Love, Kerry

PUMPKIN SPICE SPICE BABY

A DENVER EDGE SWEET HOCKEY ROM-COM

COFFEE LOFT SERIES

KERRY EVELYN

Swan Press

Pumpkin Spice Spice Baby ©2024 by Kerry Evelyn

Edited by SharpEditor

Proofed by BookNookNuts

Cover by Beck & Dot

Interior formatting by Chris Kridler, Sky Diary Productions

Paperback ISBN: 978-1-960412-17-1

Dear Reader,

Thank you for visiting Palmer City Coffee Loft! If you love a fun playlist and would like to be fully immersed in Tasha and Monty's story, check out their Spotify playlist at tinyurl.com/PumpkinSpice SpiceBabySpotify.

For all the Palmer City extras—team rosters, printable activities, recipes, and other bonus material—sign up for my newsletter at KerryEvelyn.com/links to receive the password to the Freebies tab on my website.

For more access to me, a peek into my life as an author and homeschool mom, daily posts, games, takeovers, giveaways, and more, join my VIP Crew at Facebook.com/groups/CranesCoveCrew.

Enjoy the story! I'll "see" you again after the epilogue!

XOXO!
Love, Kerry

PS: *Pumpkin Spice Spice Baby* is a childhood rivals and frenemies-to-more forced proximity sports romance with #justkisses and no swearing. It also contains scenes referencing the death of Monty's sister to childhood cancer.

CHAPTER 1
Tasha

Mid-May

I tapped my toes on the mat, the light *thump thump* of my cheer shoe muffled by the surrounding din. The team announcements were well underway, and my coaching partner hadn't arrived yet.

The cheer gym at the Plex is large and loud. And on Team Reveal Day, the sound within the vaulted ceilings over the four cheer floors and tumbling area reached record decibels on the Screaming Girl O-Meter.

Having been part of the sport of cheerleading since I was a preschooler, I was neither surprised nor bothered by the racket. I was even the one to start it sometimes. But today, I was preoccupied with Nate's absence. This would be our second year coaching together, and we had a title to defend.

What could be keeping him? I lifted on my toes to peer at the staff door for the umpteenth time.

It was opening …

There he was! *Phew!* Nate caught my gaze and waved as he squeezed along the wall toward me, absently high-fiving as he waded through the athletes and parents between us.

Wait a sec.

A few feet behind him, another guy was easing his way through the crowd of athletes of all ages, dressed in the same FireVolts tee and red shorts as Nate. His familiar blond hair and bulky build took my Nate-is-late anxiety to a whole other level.

What was Montgomery Biddington doing here? And wearing *our* team's official shirt?

I was sure he said he'd be here less often this year. Due to his new job as Number Three Ridgie, the backup to the backup mascot for Denver's NHL team, Monty said he didn't have time to coach cheer teams anymore. Private tumbling lessons only.

"Hey." Nate arrived by my side, breathing easy. "I was—"

"You're late." I shook my finger at him. "Our team is two away."

His cheerful expression dropped. "About that … I found out this morning I got the internship with one of the physical therapists here at the Plex."

"For the fall?" I asked. That was a big deal, but his tone was suspect. I lifted my chin and forced myself to smile. "Congratulations!"

Nate shook his head. "I start next week."

I pulled my lips into my teeth and waited for him to say more.

He squirmed a little. "It's full-time."

"Great!" I replied. "No more money worries, and you can still coach at night."

He blinked, then turned his head back toward the crowd.

I followed his gaze. Monty was getting closer to where we coaches stood behind the popup stage, waiting for the emcee to announce our teams.

"Tasha, I ..." Nate began. I turned my head to look at him. He was frowning. Not a good sign. "The hiring manager said that my schedule would be erratic, and he recommended that I not coach a team this year. So ... I had to give up my position coaching the Worlds team with you."

I was the one blinking now. "You're serious?"

He nodded. "They want me to work with the trainers for the Voltage."

My mouth dropped open. The Voltage was the Denver Edge's minor league hockey team, and they were based here in our hometown of Palmer City. Their practice rink was at the Plex—a hop, skip, and a jump from where we were standing.

"So you can miss some practices," I suggested. There had to be work-arounds. "I can take the athletes to the comps by myself. We'll make it work."

He shook his head. "I suggested that. This is an all-in or all-out opportunity. I'm so sorry, Tasha."

"B-but," I stammered as his solution seeped in. "Who—" I paused as he turned his head toward Monty. "No. Uh-uh. Not him. Anyone but *him.*" The hairs on the back of my neck stood up, and I suppressed a shudder.

Nate swallowed, his Adam's apple bobbing while he chose his words. He squeezed his eyes shut, then opened them, locking his gaze on mine. I saw the sympathy and regret, and I honestly felt a little bad for the guy. He knew about my past with Monty. There really *had* to be no other option.

"Tasha, he was the only one available ..." He let his

sentence trail off, unable to retrieve any additional words that might pacify me.

"Not *entirely* available." Monty stepped into place next to Nate and crossed his beefy arms over his muscular chest. "But *someone* had to get you both out of this bind. We can't be canceling our Worlds team. Not when we're defending champions. Wouldn't want to disappoint the athletes, you know? I worked too hard getting their tumbling skills almost as good as mine over the last year."

I rolled my eyes. Humble he wasn't.

"We're grateful to you, Monty. For sure," Nate said.

"Speak for yourself," I mumbled.

Monty's full lips spread into a wide grin. "It'll be like old times, Tasha. We can play Good Coach/Bad Coach just like when we used to run the summer camps."

That was forever ago, back when we were friends.

I cleared my throat and let my voice drip with sarcasm. "Sounds like a blast."

"That's the *spirit*," he chimed. "Oh, and we'll have to tweak the practice schedule. I have forty-one home games plus NHL All-Star Weekend and other team obligations. Plus Nana Booboo's rehab. She'll be at Mountainview Manor's rehabilitation facility for some time, and I like to be there for her therapy appointments. I'm a busy guy. You understand."

I softened my expression out of respect for his Nana Booboo. Monty's grandmother had suffered a stroke recently, but the doctors were confident she'd make a full recovery. I hoped so, with all my heart. She was *his* nana, but she was *our* cheer nana. Monty had started the sport not long after I had, and Nana Booboo had brought him to every camp, practice, and competition until he could drive himself.

It was at the Plex she got the "Booboo" tag to her name. Monty was always pushing himself to be the best. Every time he hurt himself, he'd run to Nana and cry, "Nana! Booboo!" and she'd kiss it better. At some point during that first year, we were all calling her Nana Booboo and asking for get-better kisses. She was always happy to oblige.

Nana was also a frequent customer at my day job, the Coffee Loft. I credit Nana for my addiction to pumpkin spice lattes. She encouraged me to apply there when I was looking for my first job, and I've been there ever since. These days, I worked the opening until midafternoon shift, then drove to the high school to coach the varsity cheerleading squad. And two nights a week, I was here. This past year, I'd coached two competitive cheer teams here at the Plex, four nights each week, and it had been too much on top of everything else. The Worlds team was relatively easy; the members were older, mostly college students and cheerleading lifers, and they took direction like pros.

"Our turn." Monty gave my bicep a gentle nudge with his elbow. "C'mon, work wifey."

"I am *not* your work wifey." I shot him a glare and focused on the emcee.

"And now, on to our final team, the FireVolts, coached by Tasha and Monty! Defending their Worlds Championship this year will be ..."

The heads of the veteran FireVolts, gathered in front of the stage, swung to Monty. I noted surprise on their faces, and rightly so. We all expected Nate to be their coach again.

Monty and I jogged up the steps to the stage as the athletes' numbers were called. About two-thirds were veterans of last year's team. Two were newcomers from a rival gym, and a few had moved up from the senior teams. Nate and I had been super selective while also recognizing potential and coachability when we were choosing the members. No bad attitudes or drama allowed.

Nate worked his way through the group that gathered around us, sharing about his new position and confidently endorsing Monty as just what the team needed to level up. Most of them knew him already and welcomed him with open arms.

But Monty wasn't experienced enough to coach a team at this level. Sure, he could tumble and partner-stunt his way to first place with my cousin Gabby, but he'd never coached a whole team of athletes around his own age, in their early to mid-twenties. We'd turn twenty-five in January. Our Worlds team featured men and women ages eighteen through twenty-seven, and they deserved a coach of their caliber to ensure their winning streak remained intact.

I snuck a glance at Monty, chest out, shoulders back, practically oozing confidence, and sighed.

"You owe me big time," I mumbled to Nate.

"You'll be fine, Tasha. And maybe you two will become friends again."

"Unlikely." That would require Monty earning my trust back.

Never. Gonna. Happen.

Nate laughed. "So there's a chance. Good." He leaned over me to get closer to my ear. "I think he needs something like this to get his mind off his grandmother's recovery. I got the sense she's not doing well."

My eyes widened, and I whipped my gaze over to my archenemy. I might not like *him* anymore, but Monty's Nana Booboo was one of my favorite people in the whole world.

If coaching a team with him could help her in any way, I'd get through it.

I might even try to be civil to him.

Might.

CHAPTER 2
Monty

Mid-June

The strong powerhouse I knew as my Nana Booboo had never seemed so small and weak, covered to her chin by her favorite quilt—a patchwork of my old cheer tees and uniform shirts. I struggled to believe this was the same woman who pulled me out of sunrise-to-sunset (as she called it) preschool and took over my daily care while my parents worked and traveled.

I scooted the plastic and metal visitor's chair as close to the left side of the bed as was possible and lifted the blankets by her hip to find her hand. It was tiny and cold, so I kept it under the covers and gave it a gentle squeeze.

Her eyelids fluttered open, and the left side of her mouth curled up into a smile. "M-my boy," she whispered.

"I'm here, Nana. Did you have a nice nap?" I squeezed her hand again, and this time she squeezed back and the side of her mouth twitched with effort to form a smile. Her face was lined from years of smiling and laughing—and probably smirking from getting her way. I longed to see those lines deepen again.

As if exhausted by the effort, she closed her eyes and sighed.

It had been a month since her stroke, and except for a brief cursory visit from my parents to set up her health-care plan, I'd been her only familial visitor. Her siblings and their families had all moved out of Colorado decades ago, and my late grandfather's family was far too busy living their high-society lives to check in on the woman who had grown his business and their money when his father struck oil all those decades ago. Their son, my dad, was their only child, and after my sister died, I became their only grandchild.

"How's ... the h-h-how-sss?"

"The house is fine, Nana." Her speech was improving each week. It had terrified me in the days after the stroke when the side of her face drooped and all she could muster was moans and grunts.

I'd moved into her sprawling Victorian out by Lake Moonshine after boarding school. Scandalizing my parents when I chose coaching over a business career, I'd taken classes at the local university instead of attending an Ivy League school. What was the point? I had all the money I'd ever need, and I for sure didn't want my dad's life.

"D-Dr. sa-says ..." She closed her eyes again and pressed her lips together. The left side of her face scrunched in determination. "Says I need ... acc ... acc ..." She sighed.

The door to her private room squeaked open. I glanced over my shoulder and greeted her doctor, a fit man in his mid-thirties who resembled a grown-up Harry Potter, circular eyeglass frames and all.

What a chump.

"Nice to see you, Montgomery." He pushed at the center of his frames. As they slid up his nose, he cleared his throat. I'd told him countless times to call me Monty, but he hadn't. Like calling me by my full name gave him an air of authority.

"How's she doing?" I asked.

"Working hard. She's strong, but it'll take time."

"The rehab my parents set her up for—can she do that at home?"

"I'm glad you asked. I was telling Nancy here this morning that we can't release her until her home is accessible."

I frowned. "What does that mean? It has an elevator." My mind flashed back to the old house. It had been through dozens of renovations over the years. The elevator was added when her diabetes made it hard for her to walk up the stairs.

He schooled his expression into what he probably thought was kind, but it came off smug and his explanation condescending. "It means an extended ramp—the one you have isn't up to code—and a bathroom renovation. An entire bathroom must serve as a shower, with a drain in the floor. Grab bars in the others." My eyes widened as he went on to list even more extensive modifications her house would need.

With seven bathrooms between the house, garage, and pool, it would probably be cheaper to build Nana a new house.

"What's the timeline for her coming home?" I asked.

The doctor explained the benchmarks required for her to leave the rehab facility. I held on to her hand as he went over the requirements that were even more extensive than the house renovation list.

"And she'll need twenty-four seven monitoring until we're confident she can be alone safely," the doctor finished.

"N-no babysitter!" Nana barked out, and I laughed. It sounded more like *nah baybahtah*, but we both understood clearly what she meant.

"Don't worry, Nana. It's just a formality to keep you safe. We'll hire a nursing agency. You'll make some new friends and be waited on hand and foot, like you deserve. Teach them how to watercolor." Nana was a masterful watercolorist, and since her dominant hand hadn't been hampered by the stroke, I assumed she retained her ability to paint.

She harrumphed in objection, but her lips twitched, so I could tell she didn't totally hate the idea.

"As for when she's going home, it's hard to say. The stroke was extensive, but she's strong and has made significant gains. It will all depend on how she continues to progress. Get the renovations done, and then we'll talk." He turned on his heel and strode out the door with an air of self-importance.

I rolled my eyes at Nana, and she gargled a laugh.

"I don't like him," I said. I leaned forward to place a kiss on her forehead. "But I love you, so I'll do what he says. What color tile do you want in your fancy new bathroom?"

THE DENVER EDGE had made it to the playoffs and advanced all the way to the last round in their quest for the Stanley Cup. The first of the two teams that won four out of seven possible games would win the hardest and most difficult trophy in sports.

They lost Game 5 in Miami, so they were back in Denver for Game 6. It would be their last home game of the season, so I was called in to don the third Ridgie costume and visit the private boxes for photo ops. The backup Ridgie was outside working the pavilion and greeting fans, and the main bear would be on the ice and in the stands during the game. Our handlers were all in touch so that no two—or three—Ridgies were seen at the same time.

Jared, my handler, and I were able to catch some of the game from inside. Our team was literally on its last legs. After a nasty shove into the boards, one of our best defensemen, Brendan Trotter, had to be escorted off the ice on one skate. His defensive partner, Trask Emerson, had left the game in the first period and hadn't been back. When Jason Dexter, our starting goalie, missed a fifth shot, his blocker fell off his hand, revealing a heavily taped wrist. He'd left the game and hadn't come back. And from the way Tasha's brother-in-law, Xavier Schwann, was skating, I wouldn't be surprised if he had some cracked ribs. And those were just the guys I knew personally.

Hockey players were nuts.

They were probably the most skilled and strongest athletes of any team sport—except maybe all-star cheer, of course—and yet they continued to push their bodies day after day and year after year to the breaking point for a trophy. And they were underpaid—the entire team together made just over what the starting center for Denver's basketball team earned.

I kind of understood their drive, though.

I'd trained to be the best in my sport, and I didn't care about the money. I donated all of my earnings from coaching and sponsorships.

If this team didn't turn this game around fast, they'd be done tonight.

It wasn't looking good.

With eight minutes left on the clock in the third period, the Miami Ice Cats called a time-out. The crowd noise increased, but I couldn't make out what they were saying. I sipped my water and almost spit it out when the cameras zoomed in on Ridgie Number One, chasing a pigeon on the landing between sections 102 and 202. From what I could gather by watching the replays, it hadn't been a problem until it had flown down to the ice and almost got smashed by a stick. The refs had chased it off the ice and up into the stands.

Up steps, down steps, back up. Jumping, swiping. Just as I was thinking he was going to hurt himself, he tripped down the steps of 202, rolling at least three times before coming to a stop on the landing behind 102's accessible seating.

"Ridgie Number One down!" Jared's radio squawked. "We need Number Three to 202 STAT. We have crying children!"

On the screen, Ridgie Number One was loaded onto a stretcher. His handler lifted a bear paw to wave at the cameras as the paramedics rolled him into the hall and out of sight. The camera then panned the crowd. Kids were crying, and the place was in chaos.

Jared assisted me in attaching my bear head, and then we booked it to 202, where I emerged to thunderous applause. I waved, took a bow and did a standing back handspring to ensure the crowd that Ridgie the Bear's booboos were all fixed.

"Rid-gie flip! Rid-gie flip! Rid-gie flip!" The crowd chanted their request, and who was I to deny them? Before anyone could tell me no, I motioned to the yellow-shirted arena staff to keep the path clear on the landing.

Then I took off.

Back handspring into a back tuck, punch front to a cartwheel, two more back handsprings and a half twist, landing clean. I raised my arms, pumping the air and clapping my paws.

The game was still on hold since the pigeon's first merry jaunt over the ice. Continuing to fly free, it had made it down to the ice again. The refs chased after it, and from the looks of it, they were trying to direct it toward the tunnel.

I remembered a prop I'd seen in the mascot closet: a giant butterfly net. I jogged into the hall, motioning for Jared to come with me.

We entered the elevator. I pressed the button to take us to ice level and told him my idea. "Ask one of the other handlers to get the oversize butterfly net and bring it to me in the tunnel."

"You think you can catch that thing?"

I shrugged. "Probably not. But me trying will provide comedy until a bird catcher can figure out what to do."

"I'll get your skates." He bolted out of the elevator, and I headed to the tunnel to wait.

A few minutes later, Ridgie's skates were on and I had the net in hand. I walked to the opening and waited for the cameras.

The announcers called attention to me, and I raised my arms, waving the net for dramatic effect.

"And there's our Ridgie the Bear! Will he succeed where everyone else has failed? Let's cheer him on!"

I skated out to center ice, where the refs were still trying to corral the poor bird. I stopped just short of them and covered my bear mouth with a paw, mocking their attempt. The crowd ate it up as the Benny Hill theme song filled the arena. The comedic tune provided a laughter-inducing soundtrack for my plight.

The refs parted, and I closed in on the pigeon, swiping at it with the net but not really trying to catch it. Farther down the ice it went, until it was right in front of the goal.

If I could trap it in our net ... my thoughts raced as they formed an idea. Slowly, I glided toward the bird, legs spread apart and arms out to the side, trying to appear as big as possible. The bird saw me and hopped back ... then back again until it was just inside.

I skated into the net and plastered myself across it in a big bear hug. The fans went wild. I couldn't see the bird, but I didn't need to. The announcers were still giving a play-by-play.

"And Ridgie effectively traps the pigeon! The little fella could escape through the bear's five-hole, but he seems content to stay in the corner, folks. Here come the referees and linesmen to assist. It looks like they're going to try to trap the pigeon in an ice bucket! Yes, ladies and gentlemen, that's exactly their plan!"

I glided backward to allow them access, and two of the officials went into the net, one armed with a bucket and the other with a poster from a fan. The bucket closed over the bird, the poster underneath the bucket, and it was trapped.

I took a victory lap around the ice, waving and pumping my fists to keep the crowd excited.

And I threw in a few back handsprings for embellishment. I'd probably get in trouble for those—and for upstaging Ridgies Number One and Two, but so what? This crowd needed a pick-me-up, and so did the team.

Play resumed, and Xavier scored, making it a 5-4 game. With three minutes left, the backup goalie was pulled, and team captain Dean Hathaway tied it up with a minute left.

The Edge won in overtime, 6-5, and we would be going to Miami for Game 7.

CHAPTER 3
Tasha

June

I breathed in the aroma of my pumpkin spice flavored coffee, letting the steam warm my face and penetrate my pores. A few years ago, I'd changed up the ingredients for max health benefits—for me—and minimum digestive issues. I mixed my own blend of spices, subbed out the two-percent milk for oat milk, and nixed the pumpkin puree and whipped cream.

Three more minutes until I'd unlock the front door to the Coffee Loft and turn the sign to "Open." I liked these early morning shifts. Setup was quiet enough that I could visualize my day, and once we opened the door, the steady stream of customers kept me busy until it was time to go to the high school to coach the varsity squad. School was out for the summer, but my job wasn't done. We had tryouts and fundraising, cheer clinics, camp, plus new routines to plan—it was never-ending.

Having three jobs could be tedious at times, but it paid the bills.

And I had a *lot* of bills.

I pushed that unpleasant thought out of my brain and thought of Monty's Nana Booboo instead. Never one to follow rules, especially when caffeine or treats were concerned, she'd been the one who'd gotten me hooked on my favorite beverage, having handed me hers during a water break at a hard practice when I was eight. I'd fallen several times already that day, having hardly slept the night before due to a stomachache. She'd told me to take a sip, and I did. Then another and another before she could pry it out of my hands. It was the caffeine jolt I'd needed, and the three sips became a before-practice ritual every fall until I could buy my own Lofty-size pumpkin spice latte.

Co-coaching with Monty had been going well, so far. As he'd suggested, we brought back our old Good Coach/Bad Coach shtick, and everything was coming together.

"It's time!" my cousin Gabby called out from behind the counter. Riva, the owners' yellow Lab therapy dog trainee, trotted out to join me on my walk to the door. The pup loved to greet guests and had a little doghouse built into the counter.

I set my Coffee Loft branded travel mug down and opened the door, peering up and down Main Street to see if any of the regulars were heading our way. The street was unusually quiet for a Monday. I shrugged and pulled my head back inside, closing the door behind me.

"No one's here yet, Riva." I picked up my coffee and bent down to pet the pup with my free hand. We crossed the store and split off, Riva disappearing into the recessed doghouse, and I joined Gabby and the owner, Jannell, behind the counter.

I loved this place: the aroma of the beans, the sugary sweetness of the treats, the bustle of locals in and out, and the new second level, an actual loft accessible by a spiral iron staircase in the center of the café. Cozy reading areas and tables provided the best atmosphere for losing oneself in a book or playing board games with friends.

In the front of the store, two large bay windows sandwiched the old saloon-style entrance. A seating area with small sofas created a comfy space by one of the windows, and on the other side, small round tables and upholstered chairs gave a cozy feel. Along the side wall opposite my station, the original mahogany bar was now lined with barstools and served as workstations. The rest of the first floor had your standard tables and chairs to seat the max capacity.

Customers began to arrive, and we fell into the familiar morning rhythm of taking and filling their orders. My sister, Penny, arrived just before one o'clock. She used to work here full-time before she married her hockey player husband. Living with Xavier erased all her bills and gave her time to focus on her music studies and harp playing.

Gabby had cut her shifts as well. She was engaged to Noel Allaire, one of Xavier's teammates, and both she and Penny had been busy supporting their guys during the playoffs.

It was rare that the three of us had a shift together anymore, and I had a feeling come next season both of them would quit entirely. Gabby and Noel were getting married later this month when hockey ended. Why would she work here if she didn't have to? At least Penny had a reason to come in; she made Xavier's good-luck toffee coffee concoction before home games. He scored a goal every time.

During a brief lull, I refilled my coffee and snacked on a slice of Sunflower Bakery's gluten-free bread. I had to be careful with my intake; the right amount of caffeine helped my systems to function. Too much would cause my IBS to flare. I also had celiac disease and dairy sensitivities. Lucky for me, Jannell kept the shelves stocked with treats I could eat and also decided pumpkin spice would be available year-round. Before that, I brought in my own coffee in the offseasons.

"One more day!" Gabby sang to Penny. "Are you packed for Miami?"

My ears perked up, and I suddenly became engrossed in my coffee. They were excited about their guys' team making it to Game 7 of the Stanley Cup final, as they should be. They weren't purposely trying to leave me out of the conversation. The series was tied 3-3, and Game 7 would be in Miami. All the significant others and their families were traveling there for this game.

"Mostly," Penny said. "I'm glad to have you and Brenna to room and navigate with. It seems like a big ordeal."

"Because it *is* a big ordeal. I just hope Noel will get some playtime. In Round 3 he was a healthy scratch every game, and he only got a handful of shifts in Game 4 this round."

"I'm sure he will," Penny assured her. "The coaches probably just wanted to make sure he didn't get hurt. He's only got one kidney, you know."

Gabby laughed at Penny's quip. "Yeah, I know."

The bell over the door chimed. I tipped my chin up and sighed. Of course it'd be Monty.

He sauntered right up to my register. I set my coffee down and peeled myself from the back counter.

"Hey, Monty!" Gabby greeted him. "Are you going to Miami?"

"Hey, Gab. I am. Thanks to my extraordinary performance in Game 6 and Ridgie Number One's broken bones and subsequent retirement, I have officially usurped the incumbent bear and achieved the position of Ridgie Number One."

"That was epic, by the way," Gabby praised. "I'm glad you're coming. You can help me calm Penny's nerves."

Huh. She hadn't suggested *me* to calm Penny's nerves. I was Penny's sister, for goodness' sake. Why would she ask Monty and not me?

Oh, right. Because I wasn't going.

Just another item on the list of Ways Gabby Annoys Tasha.

Whatever.

I tapped the tips of my short cheer-friendly nails on the counter as I waited for Monty to stop talking long enough to place his order. Finally, they finished gushing over the trip and he turned back to me.

"Key lime protein shake, please."

My eyebrows lifted as I punched in the order. Like Gabby, Monty had always drunk iced chocolate since we were kids and still preferred it in the afternoons. But during one of our cheer competition trips to Orlando, he'd gotten hooked on a particular key lime and vanilla protein powder shake. He'd made a deal with the previous owners to have key limes shipped here after he decided the drink had everything to do with his best performance to date. "A little late in the day for your morning go-to," I observed, adding a hint of sarcasm to my tone.

"I was with Nana," he retorted. "Some things are more important than the time of day I drink my protein."

My heart twinged. I softened my tone. "How's she doing?" I asked as he tapped his credit card to the payment device.

"Fine." He glanced over at Penny and Gabby. "Do you have a minute to talk in private?"

"Private?" I stepped back, surprised at his request.

He rolled his eyes. "You know, like me and you, alone. Where no one else can hear us talk."

"I know what *private* means," I shot back and flipped my ponytail over my shoulder. "I'm just surprised. We could talk at the gym. Why here, why now?"

He huffed. "Just—yes or no?" The impatient response was very un-Monty-like. I'd rarely seen him lose his cool.

"Fine. Follow me into the kitchen." I turned and called out to Gabby to make his drink, telling her we'd be right back.

Monty followed me through the kitchen to the refrigerated room. I held the big heavy stainless-steel door until he was inside and slammed it shut behind me.

"That's not locked, is it?" he asked, concern flashing across his features.

"Nope. The last place I want to be is locked in a freezing closet with *you*," I assured him.

"Same," he drawled in his deepest register, but he was smiling.

Huh.

"So, why the clandestine meeting?" I crossed my arms and tapped my foot.

His gaze lowered to my sneaker. "I'll make it quick. You have an extra bedroom. I need a place to stay while Nana's house gets up to code so she can come home."

My heart pounded in my chest. He couldn't be serious. "I'm sorry, what? You want to move in with me?"

"I don't *want* to," he replied dryly. "But it makes sense. We can even carpool to practice."

I shook my head. "Can't you stay with your parents? Or with one of the guys? Penny and Xavier have a guest room." *Anywhere but my place.*

"No. Nana specifically suggested you because she'll know Parfait le Chat will be well cared for if I have to travel."

I gaped at him. "And your cat, too?"

"*Nana's* cat, officially," he corrected. "My parents are pet-free. The guys all have their own pets or will be traveling for the summer. And Pen and Gab have enough going on to worry about caring for a pet."

"And I don't?" My voice rose at his implication that I wasn't busy. "Three jobs, remember?"

He tipped his head back and sighed dramatically. "Name your fee."

"My fee?"

"I'll pay your rent all summer."

"It's already taken care of." I didn't have proof, but I was sure Xavier had paid the rent for the rest of the year when Penny moved out.

"I'll pay you anyway."

"Nope."

"C'mon, Tasha. There must be something you want. And are you really prepared to turn me and Parfy out on the streets?"

"Pet-friendly hotels exist, you know."

He met my gaze and held it. I shivered. Darn near-freezing temp in this fridge.

Connections.

The word popped into my head, and I stewed over it. Monty now had access to guys my age that made big money. Big bankfuls of money that wouldn't even be dented by my medical bills. Nice, hard-working guys who had good enough insurance they only had to work one job instead of three. Guys who appreciated eating healthy and weren't averse to dating cheerleaders.

Surely, I could hit it off with one of them. Fall in love, get married, and relax for once in my life? I was more suited to being an athlete's wife than my sister was. Penny didn't even wear makeup, and her idea of styling her hair was braiding it.

"There is *one* thing ..." I let the sentence trail off and narrowed my gaze, still locked on his.

"Name it."

"I want to be your plus-one for all Edge-related events." His eyes widened. "Don't get excited." I rushed to explain. "I want to date a hockey player. Help me get into their world. We can start with Gabby and Noel's wedding."

He didn't speak for a minute. I waited as he pressed his lips together, chewed on the inside of his cheek, and squinted back at me.

"Deal." He stuck out his hand. "Shake on it?"

I shook my head. "Didn't mean anything the last time."

His jaw dropped, and he pulled his hand back as if stung.

Good. I spun on my heel and stalked out of the fridge before he could invent an excuse or apologize or—

I didn't care. The past was the past.

It was time to plan my future.

A future where I didn't have to work so hard to merely survive.

CHAPTER 4

Monty

Move-in Day.

 After a brutal Game 7 loss in Miami, I was back in Colorado and ready for the reno to begin so it could be over.

"Mew!"

Parfait le Chat, protesting vehemently from his soft-sided pet carrier, was my last trip. I'd set up the mackerel tabby's bed, toys, food, water, and litter box in my room and bathroom. "Almost there, boy. Just up these stairs and ... here we go."

After my sister Mindy died, Nana decided I needed a cat. My parents wouldn't allow pets at our house, so Parfait— named after Nana's favorite dessert at the time—lived at her house. Tasha and I spent a whole practice brainstorming silly nicknames. Parfy, Barfy, Parfait the Cray, Parfetta the Chetta. All ridiculous, but it was the first time I'd laughed in weeks.

"Nana says his name is Par-feh luh Sha." I stroked my new kitten *and winced when he bit me." But I can read and it says Par-fate-lee-chat. So dumb."*

Tasha giggled. I was pleased that I'd made her laugh.

"Well," she said. "We'll just have to give the little fuzzball a nick-name. How about Parfy?"

"Or Barfy!" I hooted. We collapsed into giggles as the kitten ran around us jumping and scratching and hopping like a bouncy ball in one of those lottery boxes.

"Parfait the Cray!" I could hardly get the words out I was laughing so hard.

"Parfetta the Chetta! Like cheese!" Tasha squealed.

Warmed by the memory, I couldn't help chuckling as I pushed my key into the lock and opened the door. Tasha's apartment was just off Main Street, separated by a parking lot from the back of the Coffee Loft and its neighboring businesses. It was a good ten-minute drive from Nana's, and Parfait had cried the full duration.

Montoya Construction would start the accessibility renovations on Monday. I figured with the wedding this weekend, it'd be better to move in on Friday than on Sunday. So I'd been in and out all morning while Tasha worked at the Coffee Loft. She was home now. Nowhere visible, but the aroma of something cooking gave her away.

I toed off my shoes under the entry table and slid my feet into the fuzzy slippers Tasha had given me for a high school cheer secret Santa gift. They were worn out like a well-loved teddy bear and a little too small. Trusty, dependable, broken in, a little withered and dulled by age but functional and far superior to a stiff brand-new pair. My toes peeked out the open front, but the worn-in softness and familiar comfort far outweighed the minor size deficiency.

I settled Parfait in my room and shut the door, closing him in. Best to let him get adjusted to a smaller space before overwhelming him with the full layout. I snorted. Tasha's entire apartment was smaller than Nana's master suite. The cat would be fine, but I didn't want to press my luck just yet.

I crossed the living space to the open kitchen to inspect the permeating scent. A Crock-Pot sat on the counter, and I lifted the lid. "Mmm." It was some kind of chili with veggies.

"Drop that crock cover or I'll shoot."

I glanced up, furrowing my brow as my brain registered the sight before me. Tasha, in a belted satin robe, her sandy hair in long, sculpted waves, held a squirt bottle. I couldn't help chuckling.

I replaced the lid on the pot and held my hands up in defense. "Wouldn't dare mess with your dinner. Why *are* you making dinner? Don't they feed you at rehearsals? And what's in that bottle?"

She glared at me. "Water, for the cat. If he goes where he's not allowed."

That elicited a full belly laugh, deep from my gut. "First of all, a cat is going to go where a cat is going to go. Second, and lucky for you, Parfait is old and lazy. Ancient by cat standards. And he only jumps if he's highly motivated."

The muscles in her face relaxed, and she lowered the bottle. "Fine. It's chicken and veggie chili. Gabby forgot about my dietary restrictions, and the kitchen couldn't accommodate tonight on such short notice. So, I'll eat before I go and probably when I get back. It's fixed for tomorrow, though," she added.

Tasha had always been a picky eater, and as an adult, she'd become a weirdly healthy eater. She was always refusing food at events; this had gluten, that had dairy, the other thing had cross-contamination.

"Why are you still looking at me?" she asked.

Was I? I guess I was.

"Uh … your hair looks nice." It did. I was used to seeing her in a ponytail.

"Stop it," she gritted through her teeth.

"Stop what?" I asked.

"You don't need to be nice to me because I saved you and your cat from being homeless."

I held back a laugh and pasted on a smug expression. "Noted. You've got a blob of lotion on your cheek."

"I—" Her free hand flew to her face. "Uh!"

She spun around and stalked back to her room. I chuckled. It was fun ruffling her feathers. It came naturally.

After Nana's stroke, I made a list of my regrets. Not monitoring her sugar intake as stringently as I could have. Wasting years and effort trying to get my parents to notice me. Breaking my promise to a four-year-old Tasha that I'd be her stunt partner forever.

But it wasn't enough that I'd broken our partnership after sixteen years. It was my choice for her replacement that had rubbed salt in the wound, though that hadn't been my intention, and I'd regretted it almost immediately. There was a lot of work to be done if she was ever going to forgive me. I wanted to earn her trust again as much as I wanted Nana to make a full recovery.

I just didn't know how.

Maybe that path would be revealed to me while I was staying here.

I spent the next few hours unpacking and petting Parfait. I figured I'd stay in my room until Tasha left for Gabby and Noel's wedding rehearsal and dinner. Once I finished, I relaxed on the bed. The old cat climbed onto my chest, turned in a circle, plopped down, and fell into a deep sleep.

Knock knock. I glanced at the clock. 5:07. Parfait was still snoring. "Come in," I said lightly.

Tasha opened the door slowly, revealing herself one inch at a time. Her long waves were held back with a glittery headband, and she wore a fit-and-flare yellow sundress that set off her tan. She looked like ... a ray of sunshine.

Very un-Tasha-like.

I tried not to react.

Because of the cat, of course. Didn't want to disturb the old guy.

Le Chat. I laughed internally at my own joke.

"Montgomery! You're not dressed. Aren't you coming?"

"Huh?"

"To the rehearsal."

"I'm not in the wedding," I reminded her.

Tasha's forehead knitted in confusion. "Gabby didn't invite you to the dinner?"

"She did. But I figured I'd stay here and help Parfait get adjusted. No one will miss me."

She tilted her head and frowned but recovered quickly. "That's true." But it didn't land with the usual vitriol. Was she disappointed I wasn't going?

Impossible. The girl hated me. I was only here because our arrangement was mutually beneficial.

"Help yourself to the chili. Bye."

The door clicked shut behind her, and I stroked the cat thoughtfully. Tasha had been almost civil. What was that about?

TWENTY-SOMETHING HOURS LATER, the wedding reception in Brenna Trotter's barn venue was well underway. The wedding party dances had been danced, the cake had been cut, and now it was time for my favorite part.

Line dances.

This reception was stacked with former cheerleaders and current hockey players, none of which were on the floor yet. They'd get rowdy later, but I'd be on my way home by then. I positioned myself in the center of the dance floor behind Tasha's grandmother and great-aunt as The Hustle got underway. DJs always warmed up the crowd with that one. It was old and got the Boomers on the floor. Then they'd play the Electric Slide, and the Gen Xers would join in. Depending on the event, the Achy Breaky Heart was next. Then the Macarena, the Cha Cha Slide, the Cupid Shuffle, and finally the Wobble.

I knew them all. I put my own spin into each of them. As did Tasha and Gabby. We'd been doing most of them at cheer camps since preschool.

I looked for her over the dancing septuagenarians. She stood by the dessert table, speaking to a waiter, probably asking for the ingredients. The sign *said* "Gluten-free Chocolate Cake," but as I learned from her, that didn't necessarily mean it was true, especially if it was made with or on the same equipment as the gluten-full desserts. When she turned away from him, I waved. She rolled her eyes and shook her head.

The next time I faced her direction, she'd moved, and I

located her back at our table, chatting with Brenna. I waved again and caught Brenna's attention. She said something to Tasha, then pulled her to her feet.

They were coming my way. The song faded out, and most of the Boomers left the dance floor, making room for the next generation and a handful of Millennials and Gen Zers who knew the Electric Slide.

There was room in this line dance to change it up. Tasha had been the one to teach me that. One year at cheer camp, we had to choreograph our own variation. She was a born choreographer. She not only did hers but mine and Gabby's, too.

I loosened the tie around my neck and rolled up my sleeves as they stepped into place to my left. I'd ditched my jacket as soon as we arrived at our table.

"Let's see what you got," Tasha challenged, stepping into the grapevine and turning in circles instead of sliding.

Classic Tasha.

The next move was to lean back and twist your body to the right, then roll forward to punch at the ground. This was the part where she'd had me do a back tuck and then punch forward. But I didn't have room for that here. Instead, I busted out my pop-and-lock moves and flat robot hands.

Giggling behind me encouraged me to continue that way, and by the end of the song, I'd broken a sweat. Tasha patted my back. "The kids loved that."

I lifted my brow and waited for her opinion, but of course it wouldn't come. Straight praise wasn't our thing anymore. Not for a long time. Not since—

I kept my expression neutral as more guests crowded onto the floor. Tasha danced beside me through all the dances until the Wobble ended. The DJ slowed it down with a '90s ballad, and that was our cue to head back to our table. Neither of us got into the slow dances. They were awkward and … feely.

I didn't want any feels.

"Hey," she hissed, pulling at my elbow as we waded through the lovey-dovey couples to get to our table. "Who's *that* guy?" She tipped her chin with appreciation toward a tall, pale blond deep in conversation with Xavier. But he wasn't looking at Penny's husband.

His gaze was fixed on Tasha.

"Vlad?" I asked. "Noel's friend from some European league," I said dismissively. "Signed with the Edge last week."

"So he's local. Introduce me?"

I studied her face, flushed from dancing. Exerted, Tasha was at her friendliest. Endorphins made her nicer.

Without a word, I led her over to the guy.

Xavier saw us coming and waved us over. "Vlad, have you met my sister-in-law, Tasha?"

He shook his head. "Vlad Ivanov. Pleased to meet you." He spoke carefully and deliberately, almost robotically as he held out his hand for Tasha. She lifted hers for a shake, but he raised her arm and brushed a kiss against her knuckles instead. Her left arm was still hooked into mine, and I felt her whole body shiver at his touch.

I already hated the guy.

"Vlad's Russian and working on his English," Xavier explained. "We're all helping him learn words."

"Nice of you." I turned to Tasha. "Enjoy your conversation." I smirked. I peeled her arm off mine like it was poisonous and sauntered back to our table, plopping into my seat next to Penny.

"What do you know about Vlad?" I asked.

She fussed with the baby's breath tucked into her waist-length braid. "Not much. Xavier likes him. Why do you ask?"

I thumbed over my shoulder. "Tasha likes him, too."

"Aw, are you looking out for my sister?" She smiled and patted my knee. "I knew you didn't hate her."

"Hate her?" I blinked. "I don't hate her. She's the one who froze *me* out."

"I know. But you hurt her pretty badly when you chose Gabby as a partner over her that summer before she broke her leg."

"I had good reasons."

"I'm sure you did. But it cut her deep. Especially after your pledge to be 'partners forever,'" she air-quoted. "And then she fell and broke her leg ..."

"We were *four*. Little kids make all kinds of silly promises. And most don't remember them and hold onto them their whole life."

"It wasn't silly to her, and you know it. She trusted you, Monty. It's very hard for her to trust people; always has been."

"I know." I squeezed my eyes shut. The memory of preschool me and Tasha spitting on our palms and shaking on *partners forever* haunted me. "I never dropped her, not once."

"She knows that. And I think that made it hurt even worse, especially after she fell." Penny sat up straight as Vlad and Tasha passed us, hand in hand, toward the dance floor.

"And now she slow dances," I mumbled, incredulous.

"So go cut in," Penny suggested.

I shook my head. "Doesn't bother me."

She cast a pointed look at me and patted my knee again.

"Keep telling yourself that." Xavier appeared behind her, and she stood. "Don't be so stubborn," she advised me. I averted my gaze as they made their way through the tables to slow dance to whatever lame song was playing.

Time to put in a request.

It took a fifty-dollar bill to convince the DJ to play "The Chicken Dance," especially since it was on Gabby and Noel's banned song list. Who banned the most iconic dance?

Gabby, that's who. I wish I'd had my phone ready to snap a picture of her face when it began to play. I knew it irked her, but I didn't request it to make her mad. I requested it to get Tasha's attention. Those two had been in competition since they were born.

They were both super smart and great athletes. But Tasha could also ice skate, and Gabby, despite years of lessons as a kid, was still a bender. She'd improved a bit since dating Noel, but there was zero grace in her slide. Tasha, on the other hand, could have gone into figure skating instead of cheer if she'd decided to. And with her natural ability to choreograph graceful and compelling routines, she was fun to watch on or off the ice.

I joined the guests forming a circle on the dance floor and snuck a glance in Tasha's direction. She was six people down from me, and I watched and listened while she taught Vlad the moves.

"Gabby *hates* this song!" she shouted over the music. "I had my tenth birthday at the ice rink, and she couldn't skate. But Monty and I pulled her out for this song because we thought we could hold her up. We couldn't. She fell more times than we could count!"

Vlad just smiled. Probably couldn't understand a word she was saying.

Probably didn't care, either, from the way he was looking at her.

It irked me.

I glanced at the glowering Gabby, and I smiled at the memory. Guess she never got over it. While I flapped my arms, I scanned the circle. A few people down from me were Brenna and her husband, Brendan, then Nate and his roommate, Leon. Across from me, Gabby's brother Jake and two of his college buddies were paired up with a trio of girls from the Worlds team, some hockey players next to them. Then Noel, Xavier, and Penny. Behind them, Gabby was at the DJ's booth, probably reminding him in the kindest way that he wasn't supposed to play this song.

When she looked up, I flashed a grin as I shimmied into a squat. When I wiggled back up, she was shaking her head and laughing.

Gab was a good sport.

But the joke was on me. "The Chicken Dance" ended, and another ballad began.

How I loathed weddings.

Couples getting cozy, singles on the prowl. Except for me. I didn't have time for a relationship. Since Nana had been stuck in a wheelchair, she'd been my top priority. I'd yet to find a woman who was okay with that. It was tiring, dating. And there was always that small part of me that wondered if they were more interested in my money than me. My trust fund was substantial. I drove a high-end pickup truck. I lived in Nana's Victorian mansion. And I had no plans to ever move out.

I'd given up looking for someone who was okay with all that.

I passed Tasha and Vlad as I exited the dance floor, trying

not to be a creeper. He was a charmer. She was flushed, giggling, and batting her eyelashes. It was hard to tell if she was being genuine—because, endorphins—or playing it up because she so desperately wanted a hockey boyfriend like her sister and cousin. Xavier and Noel were great, but she sure was narrowing the field. There were only a handful of single guys on the Edge, and she'd managed to catch the eye of the newest most eligible bachelor.

"Monty!" Penny waved from the table where she was standing with Xavier. Seated at it were an older couple, probably his parents, and who I assumed were his three sisters. "Have you met the Schwanns?"

I offered my hand to Xavier's dad. "Montgomery Biddington. Nice to meet you."

"Heinrich Schwann and my wife, Irina."

"He's cute!" the middle daughter whispered loudly to the youngest. I grinned at the preteens but pretended not to hear.

The oldest, who I knew to be in her early twenties from Penny talking about her, shushed them and smiled. "I'm Daniella. These silly girls are Karina and Edyta. Nice to meet you."

"Pleasure." I shook their hands and kept my face neutral as Penny used her index fingers and mouthed *she's single* in Daniella's direction.

Time to go.

"Pen, can you make sure Tasha gets home? I need to check in on Nana before visiting hours end, and I don't think she's ready to leave." I nodded toward the dance floor, where she and Vlad were swaying. He was wearing a perma-smile, and I don't think he blinked the whole time I stared at him.

What a meathead.

"Sure. Say hi to Nana Booboo for me and tell her we miss her at the Coffee Loft."

"Will do. Thanks, Pen."

I weaved through the tables to my chair, retrieved my jacket, and was out of there before the song ended.

CHAPTER 5
Tasha

One week later

I should've known better.

My stomach seized again, and tears eked out of the corners of my eyes. The projectile vomiting had ceased around 2 a.m., but my gut was still revolting from being violated.

Monty ordered food last night from Pasta Nacht's, a restaurant that was usually safe for me. I ordered the same gluten-free dairy-free fettucine alfredo every time, and it was fine. They knew me and my food issues. And just in case, I personally called in the order every time to make sure they knew it was for me and reminded them of the consequences if any of the ingredients were cross-contaminated.

Foolishly, I let Monty place an online order. I typed in all the special requests myself, and when our food arrived, the delivery driver assured me they'd been honored, pointing to the extra-long receipt with all my instructions printed on it.

Ha. What did he know?

I should have called and spoken to the manager on duty. Instead, I'd spent the night regretting every single bite, and now I was housebound and would miss Penny's only performance at the Renaissance Faire this summer.

I *hated* not showing up for her. When my sister's fingers touched the strings of her harp, I relaxed. She used to play it in the Coffee Loft, but now that she was working there hardly ever, the harp stayed at her and Xavier's apartment. He'd even made her a music room.

She deserved it. Every bone in Penny's body was nice. Sweet like the coffee she made for her husband. His hockey season was over, and next week they'd be leaving to visit his family in Calgary. I probably wouldn't see her again until her birthday in August, when Xavier flew all of his and her relatives to his family's castle in Europe. He'd inherited his grandfather's estate and title—Baron von Schwann—making my sister a baroness. Pretty much European royalty.

I pulled my legs up to my chest and texted Monty. *I'm sick. Are you going to the Ren Faire? If so, can you record Penny's performances for me?*

He responded right away. *I was just about to text you. Sounds like an animal is dying behind your door.*

Ha ha, I texted back.

For real. I need to see your face. Penny will ask why you're not there. I need proof that you're alive and it's not an imposter messaging me.

I shook my head. *Not gonna happen. So, you won't go, then?*

Maybe. If you ask me nicely.

I rolled my eyes. Normally, I wouldn't cave to such demands, but I needed this text conversation to be over so I could lie down and close my eyes again. *Will you PLEASE go to the Ren Faire and record Penny for me?*

I think I can squeeze it in. Send me the details. And text me if you need anything from the pharmacy or grocery store.

Thanks. And please let Penny know I feel terrible I can't make it. She'll understand. Tell her I said she cannoli imagine what I'm going through.

Cannoli was our code word for Italian food. Different cuisines wreaked different havoc on my systems. She'd know by the use of the word I was sick as a dog with digestive issues. I tapped out all the pertinent information and attached the Ren Faire map to my reply, then stretched out on the bathroom rug, bunching a towel under my head for a pillow and praying for sleep.

No sense in going back to bed. I'd just be back here once the current bottle of water I drank processed.

Mercifully, sleep overtook me. When I woke up, the sun had shifted. It's light no longer shone at full force through my window and the bathroom was dim. Groaning, I sat up and felt around for my phone.

4:47 p.m.

I swiped to check my texts. A few from Penny, plus a missed call and voicemail. And a whole bunch from Monty. Recordings of Penny's performance alternated with questions about my welfare.

I groaned when my phone rang.

It was him.

I closed my eyes and swiped to answer it, tapping the icon for speakerphone and laying the device on the floor by my head.

"Tasha?" Monty's deep voice dripped heavily with concern.

"Yeah?"

"Can you unlock your door?"

"No."

"I have grape Gatorade for you."

Tempting. But I couldn't muster the energy to get up and go to my bedroom door even if I wanted to.

I tried to sound like my normal self. "Put it in the fridge."

"If you don't open the door, I'm going to pick the lock. Penny said you're probably dehydrated. I'm not playing, Tasha. I *will* call EMS if you don't let me in and drink this stuff."

Ugh. I wanted to curse into the phone and tell him where to go with his Gatorade. But I couldn't, because the truth was, I was weaker than I'd been before my nap. I needed electrolytes, but for now, Gatorade would suffice.

I kicked the bathroom door closed. "Fine. Bring it in and leave it on my desk."

"Aren't you going to open the door?"

I squeezed my eyes shut. "Can't," I breathed, admitting defeat.

There was no scuffle at the door; Penny had probably told him we kept the keys to our rooms on top of the doorframes, just in case of emergencies. I pulled my knees to my chest and prayed he wouldn't try to bust into the bathroom.

I couldn't let him see me like this.

"Tasha!"

Well, I guess higher powers had other ideas. I didn't have to open my eyes to know he'd pushed open the bathroom door. And I didn't need my eyes to tell me when he fell to his knees on the ground next to me.

And I didn't need my eyes to feel his arm snaking behind my shoulders and gently guiding me into a position conducive to sipping liquid.

I couldn't have been more mortified if I'd had a wardrobe

malfunction at the top of a cheer pyramid. I'd never felt so exposed as I felt in this moment. Sweaty, disheveled, stinking like vomit and whatever else … I'd never live this down.

"Tasha." His voice cracked as he pulled my head into his lap.

"Your … thighs are harder than the floor," I gritted out. "Please go away."

"I'm not going anywhere. Drink."

I closed my mouth to protest.

He prodded the rim of the bottle to my lower lip. "And of course my thighs are hard. I work out five days a week."

"You're supposed to have rest days, dummy."

"Rest is for the weak. No drinky, I call nine-one-one."

I parted my lips in defeat. He hated me enough to follow through on the threat.

The cool grape-flavored liquid coated my tongue. I swallowed slowly, not wanting to incite another round of dry heaves.

Still with my eyes closed, I fumbled to swat the bottle away with my hand. "Enough."

"Open your eyes."

"No."

"You can't pretend me away. I'm going to help you get to your bed, and you should have your eyes open."

"No."

He sighed. "Fine."

Before I could respond, he maneuvered me so that one of his arms looped behind my back and another was under my knees. As he stood, my stomach groaned loudly.

"Down," I whimpered. "Please."

"In a minute," he cooed.

As Monty carried me to my bed, another wave of nausea

hit. My head spun, and I used every ounce of strength I could summon to keep my mouth closed. My cheeks puffed out with each burst of air from my stomach, but I succeeded in keeping the Gatorade on the inside.

Monty set me down gently on my bed, and I rolled to face the wall so my back was to him. "Please go," I whispered hoarsely, once the heaves had passed.

"Yeah ... no. Bucket's behind you." A creaking sound signaled he'd found my desk chair and was leaning back in it. "Penny would kill me if you died on my watch. You're my patient."

If I had the strength, I would've rolled my eyes, even if he couldn't see them. "I'm not going to die, and I'm not *your* anything. So, go."

"Right now, you're a pain in my backside," he retorted. "Pretend I'm not here. I'm going to read on my phone and pretend I'm anywhere else."

"Don't make me your pity project," I said through gritted teeth.

"Hard not to pity you. You look miserable. I wouldn't abandon a sick animal, even if it roared at me or unleashed its claws. So why wouldn't I sit here and get verbally abused by you?"

My stomach groaned again, and my eyes stung. I didn't answer his question. Why did it have to be *him* that was here?

Right. Because I had no one else.

Penny was at the Ren Faire. Gabby was on her honeymoon. I didn't really have any other friends. Over the years, my friend circle had shrunk to them and a few former-friends-now-acquaintances in the high school group chat. But I knew they had another chat that I wasn't a part of, for when they made plans to go to places I couldn't eat food at. For the longest time, I'd eat before I left to hang out and snack on celery and water at dinner. I guess after all the times I said no, I couldn't eat there, they listened. And stopped inviting me.

I *considered* calling my mother, but she'd overreact and baby me. I was a grown adult with a bachelor's degree in sports fitness and a master's in nutrition. I wasn't the type to call my mommy every time I had a hangnail.

I could take care of myself. I knew how my body worked. I knew what upset it, and I knew how to fix it.

It would just take a few days. I could rest until Monday, and if I had to call in sick to the Coffee Loft then, Jannell would understand. School was out, and the high school squad didn't start formal practices until the end of July. The FireVolts practiced on Tuesday and Thursday nights.

My digestive system would be back to normal by Tuesday, I was sure of it.

I must have dozed off again. When I woke up, I was curled up and facing the other direction, under the comforter. Blinking in the darkness, I waited until my eyes adjusted to the sliver of moonlight peeking in from between my curtains.

The desk chair was empty. Good.

My stomach growled a complaint. I should try to drink again. The small bottle of Gatorade was in an ice bucket on my desk, just out of reach on the other side of my night-stand. Tentatively, I swung my legs off the bed and pushed myself up to a sitting position. Taking a deep, steadying breath, I lowered my feet to the floor.

"Ow!"

"Mrow!"

I retracted my legs immediately and peered down. Monty

sat up, rubbing at the hip I'd tried to stand on as Parfait shot out of the room.

Evening my startled expression and raising my eyebrows, I snorted. "Really? That hurt?"

"You're heavier than you look."

I tilted my head to the side. We both knew that he was capable of lifting girls heftier than me into the air, fully extended, in one hand. "Are you going to move, or should I attempt to leap over you?"

The moonlight reflected in his eyes as he scooted leisurely out of the way for me. "Glad you're feeling better," he mumbled.

"Yep, no need for you to play hero—or nurse. I can drink my own Gatorade, thank you very much." I clutched my stomach as I walked the few steps to the desk. I had to pretend I was fine so he would leave. I'd need to use the bathroom when I finished the bottle, and I didn't want him here for *that*.

Monty's hands beat mine to the Gatorade. He twisted the cap off and held the bottle out to me. I took it and used my other hand to brace myself on the desk. I sipped and stopped. Sipped and stopped. Sipped and—

"Excuse me." I set the bottle back into the ice and spun around, hobbling toward my bathroom.

The Gatorade was coming up, and there was nothing I could do this time to hold it back.

CHAPTER 6
Monty

I scooted across the floor to the closed bathroom door and leaned against it. I wanted to give Tasha privacy but also be there in case she needed help. A few minutes later, when a harp rendition of "Somewhere Over the Rainbow" drifted out from under the door, I surmised she'd placed the end of her phone next to it, speaker pointed toward me, to mask any sounds coming from within.

Deciding she was probably okay for a few minutes, I got to my feet and plodded to the kitchen. Last night, I'd found her binder of recipes and thumbed through it, selecting one for an everything-free chicken soup she'd tabbed and labeled as "Recovery Option #1." She had all the ingredients for it in the freezer, most in Ziploc bags with the same label, so I dumped them all in her Crock-Pot, clipped some cilantro and parsley from the pots by the window, and turned the setting to low.

The entire time I worked, Parfait lounged on the bar. He was a counter connoisseur and particular about his flat surfaces. Since he wasn't near where I was prepping the food, I allowed it. It was a laborious effort for him to jump from the arm of the sofa to the nearest barstool and hop up. He would continue the routine if I put him on the floor. And if I shut him up in my room, he'd mew at a surprisingly loud volume and disturb Tasha, so that was out of the question.

I moved to the sofa an hour later, and Parfy shifted his position to face Tasha's door. I was able to coax him off the bar with a handful of treats, and I pulled him into my lap.

They didn't call it a slow cooker for no reason. As the ingredients mingled, the aroma teased my nostrils and airways, and by hour three I was salivating for it. I fed Parfait, washed my hands, and checked on the soup. When I lifted the cover, a cloud of steam hit me in the face.

Should've expected that.

I returned the lid over the soup and came to the conclusion I was looking forward to trying it. Usually, the way Tasha described her unusual food combinations sounded weird. But having lived with her for a couple of weeks now, and having snuck bites and tastes of her leftovers, I was discovering they weren't half bad.

I wouldn't admit that to her, though.

In a lower cupboard, I found a stainless-steel container with a lid and ladled some soup into it for Tasha to consume when she felt ready. I also scooped some into a mug for myself, my curiosity getting the better of me. I wanted to taste this concoction of bone broth, chicken, carrots, cilantro, ginger, turmeric, egg noodles, and other things I'd never considered to be included in a recipe for this American family staple.

Parfait joined me on the floor next to Tasha's door, dropping a hair tie onto my fuzzy slipper and curling up into a ball in my lap. Serenaded by another harp melody, I ate the soup, careful not to drip any of the hot liquid onto his fur. He'd already been traumatized once this morning.

Besides checking on Nana, I didn't have any plans today. I usually took her to church on Sundays, but she wasn't ready for an outing outside of Mountainview Manor yet. Maybe I'd bring her some of Tasha's soup if there was any left.

I plucked the soggy hair tie from the slipper and rolled it between my fingers. It was one of those special ones without the metal band that held the two ends together. Years ago, Tasha had switched, claiming they stayed in place better. I'd shrugged. As long as her hair wasn't in the way of my hands, I didn't mind what she did with it.

Well, I *did* like it when she wore her hair down, in soft waves over her shoulders. The competitive, persistent, and perseverant version of her softened. Even her voice changed to a lighter, kinder tone. Less about business and more ... human? Tasha was a machine in the gym and a bustling barista behind the counter. When she had time to relax, she allowed the personality traits she masked to come forward.

I liked both versions of her. She was kind and caring but not a doormat. She got things done and always put forth her best effort.

There was no one else like her.

And I hated that she was hurting. I wanted to understand why, what was wrong with her, and how to fix it. I knew about her gluten sensitivity now, and I noticed that she never ate dairy products or drank cow's milk or used it or real butter in her cooking. But she'd never confided in me why, even back when we were still friends.

I wanted to know more so I could help her and support her. My life was better with her in it, and I wanted her to feel that way about me again.

I had to find a way to get our friendship back.

No matter what the cost to my ego.

CHAPTER 7
Tasha

Like I predicted, I was feeling better by Monday but not well enough for the morning shift. I was able to switch from my opening slot to the midafternoon hours so I could rest a bit longer. Tuesday was better, and I made up my missed hours at the Coffee Loft before FireVolts practice.

Monty was already there, head-to-heads in conversation with our team captains, Amelia and Evan. They were former teammates of ours and three-time veterans of the Worlds team. Amelia coached a tiny team and a mini elite team, and Evan was on the cheer staff at the local university as a tumbling coach.

The rest of the members were standing on our designated floor. I clapped my hands, the loud sound echoing over the low buzz of athlete chatter in the gym. "Five laps. Let's go!"

All heads turned in my direction. I lifted my chin and nodded in the direction of the vulcanized rubber track that outlined the perimeter of the four cheer floors and tumbling area.

Monty wrapped up his conversation and sauntered over to me. "We still had three minutes."

I shrugged and crossed my arms over my chest.

"You know, you don't *have* to take on a bad coach role," Monty continued. He cleared his throat, and my eyes snapped up to meet his gaze. "You know what they're calling us?"

I didn't care.

He didn't wait for me to answer, probably guessing—correctly—that I wouldn't.

"Coach Monsha."

"So?" I asked.

"Sounds an awful lot like 'monster.'"

"So?" I asked again. I wasn't sure how I felt about that, but I didn't really care. "We have a job to do and a title to win. I don't care if they love me or hate me."

"Hmm." He pressed his lips together and averted his gaze, waving to our captains as they passed the starting mark. "Four more, team! Pick up the pace. You've got this!"

"They're not five, Montgomery. They don't need constant affirmation. Tell them what to do, and they do it. That strategy won them the title last year."

"So bristly today. Prickly, like a cactus."

I glared at him, silently challenging him to tell me I should've stayed in bed.

He tapped his chin with his index finger. "Like the taciveria flowering succulent you were named after."

I rewarded him with a look that could freeze fire.

"No? All right, like a hedgehog cactus then. All cute on the outside, but get too close, reach out to pet it, and ouch! Stung."

"You're not even making sense. A hedgehog cactus doesn't look like a hedgehog."

He shrugged. "So? You know what I mean."

Yeah, I did. But I didn't care.

Much.

I turned on my heel and strode to the edge of the mat at the lap mark. "Bring it in!" I pointed to the center of the mat, directing the athletes to turn as they completed their run.

Amelia and Evan led the team through stretches and warm-ups while I went over the choreography portion of the routine on my tablet. We had a week of extra practices set aside in late July to learn the entire section, but until then we'd play with bits and pieces of it. They'd learned six eight-counts of it at tryouts, and I plugged that portion into the end of the number. Nate and I had needed to see who could dance and who should be tumbling or stunting during the segment.

"We're splitting into three groups. Group One will go to the far side of the mat with Amelia to perfect and personalize the final dance segment, complete with ending pose. Group Two will follow Monty to the tumble mats to work on elements he wants to add to the big finish. Group Three will stay here with me to construct the final stunting component. Any questions?"

From the back, I caught, "Does she ever smile?" from a new member of the team. The girl he whispered to had the good sense not to answer.

"Five more laps for you," I called back to him. "To answer your question, it's not my job to smile. I'm not performing; *you* are. Get your positivity cup filled from Coach Montgomery or volunteer with a younger team."

The kid's eyes widened, and he mumbled a "yes, ma'am" as he bolted to the track for his laps.

Monty cleared his throat and shot me a grin. "I've seen her smile. It could happen."

I cast another glare at him, then turned back to the team. "Don't get your hopes up."

"Did you hear that *click*, team? New life goal unlocked." Monty turned to me with a smirky grin, but his eyes seemed ... kind. Like he actually wanted to make me smile.

Recovering quickly, I retorted, "You think too highly of yourself, Montgomery. Keep on smiling like a cheer floor jester."

"A clown, huh?" He waggled his eyebrows at me and turned back to the team, who were all watching us with amused expressions. "New life goal, point two: Unfreezing Tasha's ice face and making her laugh."

"Good luck with that." I stepped away from him to start calling the names for the groups, wanting to get this practice underway so the time would pass and I could go home and crash.

Monty must have sensed I wasn't one hundred percent, because I caught him sneaking glances at me throughout the practice. Each time, I'd narrow my eyelids to slits and look away. I hated that he'd seen me sick. Luckily, it hadn't been anywhere close to the worst I *could* get.

I prayed to all the heavens *that* wouldn't happen while he was staying with me.

One more week, the contractor estimated when she stopped in to the Coffee Loft after work today.

I was counting the hours.

Mercifully, the time passed at a rate I could handle. With twenty minutes left of practice, we brought the segments together and marked their places as a group. We ran through the routine a few times, and when I was satisfied, I called them in. Monty gave them a pep talk, and we dismissed them right on time.

I watched them file out in small groups, and I let out a long breath, allowing my tense shoulders to relax.

"You could have stayed home, Tasha," Monty said quietly. He was standing just off my shoulder, so his breath was warm on my neck.

My body gave an involuntary tremble as my hairs pricked up. "No, I couldn't. We have a fixed number of practices until the showcase. Every single one of them is planned out, and I refuse to let a little digestive issue mess with my schedule." I took a step toward the door that led to the coach's hallway, but he caught my wrist. I spun around, ready to lash out verbally. But again his expression was kind.

Concerned, even.

"I know what happened is an annoyance to you. And you're used to it. But—" He paused and looked down at his hand and its firm grip on my wrist. "Sorry. I— That was scary, Tasha. If I hadn't brought you Gatorade, you might have gotten worse. You might have *died.*"

I shook my head and reined in my tone. "I'm sorry I scared you. But honestly, that was like a three on a scale of ten. If I let every flare-up stop my life, I wouldn't be living."

His eyes widened to the point where it was almost comical. But I knew he'd been genuinely concerned, so I held back from laughing or making fun of him. It was comforting to know he had a nurturing side. I'd seen him care for Nana Booboo as her health declined, but he'd still been the same arrogant jerk to everyone else.

Well, mostly just to me.

I probably deserved it for the way I treated him. But he'd hurt me. Deeply. How did he think I'd react when he broke his promise and rejected me sixteen years later when he'd requested Gabby to be his partner?

Penny always said he must've had a good reason. I was sure he did. And if it was due to the reason I suspected, it was even more hurtful than just simply being rejected.

But maybe he'd grown up a little since then. Making sure I was okay, bringing me Gatorade, and cooking my Recovery Soup weren't requirements in any roommate agreement.

Not that we had one. Hypothetically, of course.

I gave him a nod and continued on to the door that led to the coaches' office, conference room, bathroom and shower facilities. He followed at a safe distance, and I gave in to the urge to put as much space between us as possible. Once I grabbed my purse, I all but sprinted to my car.

As I sat behind the wheel, my headlights lit up enough of the lot to silhouette Monty's exit and trek to his truck. I shifted into reverse and backed out, refusing to acknowledge the streaks of tears ribboning down my cheeks.

CHAPTER 8
Monty

I tried to get to our local hospital at least once a week to visit with the kids in the pediatric oncology unit. Each day, a different activity was planned for the patients who were well enough to walk or be wheeled to an activity room that also served as a parents' lounge.

I'd spent a lot of time in that room when I was in first and second grades.

Every time I entered this place, the memories hit like a truck colliding with a brick wall. I'd wrongly assumed it'd get easier over the years, but it never had. The ghost of my sister would forever haunt this ward. I crossed the hideously patterned carpet to the floor-to-ceiling windows and gazed out at the mountains.

Mindy had been thirteen when she'd been diagnosed with leukemia. At the time, she'd been a straight A student and at the top of her cheer game. A flyer on the Senior Level 4 team, she could also have easily been an elite gymnast. The things she could do in the air! She defied all gravity and flexibility expectations.

I wanted to be just like her.

When her leg started hurting, everyone assumed it was a cheer-related injury. But she'd never fallen. Melinda Biddington *never* fell. Even when her stunting partners dropped her, she was always able to twist in a way that landed her on her feet or in the back spot's arms, like a cat.

When the injury progressed enough that it caused her to limp, her coaches refused to let her practice until she'd had it x-rayed and brought in a physician's note that she was all clear to resume activity.

But the x-ray led to more tests, and a tumor was found. It was surgically removed, and we all celebrated. She resumed practice, and a month later, her team took first place at Summit in Orlando.

Then our parents sat us down. Things were never the same after that.

Sure, the tumor was gone, but Mindy's battle was just beginning.

It hadn't been the only tumor. But it was the only one that was operable. Removing it had allowed her to finish the season.

But now she needed radiation and chemotherapy.

Me, at seven, had heard loudly and clearly what they hadn't said: Without the cancer treatments, she'd die.

I decided then and there I would spend every minute I could with my sister. My dad's driver would pick me up at school and bring me here. I'd do my homework while Mindy napped. The cafeteria would deliver dinner for both of us. When Mindy was awake, I'd tell her about school and cheer, and she'd give me tips to improve my tumbling. My parents would take turns stopping in after work, and whoever stayed the latest would bring me home.

Nana was always here when I arrived, and she would leave just before dinner. Sometimes she'd stay longer if Mindy was having a good day. Sometimes, she'd stop knitting and pull me into her lap, and we'd sit like that for hours, watching animated movies while Mindy slept. Sometimes, on the really bad days, we'd each hold one of Mindy's hands and pray for a cure.

On days I had cheer practice, Nana would drive me. She'd sit in the balcony overlooking the Plex's cheer floors, sipping her pumpkin spice latte from the Bevvie Bar—now the Coffee Loft—and watching me flip all over the mats.

She took great care of me.

And once I was old enough, I'd vowed I'd take care of her.

"Monty's here!"

I spun around and grinned as the kids began to file into the room. First in was Britlynne, an eleven-year-old who'd beaten the disease, only to have it return two years later. She reminded me a lot of Mindy at her age, even if she was a dancer instead of a cheerleader.

A few long strides brought me to her wheelchair. I stuck out my fist and she bumped it. "You good today, Brit?"

"Slaying." She scrunched her nose. "I see you looking up at Nurse Trey to confirm. Believe me"—she twisted in her seat to look up at the twentysomething—"I'm beating this thing. Right?"

Trey grinned and nodded. "Never seen a fiercer fighter," he confirmed.

"Awesome," I said. "Save me a seat?"

She nodded, and Trey wheeled her off as four-year-old Anson entered the room, carried by his dad. His mom worked for the mayor of Colorado Springs, and they'd decided she'd keep working because her salary and benefits were better than his self-employment income. She visited as much as she could and reminded me a lot of my mom, back in those days.

Anson's dad, however, was nothing like my father. My dad only showed up when he felt obligated to and if it fit in with his client dinners, golf "meetings" and business travel.

"Ans, my man!" I held up my hand, and he high-fived it. "You just wake up?"

He nodded. "Wanna go back to bed." He turned his face into his dad's shoulder.

Anson's raspy whisper caused my throat to tighten. "Rough day?" I asked. I normally wouldn't ask such a personal question, but the man's tired eyes and several-days-old scruff tugged at my heart.

"We got through it. He keeps asking for his mom. I know it's killing her not to be here. But we need her benefits."

I nodded, wishing circumstances were different. Our family had enough money to enable our parents to be with Mindy twenty-four seven, but neither wanted to. And here was a family making impossible sacrifices so their child could receive treatment.

It wasn't fair.

Nothing about any of it was fair.

More kids, parents, and sitters filed in and gathered around the stage in the back corner. Today's activity was a puppet show. I sat by Britlynne, and we laughed at the puppeteer's corny jokes. I was there while he was setting up, and he'd asked me if I'd be willing to be part of the show. I agreed, as long as it was within the first three quarters of the performance so I had time to change into my costume before the hour was over.

At thirty-five minutes past the hour, a cat and a dog

puppet were arguing over which was the best pet, and I wondered if my part was coming. I had to leave in ten minutes.

"I think we need to ask the audience which pet is better!" the cat suggested.

The dog's face scrunched, and its eyebrows lifted. "Okay. Hey kids, who thinks dogs make the best pets?"

The kids with dogs hooted and cheered. The cat asked the same question about cats, and the noise level was pretty even.

"Hey you!" The cat pointed to me. "The super big giant kid!"

"Who, me?" I asked in a forced high-pitched voice.

"Yeah!" The dog woofed. "Which pet is better?"

I scratched my head. "Well, I have a cat ..." The cat kids cheered. "But—I don't think my roommate likes him. Very grumpy roommate." I shook my head like it was the saddest thing.

The cat puppet gasped. "What kind of person doesn't like a cat?"

"I think my cat annoys her because he acts like it's his place, not hers. We're guests while my house is being renovated," I explained.

"Your roommate is a *giiiiiirl?* Oooooooohh!" he teased. "Is she smart? Is she pretty? Do you liiiiiiiiiike her?"

I snorted. "She's both of those things. And my friend."

"Oooooh!" teased the dog. "Hey, kids, maybe we can help Monty's roommate not be so grumpy. Who's got an idea?"

All of the kids raised their hands.

None of them waited to be called on.

"Do the dishes!"

"Fix something!"

"Bring her flowers!"

"Tell her she's beautiful!"

I grinned sheepishly. "Thanks, everyone. I'll try some of those things."

The puppets moved on to the next topic, and Brit leaned over. "Make her dinner and bring her flowers. When my dad does that, it makes my mom so happy she's in a good mood for a week!"

"Noted. Thanks."

"Oh, and clean up your mess. Otherwise, she'll forget the nice things when she's cleaning the mess."

"You are wise beyond your years," I said and thanked her. "I'll be back," I whispered.

I slipped out and hustled to the nurse's station. Jared was right on time and chatting up two of the younger nurses. I slapped him on the shoulder and lifted my chin to the ladies. "Need me to take out the trash?"

They giggled, and I grinned. Jared's expression turned from flirtatious to annoyed, but I didn't care. I didn't need or particularly want his friendship.

I led him to the break room and quickly changed into the mascot costume. Jared was a college kid whose aunt worked in the Edge's front office. He was pursuing a degree in physical education, so this job was a good fit for him both because of the schedule and the opportunities to work with kids.

And he was good with kids. A natural. When I got promoted, one of my asks was that he remain my handler. Ridgie Number One's current handler wasn't happy being demoted to Number Three, but I needed someone with me who was comfortable and animated and kind to children, even if he was sometimes a stick in the mud when it came to rules.

The puppet show had just ended when I entered the room, and Jared corralled the kids into a semicircle that enabled me to easily move from one to the next. He passed out mini Ridgie bears with royal blue bows tied around their necks.

I was glad to see Vali had made it to the show. She was newish, having started treatments about a month ago, eight years old, and hard of hearing. I'd attended many of Penny's American Sign Language classes for kids at the library over the years—most recently as Ridgie, of course— and asked Penny to tutor me privately in ASL so that I could communicate better with kids who were deaf and hard of hearing.

And since Ridgie couldn't speak out loud, it was pretty special that Vali—and others like her—got a little bit of extra communication.

Hi, I signed. *Are you having a good day?*

Her eyes lit up, and she straightened in her chair. Her mother fussed over her, readjusting her blanket.

Better today. And you?

I can't complain. I pointed to Jared. *Except about this guy. He snorts way too loudly.*

She giggled. *Can you hug me? I left my teddy bear in my bed, and this new bear is too small.*

I stepped closer, bent down, and held my arms open. Vali reached up and wrapped her thin arms around my waist.

She hung on longer than usual, and a muscle in my back began to spasm. I'd have to spend a little more time on it in the gym later, but I wasn't about to push her away. My rule was, I don't let go first.

When she slid her arms back into her lap, I patted her on the head. *See you next week?* I signed.

Vali nodded. *I'll still be here.* She sniffed and rubbed her eyes. *I'll probably be here until I die.*

"Valentina!" her mother gasped. She skirted around to the front of the chair and signed. *You are not going to die. The treatments are working. You will beat this! No more negative talk!*

But I'm so tired, Mama. And the doctor said it would be a long battle.

They were both crying now, daughter in her mother's embrace. Not for the first time, I was glad they couldn't see my face.

Because we all knew the truth: Lots of kids *didn't* beat cancer.

What would I have said to Mindy if she'd said something like that? Probably something similar to what Vali's mother signed.

Maybe I could give her an incentive. I placed my paw on her shoulder.

Her mother backed away, and I began to sign in fervor.

You hang in there. Be strong. When you feel better, I'll get you and your family special tickets to an Edge game. Just tell me when. You can hang out with me before the game, and I'll get you free snacks. Deal?

She laughed. *Deal.*

I squeezed her shoulder and patted her mom's back, hoping I'd left them encouraged and hopeful. I wasn't doing my job if I didn't.

Brit had positioned herself at the end of the line. When I reached her, she pressed an envelope into my hand.

"It's an invitation to my birthday party," she told Jared, who took it from me. He opened it and pulled out a pink rectangle. "For Ridgie and your friend Monty." She giggled. "It'll be here, after activity time, in a couple weeks. My little sister misses you since she's in daycare now and you always come during the day. Mom is letting her stay home from school that day."

I hadn't ever considered that the siblings would need a visit from the mascot. I nodded my oversize head emphatically and clapped my hands, ending with a thumbs-up so she'd know I'd put it on my calendar.

As I drove to Mountainview Manor after the visit, I thought about all the ideas I wanted to propose for Ridgie. More community service, more social media, more goofy meet-and-greets. Photo ops and fundraisers with the other pro sports mascots in the area. We had the power to make people smile, and I wanted to expand our audience and fanbase. If it wasn't in the budget, I'd finance it. I'd even pay Jared more than what he earned from the team.

I needed to do everything in my power to put more happiness in the world.

Because the world could be a very sad place.

And if we weren't laughing, we were crying.

Well, maybe that was just me.

CHAPTER 9
Tasha

A week after the flare-up, I was feeling great and back to my normal schedule, which meant on Tuesday at 5:20 a.m., I was chopping vegetables for the slow cooker before my shift at the Coffee Loft. Parfait had followed me to the kitchen, mewing his demands to be fed. I dished out some kitty salmon, cued my phone up to my morning playlist—on low volume so it wouldn't wake Monty—and got to work.

I hummed along to the upbeat music, dicing carrots and cucumbers, chopping zucchini. Did I want to add steak or chicken to this one?

Definitely steak. I'd had enough chicken in my Recovery Soup last week. I set my knife down and turned toward the fridge.

"Oof! Sorry, Barfy!"

"Mew!" he protested.

"Well, don't try to trip me on the way to the fridge!" I stooped down to scratch his chin and run my hands along the sleek striped fur on his back. "Who's the ugly old kitty?" I asked in a deep, silly yet condescending talking-to-pets voice.

"It's you! You're so ugly. Yes you are, yes you are!" I touched my nose to his as he purred like a car motor. "Old fat ugly kitty!"

"His name is *Parfait,* and he's not fat *or* ugly." Monty's groggy voice carried over the kitchen island to where I was squatting on the floor.

I scooped the cat into my arms and stood to face him, momentarily frozen as I took in his morning Monty-ness. Tousled hair, sleepy eyes, minty fresh vapors strong enough to inhale two feet away. Fitted tank over his monstrous muscles.

I raised my eyebrows and glared at him while I tried to get my words to work. What was wrong with me?

I was watching too many cheesy Christmas in July lovey-dovey movies, that's what. Had to be.

I swallowed and lifted my chin. "So? He has no idea what I'm saying, do you, boy?" I rubbed my face in Parfait's neck, inciting deeper purrs. "He loves me. Always has. Right, Barfy?" I kissed him on the head between his ears. "Good boy!"

"Hmm." He blinked away his heavy-lidded gaze and cleared his throat. "Sounds like I need to have a chat with him about wolves in sheep's clothing." Monty's grogginess fell away a little bit with each word, and by the end of the sentence, his normal, arrogant tone had replaced the kinder, just-woke-up voice.

"Aren't you supposed to be moved out of here by now?" I asked. He skirted around the island and reached out to rub Parfait's head. His pale toes peeked out of his beat-up discount store fuzzy slippers like a turtle poking its head out of its shell. The sight of them took me back in time to when we were inseparable, both irking me and warming my heart.

Why had he kept them all these years when he could afford the best slippers money could buy?

"Beck said by the end of the week. There was a delay on permitting to knock down the wall around the toilet. They'll be starting that today." He held out his arms, and Parfait scrambled into them.

Good. The clock was running down on this roommate thing. Then I could blast my playlist again.

I washed my hands and collected the steak and a homemade gluten-free marinade from the fridge. Monty's gaze never left my knife as I cubed the steak.

"You don't have to wait until I'm finished," I said. "There's plenty of room in here for you to make your protein shake."

He shrugged. "I figured I'd just stop by the Coffee Loft once it opened."

I pressed my lips together, wondering why he would bother with the morning rush when he could make it himself here in the peace and quiet. I much preferred to drink my coffee at home.

I glanced at the mug of pumpkin spice that I'd been sipping. Yeah. Much better to drink here in peace than at the café.

But to each his own.

In a rare burst of kindness that even surprised me, I said, "If you come over with me when I leave, I can make it for you before the rush."

Monty lifted his head, and his eyes locked on mine. His lips parted, then closed, as if he'd decided not to say what was on his mind.

"Or not." I shrugged at his rejection. Wasn't the first time. Wouldn't be the last. Not like it was an olive branch or anything. I was just trying to save the guy the time and hassle he was setting himself up for.

"Maybe another time." He avoided my gaze and slid off the stool, setting the cat on the floor. "I, uh, have some work I was planning to do there today."

Work? What kind of work did he do?

"For the charity," he added. He must've read my thoughts. "Several Edge players want to donate to the auction this year, so I need to figure out what I want from them."

I'd forgotten about his charity. Each year, his parents held a Valentine charity gala to raise money for whatever organization was trending and needing financial support. Several years ago, Monty added a silent auction to the event to raise money for the kids in the oncology units at local hospitals. This past year, Penny had played her harp at the event, and Xavier had attended with several of his team-mates. They'd left inspired and wanted to contribute. Some of them had even joined Monty during his Ridgie visits at the hospitals.

I didn't say anything as I opened the drawer that held the various types of kitchen bags and wraps. What was there to say? I couldn't razz him over that. I dumped the meat into a large Ziploc bag and poured in enough marinade to coat the pieces. I'd run home from work on my break and add them to the pot once the marinade had time to seep in.

There were a lot of perks to living so close to work.

Montgomery Biddington being within walking distance wasn't one of them.

I cleaned up my mess and washed my hands again.

5:57.

"See ya," I said with a wave, grabbing my purse as I

rushed out the door. I didn't turn around to see if he waved back. I took the stairs faster than usual, my heart pounding.

Why was it pounding?

No need to dwell on that. I took a few long breaths as I exited the building and crossed the parking lot to the strip of buildings that lined Main Street.

I punched in the code and slipped inside the back door of the old saloon-turned-cafe and into the Coffee Loft's kitchen just as the big digital clock over the bulletin board changed from 5:59 to 6:00.

Right on time. I hung my purse on the coat rack, tied on my apron, and pushed through the swinging door to the front of the shop.

With both Penny and Gabby cutting their shifts to support their guys during the playoffs, Jannell had to hire on additional staff. Betty was one of those new hires, a mother of three in her early thirties, back into the workforce after being a stay-at-home mom for eleven years. Her three kids were spending the summer with her husband's parents in New England, and she'd wanted something to do during the day so she wouldn't miss them so much.

Betty was one of those people who made you feel at ease the moment you met her, and by the end of the first week, she'd eased into working at the Coffee Loft like she'd been here all along. She quickly learned all the specialty drinks, could fix any tech problem that arose, and upsold at least half of all the customer purchases, offering shots of espresso or a cake pop to go, or the addition of food-grade essential oils into non-coffee drinks. She was brilliant, likable, and most important, not annoying.

True to his word, Monty arrived just after Jannell unlocked the door and entered the queue, which was already about twenty people deep with our morning regulars. Betty and I worked the registers, writing orders on cups while Jannell, her husband, Marcus, and their daughter, Marie, made the drinks.

The way the line went, Monty was next up for Betty, but he gestured for the man behind him to go ahead. I handed my customer her receipt, and Monty approached my register.

"Your usual?" I asked.

He nodded. "And a Lofty-size pumpkin spice blah-te for Nana."

I tapped in the extra item, surprised at his change of plans. "I thought you were staying here to work today?"

"I'll be back. Nana's therapy was rescheduled to 7 a.m., so I thought I'd soften the blow with one of your poisonous coffees to sip on all day."

I rolled my eyes. "They're not poison. There are a lot of health benefits to coffee. Coffee beans are actually—"

"I know, I know. Coffee cherries. From the coffee cherry plant." He waved his hand flippantly. "Antioxidant, heart healthy, can prevent cognitive decline, et cetera et cetera. Whatever. There are better ways to stimulate the brain in the morning."

Yeah, if it was only my brain that needed stimulating in the morning. But I wasn't about to say *that* out loud. Monty didn't need to know anything more than he'd already gleaned about my digestive system's inner workings. He paid for the order and moved down the counter.

The next few hours flew by, and I found myself glancing at the door every time it chimed to signal a new customer.

Astoria Brewer arrived during one of the short lulls after the initial rush. She stepped up to my register, and I greeted her warmly.

"Hey, Astoria! What's new in the hockey world?"

She grinned. Hockey was one of her favorite subjects. She'd played on the Olympic team, and her dad was an NHL legend who'd played for both the Voltage and the Edge. We'd known each other since we were kids.

"Lots of fan hearts will be breaking this week. Restricted free agents can start signing contracts July first," she reported.

"What does that mean for the Edge?" I asked, genuinely curious.

She frowned. "We'll likely lose a favorite or two that are worth more than what the team can pay them. Including Dean Hathaway. They haven't been able to agree on numbers with him yet, and other teams are calling with some significantly high offers."

"But he's the captain," I said. "Wouldn't they try everything they could to keep him?"

"Maybe if they'd won the Cup." She shrugged. "But they didn't, so they'll be aggressive in making changes over the summer to build a team that's better prepared to beat Miami and whatever other teams might be in their way."

"Oh wow," I said. I hoped none of *my* favorites were leaving.

"Don't worry about Xavier or Noel," she said. "They're safe. And so is Brendan."

I let out a sigh of relief. "How can you be sure?" I asked.

"I can't tell you. But don't worry, okay?" I nodded. She handed me an envelope branded to Pasta Nacht's. She co-owned the restaurant with her dad.

"What's this?" I asked.

"A gift card and an apology. I heard about your, ah, *reaction* to our cross-contaminated fettucine alfredo. I feel awful. I know the promise of more uncontaminated food can't make up for the agony you were in, but I hope you'll give us a chance to make it right."

My cheeks flamed. Who had told her about that?

I tried to hand it back to her, but she wouldn't take it. "I'm fine," I insisted. "It happens. No need for this. Can we never talk about it again?"

Astoria tilted her head and tucked a long blond wave behind her ear. "Only if you keep it."

I sighed. "Fine. Thank you." I slid the offending gift into my apron pocket. "How did you find out, anyway?"

She glanced to her left and right, then leaned in over the register. "Penny called Brenna and asked her to check on you, to see if you were at work Monday morning. I happened to be here in line with Brenna when she called, and I heard the whole conversation." Her eyes widened as she realized what she'd said. "I wasn't trying to be nosy or overhear, promise! And I haven't said a word to anyone. My nephew has food allergies; he's the reason Brewski's turned allergy-free. I saw him react once and—" She blinked as her eyes began to water. "I never want that—or anything like it—for any of my customers. *Especially* friends and family. You trust us. We broke that trust."

I sighed. Small-town life. Everyone knew someone who knew your business. "Happens all the time," I said. "You can't ever make a kitchen one hundred percent safe because you can't control what's on the hands or clothing of your employees. But I appreciate the gesture. Thank you."

She nodded. "I know. I hate that for you. And for Benji. And for everyone else affected by it."

"Can I get you your usual?" I asked, anxious to change the subject before any of my co-workers overheard.

"Umm ..." Her gaze landed on the framed chalk menu between my register and Betty's. "Yes, but a small. I'd also like to try your Summertime Splash."

I rang in her salted caramel Frodoughchino, a frozen coffee inspired by our salted caramel doughnut, and the new Citrus Twist, a lemon-lime juicer infused with one hundred percent certified pure citrus essential oils. She paid for the order and scooted down the counter.

How embarrassing.

The door chimed again, and Liam Brewer entered. *So many Brewers in this town!* As a Palmer, it was annoying. But the Brewers were all so *nice*, it was hard to dislike them.

Liam turned his head, scanning the tables as he walked up to the counter. I stepped back so Betty could take his order, but he walked straight to me.

"Is Monty here?" he asked, pointing upward to the loft seating area on the second level.

I shook my head. "No, but he's due back soon. Said he was coming to work after Nana Booboo's therapy."

He pressed his lips together and nodded as he pulled out his wallet. "I have some bad news for him. What can I get him to soften the blow?"

My heart rate kicked up. "What bad news?" I might not like Monty, but bad news was never a good thing. "About the house?"

Liam rubbed the back of his neck. "Beck found a bad pipe."

"So? She can replace it, right?"

He shook his head no, then nodded yes. "It's a little more complicated than that."

What he wasn't saying was that Monty probably wasn't moving out next week. "How bad is it?" I crossed my arms over my chest. Liam was an architect, and if he was worried, I was worried.

The door chimed, and Monty strode in, straight toward us. "I got here as soon as I could," he said. "What's the issue?"

Liam looked from him to me and back to Monty. "The whole house needs re-piping. And we can't start until at least September first because the plans and all the permitting for something this extensive have to be approved through the town's Historic Preservation Board. I'm sorry, Monty. But it's good she found this now, before the winter. Those pipes are in pretty bad condition. They've been rotting for decades."

No no no. Another two-plus months of living with this guy?

I could kick him out.

Couldn't I?

I totally could.

But that would be mean.

I probably shouldn't.

But ... I looked at Monty. His eyes were fixed on me, waiting for my answer.

I closed my eyes and dragged my hands down my face. "Fine," I acquiesced. "Stay as long as you need to."

He let out a long breath and nodded and, for once, didn't add a snappy or insulting retort. I rang up their drinks and handed Liam his receipt.

How was I going to get through almost three more months of Monty?

CHAPTER 10
Monty

J annell handed me the small iced chocolate Liam guilt-bought for me, and I followed him up the winding iron steps to the loft above the café.

He explained the difficulties and intricacies of re-piping a historic home like Nana's, and thirty minutes later I was driving back to the rehab facility to break the news to her that she wouldn't have a home to come home to until fall. It had been almost two months now since her stroke, and I wanted to bring her home more than anything.

I found her in the dining room, sitting across the table from ninety-one-year-old Clarice, our town's retired librarian. The two were deep into a game of Rummy 500 when I approached.

"Hey, Nana." I dropped a kiss to her cheek and pulled a chair from the next table over and straddled it backwards. I winked at her and leaned toward Clarice like I was making a play to look at her hand.

She smacked my shoulder good-naturedly and grinned

widely, her eyes closing and almost disappearing in her wrinkled face. "Monty, how many times do I have to tell you cheating won't even help your Nana beat me?"

Nana humphed. I knew for a fact she lost on purpose because she legit beat me every time we played in her room. She spoke slowly, her speech still slightly impeded from the stroke. "N-nope, there's no hope for me. This old b-brain just isn't what it used to be."

Clarice laid down a set of aces. "Sixty points! Doesn't take brains to get a good hand." She wrote her score on the notepad in front of her. "But maybe next time don't put an ace in the discard pile if there's already one there."

I couldn't stop my lips from twitching, so I pressed my teeth together and covered my mouth with my hand, thinker-style, and pretended that was the best advice I'd ever heard.

"Brilliant point, Clarice," I agreed, stroking my chin. "Nana, we'll have to work on your Rummy skills next time I come by."

She heaved a sigh as she drew a card from the deck on her good side. Her weaker hand, positioned against a small rice-filled pillow, held her cards. Thanks to the best speech therapist money could buy, her stuttering and pauses were almost completely gone. I was so proud of her perseverance and progress. "I suppose it c-couldn't hurt." She added the card to her hand and set down the king of diamonds. Two cards down was the queen of the same suit, and three over from that was the jack. "How is our dear Parfait le Chat? Have you found a way to sneak him in to see me yet?"

I shook my head as Clarice gleefully swept up the cards. "Not yet. He's good. But I have some bad news about the house."

"Bad news? What could be worse than me losing to Clarice *again?*"

"Jack, queen, king, plus I'll take that five of clubs to finish this set." One at a time, her mouth spreading wider with each card, she placed the three, four, five, six, and seven of clubs on the table. "Fifty-five points!"

"Hmm." Nana frowned and slid the top card from the deck. "Ha!" She placed it on the table and slowly used her left hand to extract two cards from her right hand. "Three tens! That's … ten, twenty, thirty points!"

"Glad to see your math is still sharp, Nancy. Now we just need to work on your observation skills." Clarice spoke with an air of authority as she recorded Nana's points. She pointed to me. "What's your bad news, Monty?"

I turned to Nana. "Beck's crew was re-piping the bathroom and discovered the pipes were significantly rotted. She was going to just replace the ones that were bad but decided to take a look at other piping throughout the house that was relatively accessible. It's not good, Nana. She said we're one or two winters away from a disaster of epic proportions."

"Pipe-ageddon!" Clarice shouted, then whistled. "You have the dough to fix it, right?"

I nodded. "It's going to be expensive, but the worst part is since the house is a designated historic home, permitting is going to be a process. We'll have to get the approval of the Historic Preservation Board. They meet once a month, and a review can take time. And even if it didn't, Beck has another project coming up with her plumber and can't start on our house until September first at the earliest."

Nana tilted her head in thought. "We've dealt with them before. Not so bad. I like it here. It's kind of like an all-inclusive resort. Plus, I need to keep Clarice busy. She's *old*, you know. Might not have much time left."

My eyes widened, but the ladies just laughed.

"Oh, Monty, don't look so scandalized," Clarice scolded, taking a card off the deck and discarding it right away. "I've outlived everyone in my family, including my kids. And some of their kids, sadly. I'm ready to go whenever the good Lord takes me."

"Hopefully not before the end of this game." Nana took the card she discarded and set down the other three jacks. "We're almost tied up!"

"Not quite," Clarice corrected. "Plus, I'm one hundred twenty-five points ahead from the last two rounds."

Nana shrugged and shot me a grin. "I haven't beaten her yet!"

"We-ell," Clarice dragged the word out as she considered Nana's observation. Ever the upbeat encourager, she softened. "You're doing okay, considering your stroke wasn't that long ago. You'll probably win a round soon."

"I appreciate the sentiment," Nana replied. I shifted in my seat so I could see her hand as she took the top card from the deck, which she immediately placed in the discard train, missing the opportunity to set out a five-card run.

This time I couldn't hide my smile as Clarice swept it up mirthfully and laid out the rest of her cards with a flourish, ending the game and leaving Nana with almost as many points in her hands as her total on the scorepad.

"One more round?" Nana asked.

"Hold on, doing the math." Clarice hummed as she counted the value of her cards and Nana's and did the calculations. "Yes, I'm afraid so." She chuckled. "Just one should do it. I'm ten points from five hundred. You, on the other hand ..."

"No need to tell me how bad it is," Nana interjected, using her good hand to push her cards to the center of the table.

"Can I shuffle?" I asked.

Both ladies nodded, and I gathered up the cards, pulling them into a tight pile. Nana had taught me to shuffle when I was a preschooler, and by kindergarten I was executing moves like a Vegas dealer. Once, I considered moving there to do just that. But I couldn't imagine living that far from Nana, especially after my grandfather died.

She'd taken care of me my whole life, and I'd promised her when I was young that I would take care of her when she was old and in a wheelchair.

How prophetic those words had been.

A few years ago, her sweet tooth had caught up with her, and complications with her diabetes made it too hard for her to walk. Installing an elevator in the house had been a Band-Aid to the problem, but even having to use a wheelchair hadn't dissuaded her from her desserts. One good thing about her being here at the facility was that all the desserts they served her were sugar-free, and the security made it nearly impossible to sneak in sugar-rich foods. Even birthday cakes had to be preapproved and monitored by staff so that the recipient didn't inadvertently—or purposefully—share it with a patient with dietary restrictions.

I handed the shuffled deck to Clarice.

"So," Nana said as Clarice dealt the cards. "I assume you'll be staying with Tasha until the work is done? She doesn't have a new roommate lined up, right?"

I shook my head. "Nope, she doesn't. She wanted to keep

the extra room open for Penny to stay over when Xavier travels. He said I can stay at his place on those nights, if I want. I might just sleep on the sofa, though."

"They might like their girls' nights male-free," Clarice said.

I hadn't thought about that. "Good point."

Clarice beamed. "Just common sense."

CHAPTER 11
Tasha

By the grace of God, July flew by. Monty did his best to avoid the kitchen when I was in it, but I'd often spy him taste-testing my Crock-Pot creations when he thought I wasn't looking. With him eating half the leftovers, I had to cook more often, but I didn't mind.

It gave me more chances to experiment. Monty made up for eating my food by regularly having groceries delivered, which decreased my trips to the wholesale club and farmers' market, and there were always more than enough ingredients in the orders for whatever I wanted to make. I suspected he'd raided my cookbook. How else would he have known to order some of the obscure items I regularly kept on hand, like specific gluten-free snacks and rice paper wraps?

One Saturday in August, I was in the kitchen chopping veggies when he walked through the door juggling multiple empty boxes I'd just unpacked and set in the hall for my next trip down to the dumpster. A huge smile was plastered on his face. He let the boxes fall to the carpet as Parfait ran to greet him. He scooped up the cat and carried him to the bar that separated the kitchen from the living area.

"*Do not* let him on the counter," I warned. The cat liked to drink from the running faucet. I'd given up trying to train him not to, but I drew the line when his fluff was close enough to shed on my food.

"Wouldn't dream of it," Monty said in the bored tone he liked to use with me.

"And *why* did you bring the trash back in?"

"I had an idea for a project. What are you making today?"

Monty was always collecting odds and ends the kids at the children's hospitals could use in arts and crafts projects. "I thought I'd try out a chicken curry recipe. One that's not too spicy."

"Sounds good." He tipped his chin toward the bundle of carrots next to the cutting mat. "You ever going to open up that restaurant you dreamed about when we were kids?"

I stiffened. That dream had died long ago, and it hurt to think about it.

"Palmer City has enough restaurants," I said tightly, increasing the pressure on the knife. A carrot tip went flying across the counter, causing Parfait to paw at Monty's arms to let him go so he could chase it. But Monty held on, his ridiculously big biceps twitching ever so slightly.

I looked away. From the muscles, and from the man whose pitying gaze was fixed on me.

"None of the restaurants in Palmer City are *safe* restaurants, though," he said softly.

I shrugged. "The world isn't safe. When my time is up, it's up. Like I told Astoria last month, no restaurant can be completely *safe.*"

"But the food can. Have you thought about opening a meal prep service?"

Had I thought about it? Only every other day.

I shrugged again. "Yeah, but I don't have the startup cash. Never will."

I pushed the diced carrots to the side of the mat and snuck a glance up at him. He looked thoughtful, watching me as I pulled the chives into my cutting space. I hoped that meant he was done speaking.

When I got to chopping the fresh coriander, I couldn't take the silence anymore. "What?" I asked him.

"Huh?"

"You've been staring at me."

He adjusted Parfait so the cat's front paws were over his shoulder. "I like watching you work. You're so good at it."

Compliments from Montgomery Biddington were few and far between.

I almost smiled.

But my cheeks heated, and that was enough. He couldn't know that the compliment affected me deeply.

"Thanks," I squeaked out, my head still down.

He was quiet for a few beats, then blurted out, "I want to invest in your business!"

My head jerked up. "What business?"

"Your safe meal prep business. You have to do it, Tasha. People need it. And you're the perfect person for the job. I bet you could put together the most amazing sugar-free dishes and desserts for Nana that wouldn't send her A1C through the roof."

I laughed. He really had no clue what it was like for anyone who didn't have money coming out of their ears. "Montgomery, I can't *ever* own a business. I need a job with insurance. Right now, my only dream is to pay my medical bills so I'm not dependent on my parents forever. They work too hard to work for my digestive problems."

The look that crossed his face was one of confusion, then pity. "Well," he said, "if that isn't one of the most depressing things I've ever heard."

"Yep, it stinks," I said through my teeth. "But I don't want your pity."

"I don't pity you," he said in a surprised tone. "I admire you."

"Yeah, sure." I waited for the rest of the statement, the part where he would leave a jab that was worse than the first part.

But it didn't come. I continued prepping the food for the Crock-Pot and tried to ignore the tension in the air.

"What if we were partners?" he said slowly. "I can invest the initial startup costs, and then, once your business takes off, you'll be making enough that you won't need insurance and can pay cash for all your expenses."

My heart warmed at his confidence that I could ever make enough money to cover my expenses. I had more medical debt than college debt at this point, and the only way I'd ever erase it was to marry a millionaire.

I shook my head. "It won't be enough."

"How much money could you possibly need? Let me take care of it. It's the least I can do for you letting me live here."

I gaped at him. "I'm not a charity case! I don't want to be another of your pet projects."

Monty set his shoulders back in defense. "My Cheerdanas have made me enough money to retire *and* fund Christmas gifts for pediatric oncology units at three hospitals." He spoke plainly, not bragging. I could tell he was both proud of his achievement and wanted to keep private about its success.

I set the knife down and met his gaze. His sweat-wicking, stretchy, and easily folded bandanas were perfect for cheer athletes and stayed put through the most grueling practices. "That's wonderful for you. I love that you've made your own money and aren't dependent on your parents. That must be ..." I swallowed and fought back the lump forming in my throat. "Such a relief and ... freedom."

I averted my gaze, not wanting any more of his concerned look casting on me. Some people were born with silver spoons in their mouths. Others weren't. It didn't matter that my ancestors had founded this town. Their fortune was gone, and I was on my own.

"I can help you get that, too," he said softly. "What's the point of having all this money if I can't help my friends?"

He considered us friends? I turned away, not wanting him to see the water that was rimming my eyes. I walked to the fridge and did some rearranging, calling over my shoulder in as cool of a voice as I could muster. "I appreciate your offer. I do. It's generous and kind. But I just can't accept."

"If you change your mind—"

"I won't!"

I closed the fridge and straightened up, setting my shoulders back and taking a deep breath, steeling myself to continue the conversation.

But Monty wasn't at the bar when I returned to my cutting station.

And, if I admitted it to myself, I was kind of disappointed he'd given up on persuading me so quickly.

CHAPTER 12
Monty

Mid-August

I shook my head and pulled Parfait into my lap. It was just us in the apartment. Tasha had been in Europe for the past week, celebrating Penny's birthday at Xavier's family's castle. They'd invited me, too, but I declined, citing Ridgie engagements. I could have rescheduled them, but the truth was, Tasha needed space from me. I could sense it from the ways she went out of her way to avoid me and barely spoke to me directly at FireVolts practice.

She was due home tonight, and I'd reached out to Fyvie from the bakery to help me make gluten-free dairy-free alfredo that would be ready when Tasha arrived. I figured she'd have to be starving. What airline could accommodate her food issues? And if they could, was the food even edible?

Fyvie had moved here from Ireland permanently a few years ago after a stint with her college's exchange program. She ran the bakery now, and though that was primarily breads and sweets, they always had a booth at community

events, offering various savory items and hand-crafted choco-
lates. I knew she could make a mean shepherd's pie. Surely,
she could follow Tasha's recipe, so I hired her to come to the
apartment and help me create it.

"Ye couldn't've done this yerself?" She stared me down,
wiping sweat from her brow and winding a loose strand of
curly auburn hair back into the messy bun atop her head.

"Why take the chance?" I needed this to be perfect the
first time. I only got one shot.

She shrugged. "Ay. Well, 'appy to take yer money." She
patted the counter. "It's good ter go."

She'd left an hour ago, right after we'd added the noodles
into the mixture of plant butter, oat milk, and broth. The
trick was not to add them too soon or they'd become over-
large and mushy.

My phone buzzed. I pulled it out of my pocket and swiped
to open the international chat app.

The message was from Penny. *They're on their way.*

I'd asked her to text me when her parents and Tasha left
the airport so I'd have an ETA. I thanked her and dumped
Parfait off my lap and onto the adjacent sofa cushion. "Sorry,
boy."

Originally, I'd planned a big, fancy welcome-home
dinner at the dining room table. But after I'd set it up, I
realized it might send the wrong message, and I didn't need
Tasha hating me again, especially when I felt like we'd made
great strides to repairing our friendship over the last two
months.

Instead, I'd arranged two place settings at the bar and
trimmed a dozen peach carnations, her favorite, arranging
them inside a large mason jar I'd found in the pantry.

Informal, but slightly zhuzhed up to indicate this wasn't

any old dinner. I was glad she was back, and not just for coaching reasons.

I'd missed her.

I would never admit that to her, but Parfait and I had felt her absence. While she was gone, I also had a cleaning service come in and detail the common areas and bathrooms. I appreciated her taking in Parfait and me, even though I was the last person she'd ever wanted to room with.

When her key clicked in the lock, I pulled Parfait back onto my lap and pretended to scroll my phone, looking as bored as I could muster.

"Hey," I said as she pulled her suitcase inside and closed the door. "Dinner's on the counter."

I raised my eyelids only enough to catch her expression. Surprise crossed her features, but there was something else there, too.

Exhaustion.

"Thanks," she murmured, turning toward her room and stopping abruptly. "What"—she pointed past the dining table to the collection of boxes stacked in the corner—"is that?"

"That," I announced proudly, "is Parfait's new cat castle."

"You made it out of product boxes from Costco?" she asked, bewildered.

"I did. Thirty-seven of them." The boxes stretched out from the corner and lined the back and side walls for about three feet in each direction.

She blinked at the structure and sighed. "It's … nice."

I pushed Parfait off my lap and stood. He mewed in protest. "Sorry, boy." I crossed the room in long strides to get ahead of her. "Stop."

Tasha narrowed her eyes. "I don't have the energy to fight with you. Please, move."

I shook my head. "Eat. I'll shlep this to your room. Want it on the chest at the foot of your bed?"

She pressed her lips together, considering, then nodded. "Yeah, thanks."

When she let go of the handle, I stuck my arm out for her backpack. She shrugged it off her shoulder and turned toward the kitchen.

After setting her suitcase on the bench and the backpack on her desk chair, I joined her at the bar. A scoop of fettuccine was on her plate, but she wasn't eating.

"It's safe, I promise." I slid onto the barstool next to her. "And Fyvie oversaw the whole process so I wouldn't mess it up."

"Fyvie was here?"

I nodded, spooning a heaping portion of noodles and cheese onto my plate.

"Did she bring the flowers, too?"

I shook my head. "Nope, that was me." Taking advice from Britlynne, but I left that part out.

Tasha regarded me curiously, and her cheeks pinked just enough for me to notice. Then she gave a half smile.

Would you look at that? I thought. I'd have to let Brit know the flowers worked.

Tasha turned back to her food and picked up her fork. Slowly, she wound the long noodles around the tines. "Penny's pregnant."

I swallowed my food and watched her carefully, not wanting to say the wrong thing. She was hunched, shoulders slumped. Her words carried a happy tone, but her body language told a different story.

"So, you're going to be an auntie," I said lightly. "Congrats."

"Thanks." She brought the fork into her mouth and chewed her noodles for what felt like a long time.

I did some mental calculations. "May?"

"May you what?"

"No, May. The baby's due in May?"

"Oh. Yeah. Right during the playoffs. They didn't plan it."

I believed that. I hadn't been in the hockey world long, but even I knew players and their wives did their best to plan summer births to avoid the playoff madness.

"She won't be able to travel to away games if the Edge make the playoffs this year."

I wound up a section of noodles for another bite. "And there's a good chance of Xavier missing the birth if they do."

"Yup." She popped the P. "But Auntie Tasha will be here. Or wherever I'm living at that point."

"You won't be here?" I asked.

She shrugged. "Depends if I find another roommate. But I was thinking it might be better if I moved home. Not having to pay rent is helping me make a dent in my bills."

"College loans?"

"Those are almost paid off. It's the medical bills. As long as I can manage to stay out of the hospital, I should catch up in about two or three years."

I was sure my eyes bugged out. "Two or three *years?*"

"What can I say?" She shrugged. "This body"—she used her free hand to make a sweeping motion from head to toe—"is expensive to maintain."

I struggled not to show my utter surprise. "And that's with insurance?"

"Yup. Mine from the school and my parents'. But that runs out the day I turn twenty-six."

Which wasn't that far away. I didn't know what to say, so I took another bite of noodles.

"Thanks for making dinner," she said. "That was nice of you."

I nodded. "You're welcome. Your recipes are really great." That gave me an idea. "What about a cookbook?"

"Huh?"

"If you can't open a restaurant or meal-prep service, what about writing a cookbook?"

The corner of her mouth lifted. "What, and sell all my secrets?"

I nudged her side lightly with my elbow. "I bet it'd be a bestseller."

Tasha's lips pulled into a full smile, but it didn't reach her eyes. "I love the confidence you have in me."

Her smile fell, so I spoke candidly to entice it back. "I've known you almost our whole lives, Tasha. You've always accomplished every goal you've set. Why *wouldn't* I have confidence in you?"

The smile didn't return, but she lifted her noodled fork and stabbed the air in my direction. "You forget I lack the trust fund to get any monetary dreams off the ground, and I don't have any connections in any industry—except cheer—to even have a chance."

"I can handle that part. Honest. And—" I nudged her again. "I'd work for free."

She stiffened. "I told you already that I don't want to be your charity project."

"But—" I tried to think quickly. "I'm not supporting *you*, per se. I'm helping to get a service or a tool into the hands of people whose lives your knowledge could improve. Why *wouldn't* you say yes to an opportunity that could help thousands of people better their lives?"

I had her there.

Tasha gathered the last of her noodles and twirled them onto her fork. "I wouldn't even know how to start."

I pointed to her recipe binder on the far counter, nestled between the microwave and knife block. "Type that up. Take pictures of your food. Put it all in a doc. Then give it to me on a thumb drive. I'll keep it safe and make sure only the right hands have access." I spoke that last sentence in a teasing tone, hoping to lighten the very big offer I was making.

"You're serious?"

"Cross my heart."

"And hope to die?" she filled in with just a smidge of snark.

"Let's not go *that* far." I ran my fingers through my hair and made a show of patting it all into place. "The world needs Montgomery Biddington alive and in studly form, thank you very much."

Tasha rolled her eyes, and I let out an internal sigh as she slid off her stool and carried her plate to the sink. She hadn't said yes, but she hadn't said no, either. Not *really*.

"Are you done?" she asked, turning the water on and rinsing the fake cheese off her plate.

I looked down at my dinner. One forkful left. I twisted it up and handed her the plate. Parfait hopped up onto his vacated stool and leapt onto the counter, beelining straight for the running water.

"Your cat has the rudest habits." She took the plates to the dishwasher and loaded them in with her fork.

I joined her in the kitchen and slid my fork into the utensils basket. "I got the cleanup. Go wash off the airplane ick and get to bed. We have Saturday practice tomorrow."

She groaned. "Right. At least it's at noon. Jet lag is going to be awful."

"Lucky for us, the team can nearly coach itself."

"Nearly?"

"They could probably stunt okay without us. But no one can choreograph like you, and none of those tumblers could touch me on the floor."

"Yet. It won't be long before the students surpass their teachers. Like we did ours." Tasha gave a small smile. "Thanks for dinner, Monty."

She turned and set off toward her room, leaving me stunned.

Tasha hadn't called me Monty in *years*. Did she even realize?

Probably not. She was beyond exhausted. Her brain likely reverted to its original setting.

I rubbed the back of my neck and watched her until she closed the door. My mind started to spin with ideas for how I could keep up the level of camaraderie we had tonight.

I missed the old us. For sixteen seasons, we were stunt partners and best friends. When I chose Gabby as my stunt partner over Tasha, I never for a minute even dreamed I'd lose her friendship. Our rivalry heated up after that, and it was in the process of trying to outdo each other that she'd gotten hurt. Her stunt partner hadn't known her like I had. Couldn't anticipate her moves and quirks like I could, and he hadn't had the experience to improvise quickly if something was off.

All these years, I blamed myself for Tasha's fall and subsequent departure from competition. I knew she blamed me, too. And it was easier for both of us to act like it didn't matter.

But I knew it did. To both of us.

I wasn't sure if I could ever make it up to her. Not with investing financially or even helping her coach her team to another championship. But I sure would try with all my resources—and heart—to get my old bestie back.

It didn't take long to scoop the leftovers into a container and load the cookware into the dishwasher. Her model was older than Nana's. I read the faded instructions on the inside of the door, loaded the soap, and pressed start.

Sleep came fast and was filled with flashbacks from our childhood. I woke up smiling.

Until I registered the banging on my door followed by Tasha's angry voice.

"Montgomery! You get in the kitchen NOW!"

CHAPTER 13
Tasha

What. An. Idiot.

I spun on my heel and stalked back to the kitchen with my phone to my ear. "Thanks," I told my landlord. "We'll have the bubbles cleaned up by the time the plumber arrives."

Nothing like getting an early-morning call from your sweet elderly downstairs neighbors about a ceiling leak in their kitchen on the rare morning I could sleep in. I'd quickly apologized, run to the kitchen and ended the call with them to dial the landlord.

"What happened?" Monty sauntered out of his room, bare-chested and sleepy-eyed, wearing those beat-up slippers.

"Floody bubbles! Go put a shirt on and grab all the towels in your bathroom. This better not make us late for practice! And where are all my hair ties?!"

I glanced up the bar. Parfait lay on his side, licking his paw like he had no care in the world.

Just like a cat.

"Barfy! This isn't funny!" I marched over to him and ran my hand underneath his massive belly. He pawed at me but didn't move out of the way. "Aha!"

I pinned him with a hard stare and retrieved three of the covered elastics while he glared at me like I was a lunatic.

Sighing, I pulled my hair into a ponytail and Parfait resumed licking his paw, completely uninterested in my frustrations.

It was only a little bit past eight. We had plenty of time, and we could always shower at the Plex if we needed to. But I didn't want to.

The kitchen was a good two feet deep in sudsy bubbles. The dishwasher was running, which wasn't good, especially if Monty had started it last night. In my urgent rage to get him up, I'd been too overwhelmed with panic that I hadn't thought to turn it off until now.

I placed my phone on the bar next to an annoyed Parfait, whose food dishes were drowning under the suds, and waded through the bubbly clouds to turn the machine off.

But the blasted bubble maker had its own ideas and continued to ooze no matter which button or combination of buttons I pressed.

"Come *on*," I pleaded with the button. "Turn off!"

This dishwasher was a bad listener and needed a time-out. Maybe Monty could figure out how to end its production of suds. Although, from the appearance of things and the familiar scent of my Tia Gia's limoncello dish soap, I didn't have high hopes since it appeared he couldn't tell dish-washing soap from dishwasher fluid.

Frustrated and wet, I swatted the clinging suds off of me and carefully stalked across the slippery floor to the carpet and my room to get my own towels.

Back in the kitchen, I immediately set to work on my hands and knees on the tile. Lucky for us, it hadn't reached the rug in the living area.

"Whoa." Monty let the word drag like a surfer impressed by a bodacious wave.

"'Bout time you showed up!" I growled from the sudsy mess. I craned my neck to find him standing barefoot on the carpet at the edge of the tile, armed with a load of pink towels Penny left behind when she moved out. He'd donned his FireVolts Dri-Fit tee and pulled track pants on over his shorts.

Good. Still, my traitorous eyes lingered too long on him for my liking.

Wordlessly, he knelt beside me and imitated my movements. I was just doing my best to move the bubbles and trap them. If there was a better way, I didn't get the memo. We moved side by side, corralling and popping the bubbles as best we could toward the offending machine.

Over and over, I pressed the now soaking-wet towel over the bubbles to tamp them down. Bubbles popped and suds flew, and soon I couldn't see Monty, who had to be close by. I looked behind me at the clear path we forged and decided to venture back to the rug for a fresh towel. Carefully, I rose to my feet and traversed the slippery floor.

When I turned back, dry towel in hand, I hit a Monty wall. My feet began to slide … slide … slide …

"Eep!" Strong hands closed around my upper arms, but it wasn't enough to keep me from going down … down … down …

It all happened so fast.

I slid.

Monty slid.

He twisted me around as we fell. We hit the floor—hard —and slid across the tile, coming to a stop, Monty's head first, against the fridge and sending most of the suds we'd corralled in every direction.

For a fraction of a second, I registered my cheek coming into contact with his full lips; not a kiss, but a quick brush of featherlight contact. I immediately snapped to attention, mindful and mournful of the loss of the warm and unexpected caress.

My first aid training kicked into high gear. "Oh my gosh! Are you okay?" I pressed my hands to his chest and pushed myself up, trying not to think about the fact that I was straddling him in a very inappropriate position. But it gave me the best trajectory to examine him for a concussion.

His bright baby blues blinked up at me. Then a disembodied arm appeared through the suds and his hand found the back of his head. "I think so."

I leaned in closer and held up my index finger in front of his face. "Follow my finger." I traced the air in an arc.

He sighed and did as I asked. "I'm fine. Just a little bump." He narrowed his gaze. "No concussion protocol needed. Are *you* okay?"

"Yeah. Though my pride has taken a hit. Thanks for, um ..." I gestured wildly. "Breaking my fall."

He grinned. "It's been a long time since I was there to catch you. And been in this position. Kinda miss having a mat under me, though." Monty rubbed his head and grinned again.

So much grinning.

Stop the grinning! Stop being so nice! Stop being so un-Monty! I don't want to like you!

Cheeks flaming, I sprang to my feet. At a loss for words, I

held out my hand as he sat up. He didn't need my help to get to his feet, but he placed his fingers in mine anyway as we both stood up.

Monty didn't let go of my hand, and the strangest zingy tingles shot up my arm and raced through the rest of me, like I'd been shocked by a faulty electric outlet.

Our gazes locked. He was so close.

I gulped for a breath of air.

Why was I reacting like this?

Monty squeezed my hand, and I hastily let go, stepping back from him instinctively. His arm shot out for the second time to stabilize me as I found my footing a good arm's length away.

I covered my face with my hands. *What a disaster.*

"We should, um ..." I slowly peeled my hands off my face and gestured to the floor.

"Yeah, let's finish this up," he agreed. "When's the plumber due?"

I glanced at the clock on the stove. "Nine o'clock. We're her first stop."

It didn't take much longer to clear the rest of the suds. The dishwasher continued to pump out more, but at a slow enough rate that made cleanup manageable. When the doorbell rang at nine, we were soaking wet from head to toe, and the dishwasher was continuing to pump out suds.

"Come on in, Yvonne." I pulled the door open wide for the plumber, an old friend from high school.

Her eyebrows lifted as her gaze swept me from head to toe. "That bad, huh?"

I gave her a weak smile. "We couldn't figure out a way to turn it off without cutting the power or busting a hose, so it's still oozing bubbles like one of those fake snow machines you see in Florida."

Yvonne snorted. "I'll take care of everything." She patted my shoulder and looked past me to where Monty was standing next to the bar. "Wow, he's aged well. That's your old partner, right?"

"Yes," I said tightly. "We're currently coaching together, unfortunately." Yvonne was single, so it shouldn't bother me that she was appreciating Monty.

Why *did* I care?

I swallowed. "Still single, too," I added, loud enough for Monty to hear me. "But he's a preener. Thinks he's hot stuff. Super annoying. Counting the days till his house is done and he can move out."

She chuckled as she tracked him. "He *is* hot stuff. Let him preen. He obviously works hard to look that good."

I needed to end this conversation *now*.

"Kitchen's all yours." I stepped back for her to have a clear path to the mess.

"Does it come with him?" She winked. "Just kidding. Hey, Monty."

Monty waved at Yvonne and skirted around her on the way to his room. I felt a twinge of satisfaction that he hadn't taken the opportunity she'd so clearly presented to chat or get her number.

"Go get changed," Yvonne said. "Then scoot out of here if you need water and electricity. I'll be playing with both sources for a bit."

"Thanks." I sighed. Guess I was showering at the Plex.

Fifteen minutes later, wearing dry clothes and armed with my toiletries, makeup, and hair supplies, I headed out with Monty.

He handed me his keys. "I'll drive. Start it up while I pick up our coffee order?"

"*Our* coffee order?" I asked.

"Was I wrong to assume you didn't get to make your morning pumpkin spice blah-te?"

"No, I—"

"I'll be at the truck in a jiff." He flashed a smile and jogged in the direction of the Coffee Loft.

Shaking my head in disbelief at his kind gesture, I lifted my hand to my brow to shield my eyes from the sun while I scanned the parking lot for his vehicle. Our apartment came with two reserved spaces, but he'd told the trio of elderly sisters downstairs they could have his spot. Elaine, Janice, and Joy had been elated and left him a batch of jellied thumbprint cookies at our door. The next batch that arrived had come with a note: *Monty, Tasha's recipe substitutions made these even better! We hope you both like them. With love, Elaine, Janice, and Joy.*

That was sweet of him to share my recipe and the cookies. And further confirmation he was poking around in my recipe binder again.

I located his truck in the back and trekked across the lot. After starting it up, I settled in the passenger seat to text Penny.

Monty used the dishwasher for the first time last night. I attached a picture of the kitchen in the state I'd found it when I woke up and hit send.

The driver's side door opened, and Monty climbed in, balancing a drink carrier laden with two to-go cups and paper bag in one hand.

"That was quick." I dislodged the hot cup from the tray

and set it in the console's cup holder, then did the same with his plastic cup.

"Thanks," he said, lifting the bag and tossing the empty drink carrier into the back seat. He pulled a wrapped cylinder from the bag and held it out to me. "I ordered ahead. Bacon and avocado in a fried egg wrap?"

"Yes, thank you," I said, taking the proffered food and unwrapping it. This man's generosity and memory were next-level. He'd make a great husband.

For someone.

Someday.

"It's the least I can do after the Great Dishwasher Debacle."

I almost chuckled. "Is that what we're calling it?"

"To call it anything else would reflect badly on me, so yeah."

I shook my head. "And we wouldn't want *that*. My gosh, if the people knew you were only human ..."

A funny look crossed his face. "You're being awfully gracious about this. I disrupted your morning and probably lost you your security deposit." He paused, and the sincerity in his expression nearly undid me. "I emailed Yvonne to send me the bill."

I shrugged, doing my darnedest not to react to another kindness from the man I had to keep reminding myself I was supposed to hate. "Management—and I—appreciate that. Thanks."

He nodded and turned back to his breakfast, same as mine, and quickly wolfed it down. And two more after that.

The cheer coaches' locker room/bathroom was co-ed, which normally no one minded, as the shower and changing stalls featured eight-foot-high walls and doors with double bolts. Today, after the tense morning with my unwanted house guest, I was both aware and on edge to be getting ready three stalls down from him.

Always one to put his talents on display, Monty treated me and the coaches who popped in to his rendition of "I Hate Myself for Loving You" while he showered and dressed.

"Behind my back you wanna mess around … so not jealous but he's a clown. You're on my mind ev'ry night and day, stealing my heart and pride ah-way-ee-ay-ee-ay-ay-ay."

It only got worse from there.

"Hey, woman, it's not right, and you know that I missed you last night. C'mon over and we'll drink some Sprite …"

The effort might be endearing if it was *anyone* else. He could sing, but he really should learn the lyrics if he was going to bust into song in a public place.

"Hating myself for my love of you, there's no breakin' free from chains to you … can't walk away so I tumble to you …"

The words ended, and he hummed the rest of the song. When he joined me at the sink to brush his teeth, the quiet in the room was both welcome and … unsettling.

"Terrible rendition," I announced. "Those aren't even the words."

"So?"

I rolled my eyes, and when I glanced his way, he caught me looking. With his best Finnick Odair smirk impression, he found my eyes in the mirror as he inserted the high-end electric brush into his mouth.

I almost swallowed my toothpaste under the intensity of his stare.

I quickly looked away and finished up, anxious to dry my hair and get out from under the weight of his presence.

Aware that he'd stopped brushing his teeth and was

watching me section my hair and clip it up, I found myself wishing he was singing again, if only to keep me distracted from watching him watch me.

Why *was* he watching me?

"Why are you watching me?" I clipped the last section and reached for my hairbrush to smooth out the strands of hair I'd left loose. "You're creeping me out."

A muscle in his jaw ticked, and he seemed to remember he had a mouthful of toothpaste. He bent at the sink to spit it out and turned on the water to rinse it away. "I don't know, Tasha. Sorry." He zipped his toothbrush into his case and pulled out his shaving gear. "Want me to do this somewhere else?"

I suddenly felt bad. Had I spoken too harshly? If so, he should be used to that. But he was acting as if I'd hurt his feelings. He hadn't even offered a snappy comeback.

Monty was being very un-Monty-like today.

It was unsettling.

As he shaved, I dried my hair one section at a time, trapping each long lock between the brush's base and the barrel of the hair dryer.

The air was thick, and not just with humidity.

Monty and I snuck glances at each other as we did our morning rituals, but neither of us spoke. Getting ready next to him felt intimate yet comfortable, despite the fact that I was growing increasingly *uncomfortable*. With anyone else, I probably would have taken them up on their offer to shave elsewhere.

But I'd known Monty since we were four years old. We'd been the best of friends and respected and taken care of each other. And these last few years, even though we hadn't gotten along because he'd hurt me deeply and I hadn't been able to forgive him, he'd never disrespected me or ogled me in the ways other guys had.

I hadn't realized how much I missed what we'd had until this moment.

"That's an awful lot of work for cheer practice," he commented quietly after I turned off the hair dryer. "Looks nice."

I shrugged, not sure how I should react to his compliment and still keep a cool head. "It's Saturday."

"You've rocked a pony on Saturdays before." He pointed to the FireVolts cheer bow clipped to my backpack.

"I might go out later, and it takes a flat iron to smooth out a ponytail bump. If we don't have electricity—"

"Ah. Right." He ran his fingers through his damp hair. "You have plans tonight?"

"No, but I might." It was none of his business, but I answered him before I thought.

"Well," he said slowly. "If nothing comes up, would you like to join me and Nana for dinner? It's steak night at Mountainview. And they can accommodate any food requests."

My throat tightened at his offer. I'd missed seeing Nana in the Coffee Loft and was sure he knew it. "How do you know?"

"I asked."

Now there was a lump in my throat. Had he been planning to ask me before this moment? Why else would he have inquired about dietary options? Unless Nana had more issues than I knew about?

I breathed in through my nose for a count of ten before I answered. "Okay, then. Thank you for the invitation. I'd love to see Nana Booboo."

Well, that hadn't come out as chill as I'd hoped.

"Great." He settled back on his heels and tried to play it cool, but I knew him well enough to tell that he was pleased I accepted his invitation. "We'll stop home after practice to change and then head over. That work for you?"

I nodded. What in the freshly ground beans was happening between us?

CHAPTER 14
Monty

Dean Hathaway, captain of the Edge, held a Back-to-Hockey gathering the Saturday before training camp started each year. All the players, prospects, coaching, medical, and front office staff were invited to his mountainside resort of a home outside Denver.

Nana's house was bigger and more tastefully decorated, but I digress.

Per our arrangement, Tasha attended as my plus-one. Xavier and Penny waved to us from a bank of six lounge chairs on the upper deck on the far side of the pool. I followed Tasha around the perimeter and up the steps, carrying all of our stuff, as Zaki Marsh, one of the alternate captains, welcomed everyone from the mic at the DJ's booth.

"This party almost didn't happen," Zaki was saying. "Our GM wanted to lowball our captain, and that's not right." A boo went up from the guests. "I couldn't let that happen. Mostly because *I* don't want to host these parties. Luckily, he and I and Dex have the same agent, and since we all have more money than we could ever spend, we settled for team-friendly contracts to keep him here for another year." Zaki swept his sculpted, tattooed arm in an arc in front of him, gesturing to all the guests. "You're welcome."

He bowed theatrically to the applause and cheers, but he wasn't done yet. "On Dean's behalf, I'd like to say—hey!"

I turned to see what had interrupted him. Dean's wife had taken the mic. "Dean can talk for himself, when allowed." She smiled and shook her head at the younger man. "Welcome to our home, everyone. Have fun, be careful, and if you need anything, ask this guy." She poked Zaki in his bicep. "Now, let's give a big cheer for Cappy, my man and everyone's favorite forward!"

While Dean gave his welcome speech and preseason pep talk, Tasha and I reached the upper deck. Noel and Gabby had arrived a beat before us, taking chairs next to Xavier and Penny and leaving two chairs open on Gabby's other side. Tasha pulled her sundress over her head, revealing an apple green tankini, and tossed her dress on the lounger adjacent to her cousin's. She shot me a look that was hard to read. Was it a reaction to the way I was looking at her? —I hoped not—or was it a stick-it-to-me for forcing me to an outside chair instead of the one next to my former partner?

I set our bags down, shook off my slides, and pulled my FireVolts tank over my head.

Time to remind us both that we were supposed to hate each other.

I padded to the edge of the decking. There was about four feet of brick pavers jutting out below.

I could make it.

After making certain the deep water was clear, and any potential child copycats weren't paying attention, I walked back to my chair and spun on my heel. "Watch this," I said to Penny.

With a wink to Tasha, I hopped in place, ready to execute a move she was familiar with from years past.

"DO. NOT," she warned. "This is not a diving platform!"

I shrugged. "It can be."

With that, I was off and running. I cartwheeled into a round-off and vaulted myself off the deck and into the air, revolving into a full twist before I hit the water feet-first.

I surfaced to loud cheering and waved to the unsuspecting audience.

Ryleigh Spencer, Trask Emerson's stepdaughter, dove into the pool and swam up to me. "Can you teach me how to do that? I play hockey now, but I cheered when I was little."

When she was little? The girl was maybe fifty pounds soaking wet and, at most, eight years old.

"Please?" she pleaded. "You see that *boy* over there?"

I followed the trajectory of her finger to a kid about her age standing, arms crossed, with other boys at the side of the pool.

"Yeah, I see him. Friend of yours?"

"Nope. We used to be teammates, but he moved up to the U10 team. *I'm* still in U8." She said it like it was the worst thing in the world.

"Are you even ten?" I asked.

She shook her head. "No. But neither is he. I'm eight, and he's nine. But his birth year is the one before mine. Stupid December birthday. Mine's in the spring, so he moves up first. *So* unfair."

I loved her competitiveness. Too bad she didn't cheer anymore.

"Can you do a round-off back handspring?" I asked.

"*And* a standing back tuck," she said proudly.

I was impressed. That was a big skill for an eight-year-old.

"Okay," I said, and she brightened. "But *only* if your mom says it's okay, *only* on the lower deck, and *only* if you let me spot you."

Ryleigh nodded and held out her hand for me to shake. "I agree to your terms!" I shook her tiny hand lightly, and she swam away, leaving me shaking my head and hoping I wasn't breaking any big rules by offering.

I swam to the side and pulled myself out of the pool. A scrap of fabric landed on my head. I pulled it off and looked up.

"You're scaring the children!" Tasha adjusted her hat as she leaned over the side.

I grinned and pulled the tank over my head. "You just can't take all of this!" I flexed my biceps and ran my hands in the air down the sides of my body.

"More like I can't take your blinding paleness!" she retorted.

I snorted. I wasn't pale. I spray-tanned year-round, and she knew it.

Now things felt back to normal. "Can you toss down my towel?"

I caught it just before it landed on my head and laid it at the edge of the pool, smoothing out the air pockets and wrinkles so Ryleigh would have a non-slippery spot to launch from. But first, I'd stand on it and toss her in, just to make sure she was capable of doing everything she claimed.

"Mr. Monty?" I turned to find her at my side. "Mommy said yes, but Daddy Trask said if I get hurt, he'll body-check you so hard they'll need to find another new Ridgie."

I glanced over to her parents. Trask was bouncing her

two-year-old brother on his knee. He lifted the baby's sippy cup in the air with his good arm and grinned. Poor guy was just out of a sling from fixing his torn rotator cuff. Well, I was happy to throw his kid around until he was up to the task again.

I waved and bent down to Ryleigh. "Well, it's a good thing that's not going to happen. Trask is one tough guy."

She set a hand on her hip and appraised me from head to toe. "You're bulkier. You could take him."

Bulkier? I loved this girl. Delivering insulting compliments like a pro.

"Let's start with a standard backflip into the water." I linked my fingers together and squatted down to her height. She placed her hands on my shoulder and counted down from three. I tossed her up, over the water. On her first attempt, she circled fully around and her feet slid into water like a pro diver.

She was back at my side in seconds. "Can I try the twist now?"

I nodded and explained the technique. She managed to twist 180 degrees on her first attempt.

"Not bad," I said, holding my hand out for a high five. I gave her another tip to straighten out her form, and the second one was perfect. Next, I talked her through the round-off on a wet surface, making her promise not to try this without a trained professional in a controlled situation. After one round-off back tuck into the water, I determined she was ready for the twist.

"Let's get you some extra height on this one." I glanced over at the boys, who'd stopped laughing and pointing and were now watching with their mouths hung open. "Put it all together. Do you think you could round-off into my hands?"

"I was waiting for you to ask me that! Let's do it." She turned away to take her mark for the running start, tossing a glance at her adversary on the way.

Ryleigh was a natural. "Why did you quit cheer?" I asked after her second—and perfect—dive.

"Mommy said I had to choose 'cause she's only one person and club hockey and elite cheer are both full-time jobs."

I laughed. "That is true. What about tumbling in your spare time? I could help you perfect the full twist, add a kickout or whatever else, and by next year you can *really* wow those guys."

Her eyes widened. "I like that idea!"

"Great. Tell your mom to call the gym and we'll get it scheduled."

"Cool!" She tipped her chin toward the boys, who were now cannonballing and whatever else into the pool. "Can I go one more time?"

"Sure," I said. Most of the other kids of impressionable age were near the zero-entry end of the pool or using the waterslide. "How about two more times?"

"Yes!"

Off she went. As she swam back to the side, I caught a familiar accented voice above me.

Vlad.

I stiffened as I listened to him greet Tasha, Penny, and Gabby. Then, instead of talking about hockey—or anything else—with Xavier and Noel, he commented on *me*.

"He is good with the children, no? Makes a good bear."

"*So* good," Penny replied. "Not only has he coached kids at the gym, but he's visited the kids' cancer wards in local hospitals for years."

Good ol' Penny. If I ever needed encouragement, I knew who to call.

"One more?" Ryleigh called.

"Definitely," I said, leaning in conspiratorially and dropping my voice. "They're looking again. Make it good."

She nodded. "It's not hard. They look like a bunch of kids playing around compared to me."

I laughed. That was exactly what they were.

She set off and this time twisted a perfect 360 degrees on her way into the water. I shook my head. There was so much confidence and natural talent in that little frame. I hoped she did take me up on my offer for tumbling coaching. She reminded me so much of Tasha at that age.

Ryleigh waved and swam toward the waterslide. I turned toward the stairs and did my best to overhear Vlad, but he was speaking too low. From his perch at the foot of Tasha's chair, he regaled her about his summer overseas.

Chump.

I flopped into my chair and made a show of digging my earbuds out of my bag, making sure he noticed me putting them in.

I didn't turn them on, though.

Was that wrong? Probably.

But someone had to look out for my roommate. She was doing a terrible job of it herself, and her family didn't even seem to notice. I adjusted my chair and leaned back.

"Your date is giving me—how you say it?—the evil eye," Vlad observed. His upbeat tone and stilted English grated my nerves further.

"Oh, him? He's not my date." Tasha glared at me.

I winked at her.

"Then, what? You were at a wedding with him. You are here now."

"I danced with you, remember. Monty and I are just friends."

Friends, huh? Progress!

"Friends who date?"

I coughed. Tasha glanced over at me before shaking her head vehemently. "We're not even friends, really. We just work together."

Ouch.

"And live together," Vlad observed.

"Temporarily." The word was spoken with emphasis.

"He is quite a showman, no? And handsome."

Right on both counts, Vladdy. Was he really that thick he had to beat the subject like a dead horse? Tasha had made it perfectly clear she had zero feelings for me.

Tasha smiled sweetly at him. "I promise you, there is nothing-nada-zip"—she popped the *P*—"going on between me and Monty, now or ever."

Yes! She called me Monty.

Out loud. In public!

And she didn't refute my good looks like she was prone to do.

"Well, that is good. Because Vlad does not like to share."

You've *got* to be kidding me. He was referring to himself in the third person?

How tacky. I wished I'd thought to put my sunglasses on so I could hide my eye roll.

But Tasha was giggling like it was the funniest thing she'd ever heard.

Vlad had charm, I'd give him that.

"So then—it is okay I ask for your number?"

I could actually *hear* the breath she sucked in.

Give. Me. A. Break.

"Fine by me," she squeaked. Vlad's mouth widened into a smile. For someone who'd claimed not to know a lot of English only two months ago, he sure had the pickup convo down.

Tasha pulled her phone out and handed it to him. He took it and tapped the screen. Gabby looked over, and I caught her gaze, then inclined my head toward Vlad, who was now asking Tasha to accompany him to the buffet.

Gabby frowned as Vlad stood and offered Tasha his hand. When their backs were to us, Gabby slid over to Tasha's chair. "What's that about?"

I shrugged. "It's time she dated again. But *that* guy?" I shook my head. "He looks like an untanned Ken doll, and you can barely understand a word he says."

"Xavier likes him. Noel hasn't decided yet."

"Well, *I* think he's a chump."

She laughed. "Monty, you've thought every guy Tasha has ever dated was a chump."

I shrugged. "That's cause they were."

"*All* of them?" she challenged.

"All of them," I confirmed.

She settled back in the chair. "I'm going to need more than that. What was wrong with Sam?"

"He chose baseball over her."

"Marner?"

"Let her split the check."

"That was probably her request."

"A real man would have found a way to pay the whole bill."

She rolled her eyes. "Rafael?"

"How can you take anyone seriously who was named after a Ninja Turtle?"

"We don't know that for sure. His parents are artists. That all you got?"

"He had a unibrow. Bugged her to no end."

Gabby snorted. "I remember. And he said he'd never pluck it because society wasn't going to tell him how to groom himself."

"See?"

"Okay, what about DJ?"

"I didn't have a problem with him. Until they started dating."

"Broke the Bro Code, eh?"

I whipped my head around to her and scowled. DJ had been my so-called best friend from prep school. He began dating Tasha following our falling-out. "No. We would still be friends if I didn't have to hear all the sordid details of their dating life. Ew. She was like a sister to me."

"Uh-huh." She swatted me with her magazine. "Keep telling yourself that."

I would.

I *had* to.

Or I'd go crazy.

CHAPTER 15
Tasha

Sunday morning after the early service at St. Mary's, I hummed to myself as I boxed up the sugar-free dirt cake I'd baked for Nana Booboo. I'd had a glorious morning to myself, choosing to skip family brunch at my grandparents' house. Monty had left early, leaving a note behind that he was going to the Plex to work out before his private coaching sessions.

Good for him. He'd been irritated since yesterday afternoon. I sometimes wondered if the reason he was so built was because of vanity or working off steam. When we were younger, the more his parents neglected him, the more time he spent in the gym.

Maybe it was a mix of both.

And he didn't seem to like Vlad. Surprising, because the whole team seemed to love him. Zaki hadn't even pranked him.

"Stay away, Barfy!" I yelled to the cat, who'd moved from his perch at the bar to the counter where my frosting bowl sat unattended while I'd been boxing up individual slices of cake for Nana and her friends.

"Mew!" he protested as I gave him a squirt with the spray bottle. "Sorry, but chocolate isn't good for cats. Even the fake kind."

He glared at me and jumped down, flicking his tail in defiance as he sauntered around the counter and into the living room.

"You'll thank me later!" I called after him.

Cats.

Funny little things. I wouldn't admit it to Monty, but I loved his cat. Always had. I even left the door to my room cracked at night sometimes. He slept with Monty all night long, but shared the love. I kind of liked being woken up early with a wet nose pressed to mine.

I sighed. I was dying for physical affection. Maybe Vlad would work out. But if not, Parfait was here for at least a few more weeks.

There had been another delay on the house. The repiping wasn't scheduled to start until late September now.

It was fine.

Everything was fine.

Twenty minutes later, I checked in at Mountainview's reception desk. I handed the woman a list of the ingredients in the cake. She smiled and escorted me back to Nana's room.

The Biddington wealth had bought Monty's grandmother a private corner room at the back of the building with a breathtaking view of the mountains. I slid my tote off my shoulder and set it on the chair so I could have both arms free to show her what I brought.

"I'm g-glad you took me up on my offer to v-visit. And

not just because ... I knew you'd bring me ... *treats.*" She grinned, her smile noticeably lower on her weak side.

I returned her smile and peeled the plastic cover off the top container. Her speech was almost back to normal. "Sugar-free dairy-free gluten-free nut-free dirt cake."

"Did Fyvie ... make this?"

"Nope," I said. I set the other containers down on her dresser and retrieved a plastic spoon from my tote bag. "But you'll have to tell me if it tastes like hers. I got this recipe from the Creekside Inn. Bailey Dexter-Brewer mentioned Tabbi was the original creator of the bakery's version, and that she created a sugar-free version for a diabetic regular, so I went over there and asked Tabbi if she wouldn't mind sharing it. I tweaked it a little, though."

Nana waggled her eyebrows. "Mission accepted."

I stabbed the spoon into the cake and used the side of it to push off a small bite-size piece. "Open up."

"I can ... feed myself," Nana protested. She grabbed for the spoon, and I guided it to place it in her fingers.

"Of course you can," I replied softly. "But why should you when I can do it for you?"

Her hand shook and I gently took it back before she could drop it. She sighed in defeat.

"Let me get it for you this time. I can tell they worked you hard this morning. This isn't a therapy session, and *you* are a queen. Let the peasant serve you."

The side of her mouth twitched. "You are ... far from a ... peasant."

"Well, thank you," I replied, holding up the spoon. "Ready?"

I was happy that she complied. I carefully placed the spoon on her tongue and kept it there until her mouth closed firmly around it, then scooched it to the left to pull it out on her stronger side.

She chewed slowly and swallowed. I set the container on the rolling tray, then held her glass of water out to her to rinse it down. She sipped at the straw, waving me away after a moment.

I returned it to her side tray. "What's the verdict?"

"Can't tell the difference … between that and the real thing."

"Really?" I cocked my head to the side.

"Yes. You should … put it in your … c-cook … book."

"I'm not doing a cookbook, Nana." But I was flattered that Monty thought it was a good enough idea he'd told his grandmother about it.

She set a hard look on me. "I will … invest."

"That's sweet of you." I picked up the container of cake. "More?"

"D-don't … try to … distract me."

"That's exactly what I'm doing. Open up."

She pressed her lips together.

I chuckled. "C'mon, Nana."

She shook her head.

I sighed. "Okay. I'll think about it."

"Good." She opened her mouth.

I smiled. While I fed her, I told her about the Back-to-Hockey gathering, including getting to know Vlad and detailing Monty's antics with Ryleigh.

I held the last bite poised while she sipped her water when Monty entered the room with a new backpack slung over his right shoulder. It was … moving?

He shushed the bag and closed the door behind him.

"Nana, I finally found a way to—Tasha, what are you feeding her?"

"Dirt cake," I said, placing the spoon inside Nana's mouth.

His eyes widened, and his face turned really red, really fast. "She can't have that! She's diabetic! You know that! Why would you—" He pressed his hands to the side of his head and took two long, deep breaths. "Why would you bring that?"

I looked at Nana, who was trying not to laugh, then back at him.

"Quiet, you'll make her choke," I chided him.

"But—"

"It's sugar-free, and I got it approved." I smiled, satisfied. "She likes it so much she wants to back my cookbook. Isn't that nice? I didn't even know I was writing one."

"She—you—Nana?"

He was almost cute, the way he pulled at his hair and looked to Nana to confirm my words. I did love that he was so protective of her.

"Monty." Nana pointed to him with her good arm.

"Yes, Nana?"

"A-pologize. Now."

"I'm sorry, Tasha. I—shouldn't have assumed." He unzipped the backpack and turned back to Nana. "I, um, brought the cat."

Nana's face lit up with glee. "Puh-puh … Parfait!"

"Mew!"

I slid off the bed to make room for Monty and the cat. He sat the old kitty on the bed, and Parfait immediately set to work sniffing every inch of the bed and Nana before putting his paws on her chest and rubbing his cheek against hers.

It was a sweet reunion. When Nana teared up, so did I. As far I knew, it had been months since she'd seen her cat.

Someday, when I was old, I hoped I had a grandson—or granddaughter—who loved me as much as Monty loved his Nana. This grown man not only loved her deeply, his actions exemplified that love.

I walked around to the other side of the bed. "I should go. It was great seeing you, Nana. I'll come by again next week."

She smiled up at me as she stroked Parfait's back. "You have ... a good time tonight ... on your date."

I smiled. "Yes, ma'am." I bent down and placed a light kiss on her forehead. "Bye."

With a wave to Monty, I skirted back around the bed, collected my tote, and scooted out.

I had a date with a gorgeous and sweet hockey player to get ready for.

Why didn't that excite me as much as it should?

CHAPTER 16

Later that evening, cat in lap, I was dozing off to *Air Disasters* when the door to the apartment opened. Parfait raised his head.

"Time to go to bed, Montgomery," Tasha sang. "It's past your bedtime."

I regarded her warily. "You're the one who has to be at work in six hours." It was almost midnight.

"What can I say? Long date."

"You don't sound smitten."

She shrugged and sat on the far side of the sofa. "He's nice. But his English is limited."

"Huh. Seemed pretty fluent yesterday." My tone held an edge of cynicism.

Okay, a *lot* of cynicism.

"Maybe," she conceded.

"So, did you have a good time?"

"Why do you care?"

Good question. "Because you're keeping me up late."

"Aw, you can't go to sleep till I get home? How *parental* of you."

"Yeah, well, I have to make sure you remember to lock the door and all that."

"You sound like my dad. Kinda look like him too, with those plaid flannel pajama pants."

"What's wrong with my pants?"

"They're *so* last century." She pulled a throw pillow into her lap and hugged it. "I'm a big girl, Monty. I've been taking care of myself for a long time."

That I knew. And she did a great job of it.

"I googled him," I announced. "Did you know his mother's last name is the same as a suspected spy family? I'm tempted to hire a private investigator."

She rolled her eyes. "'Night, Montgomery."

Soooo we were back to using my full name. I sighed, then masked it with a stretch, and before I said something too sentimental, I nudged Parfait off my lap and stood up to make a show of checking the locks. "'Night, Tasha."

"Mew!"

Parfait trotted behind me. Once on the other side of my closed door, I sank into the desk chair and opened my laptop. After Tasha left the facility yesterday, Nana had told me she seemed open to the cookbook idea.

But Tasha had very little free time. Earlier this evening, I'd brought her recipe binder into my room and started typing it up. I figured it would be harder for her to say no if the big part of the job was done and I presented her with a document to edit in her leisure time.

But she had so little of it. The high school team had already been practicing daily for weeks, and her Friday nights or Saturday mornings were shot because of the weekly football games. Her *only* full day off was Sunday, but after church and family brunch, it didn't leave her much time for a passion project.

I'd returned the binder at nine o'clock, wrongly assuming her dinner date would be over and she'd be home for bed by her usual turn-in time of 10 p.m.

How wrong I'd been.

But at least I'd had the foresight to snap pictures of a bunch of recipes. I pulled up the first one on my phone and got to work.

There was no way I'd be sleeping anytime soon.

Maybe not at all.

MASCOT MEDIA DAY was a league-wide event, and the Edge's social media team had set up some wild and wacky photo and video shoots for me. A little groggy on my five hours of sleep, I sucked down the last of my second key lime protein shake after I parked at the practice facility in Denver. Jared and I would start here and drive to the arena after lunch.

He pulled in next to me and waved. I sighed at the realization of being stuck with him all day. I stretched my lips into a smile over my pressed-together teeth and saluted him.

It wasn't that I didn't like him. I did. I just hated that he was a rule-follower and was constantly reminding me of what Ridgie could and couldn't and should and shouldn't do.

Lunch was provided, and when Jared took off to find his aunt, and probably someone to schmooze about a better job,

I parked myself on a bench in the training room and zeroed in on Vladimir Ivanov.

In the most nonthreatening way, of course.

I had to send him a message that I would protect my roommate at all costs.

Xavier was spotting him on a weight bench. When they looked my way, I held up my chicken Caesar wrap in acknowledgement. Xavier leaned down to speak to the chump, and I smirked when he added additional weights to each side of the bar.

If he was trying to exert dominance, he'd need to lift more than 225 pounds.

The chump struggled with his tenth rep, and Xavier had to help him replace the bar on its rests. I made a show of yawning and feigned surprise when Vlad waved at me. I held my hand up and quickly looked away, as if he was the least of my interests.

Xavier moved on to a leg press, and I was annoyed to find Vlad striding straight for me.

"Don't drip your sweat on my lunch," I warned as he sat —too close—to me on the bench.

He pointed to my wrap. "Looks good. No carbs for me. Hurts definition."

I lifted the bottom of my shirt and sucked in my abs to show him *my* max definition. "Doesn't affect me any."

His eyes widened. "Perhaps you might share your secret?"

"Perhaps," I mumbled, then took a bite. It was no secret. I just ate a balanced diet and worked out.

A lot.

"What?" I asked. I didn't like the way he was staring at me.

"Tasha—you care about her."

"I *look out* for her," I corrected. Firmly.

"She … We have a hard time communicating. My English is not well."

I raised an eyebrow. "Sounds fine to me. And you look good. Why do you need to open your mouth?"

He laughed. "I am not interested in being loved for body. Although …" He curled his arm and flexed his bicep. "It *is* extraordinary."

I scoffed. "You say words like 'extraordinary' and expect me to believe you're bad at English? Do I look stupid?"

He shook his head. "No. I think you are very smart. Which is why I would like to ask your help."

"My help?"

He nodded solemnly. "To woo Tasha."

I regarded him with a hard look. "She can decide for herself if she wants you to *woo* her."

"Yes, but I have idea to move process along, and it requires, how you say, *finesse.*"

This guy's propensity to go from speaking well to broken English on a dime rubbed me the wrong way.

"And *no one* else can help you?" Surely, one of the guys on the team could help. Jason Dexter had two college degrees and read as much as a bookstagrammer.

He shook his head. "I asked Xavier. He said you were the guy, since you know her best."

"What exactly do you want me to do?" I pushed the last bite of the wrap into my mouth.

"I want you to translate—no, embellish?—my love letters."

My gag reflex kicked in. I grabbed my water bottle and took a swig before my choke was noticeable.

"Your *love letters?*" He couldn't be serious.

"Yes. You have never written love letters to woo a woman?"

"Heck no. What is this, the sixteenth century?"

A patronizing look crossed his face. "Dear Monty—"

"Don't call me that."

"Montgomery," he corrected. "Love letters work. Every time."

"Work for what?" And how many women had he written love letters to? "What's your goal?"

"With Tasha? Everything."

"Why?"

"Why not? She is beautiful, smart, talented, and citizen of the greatest country on earth."

And there it was.

"You want to marry her so you can stay here?"

He nodded. "Someday, perhaps. She is easy to love, no? And her sister is married to my friend. She is perfect."

"You don't even know her," I said, unhappy that a bitter tinge carried on my tone.

"I know enough to see that we could be good together. And make beautiful babies."

This guy was the Russian Gaston. Tasha was more than a freaking trophy wife.

"You're serious?" I asked.

He nodded. "Unless ... unless her heart lies with someone else?"

I shook my head vehemently. "She hasn't dated in a year. She's a bit prickly, if you haven't noticed."

His face lit up. "I like that about her. So, will you help me?"

"Can't you use Google Translate?"

He sighed. "It does not have personal touch that you, knowing her all life long, could add."

"And *why* would I help you?" I asked. This guy had nerve.

He regarded me curiously. "Don't you want your friend to be happy?"

I shrugged. "Not with the wrong guy."

"How do I become the *right* guy?"

"Seriously?" My face heated at the rate of an Instapot. "You either are, or you aren't."

A thought zipped to my brain just then. What if I *could* mold Vlad to be the guy Tasha needed? Maybe her ice would thaw and we could be friends again.

It couldn't be too hard. I'd rewrite his letters and add a bit of flair that would resonate with her.

I knew her favorite color, what flowers she liked. I knew she spent a small fortune every Easter stocking up and hoarding Cadbury Creme eggs, hiding enough of them in her room to last a year of stressful days, despite the fact that they turned her stomach. I knew now what she could and couldn't eat, even if she wouldn't share her diagnosis.

And I knew what *not* to say to her.

"If you want to win Tasha," I said slowly, "you have to do more than *woo* her. She's smarter than a puck bunny and won't be told what to do or how to live her life."

"Just what I am looking for. An independent voman!" Vlad grinned in a way that made me instinctively recoil. I didn't think he had nefarious intentions, but the guy seriously didn't know what he was getting himself into.

I *should* help him, for both their sakes.

Tasha deserved to be happy. She shouldn't have to live under the weight of her medical bills. If things went well with Vlad, maybe they'd get married and she could relax.

I wanted her to relax. She deserved to relax.

"Okay," I said. "I'll help you. But you can't tell anyone. It'll make us both look bad. I have a reputation I'm trying to build."

"Ah, yes. Best bear ever."

I cringed. "NO." I stood up and pretended to itch a spot on my upper abdomen so I could lift my shirt to remind him I was bigger and *bulkier*, as Ryleigh had put it. "As a helper. The bear is just the vessel. And you can donate a thousand dollars to the children's oncology unit for each letter I 'help' you with."

"Right. Deal. Do you have paper?"

I stared at him. He was awfully presumptuous. And what *was* this? The twentieth century? "Text me what you want me to translate."

While he went back to the locker room to grab his phone, I threw away my trash and tried not to regret what I'd promised. If Xavier liked the guy, that should be enough.

But still, it didn't feel right to me.

Tasha hadn't come home in that I-had-the-best-date-ever euphoria that women were prone to do. She didn't hum or smile or gush about Vlad. Maybe she did to Penny or Gabby, but I'd seen at the party how cool they'd been with each other: No visible chemistry *at all*. No secret glances, no heated stares, no private jokes or laughs.

It wasn't any of my business. But I'd help, see where it went. And be there for her when it didn't work out.

Because it never worked out. Because Tasha had a talent for only attracting chumps.

Vlad returned, and we exchanged numbers. Then he texted me what he wanted to say to Tasha. "I ran this in translate app, but it didn't convey the right tone."

I looked at the message. *My sweet Tasha. In cloudy sky, you are the sun, brighten and shine up my day and my path. You make my heart large with love every time I see you.*

I cringed. "How about this?"

In a cloudy night sky, 'tis you who light my way. The moon and stars are dulled by your shine, shining and sprinkling light on all that is dark in my world. Truly, my beating heart swells with every smile you bestow upon me. Your joy fills my soul and fuels my need to prove to you that I am worthy of your radiance.

Maybe I went a little overboard with the flowery prose, but Vlad wasn't likely to care if I got carried away, only that it was effective and hit the mark.

I didn't like the idea of Tasha being a *mark.*

Not my problem though. I hit send and waited while he read it, watching his smile widen each time his thumb flicked the screen to read more.

"This is perfect! *Shedevr!* A masterpiece! Exactly what I need." He wrapped his arms around me. "Thank you!"

I stood, slipping out of his clammy appendages. "I also sent you the link to my foundation. I expect two thousand dollars to clear before I translate another one."

"Yes, yes." He stood up and held out his hand for me to shake.

Against my better judgment, I took his proffered hand. "See you around."

"See you!"

I wanted to stay and scream at him that Tasha wasn't the kind of girl a man with an empty brain could woo with good looks, charm, and purple prose. But I'd play the game, and when she realized he was a fraud, I'd help her to rebuild her confidence, like every other time.

Well, except that last time. The DJ thing had been a hit to

both of us. I'd put money on the fact that she also felt relief when he'd taken a job in California and we weren't running into him on a daily basis anymore.

Maybe things *would* work out with Vlad, like the pieces had fallen together for Penny and Xavier. Theirs had been a marriage of convenience, born out of a need for him to marry to save his inheritance. But they'd been friends first.

Tasha and Vlad didn't know each other.

I suited up with guilt, wondering if I'd just set my coaching partner up for the biggest mistake of her life.

CHAPTER 17

Tasha

"Soooo ..." Penny sidled up to me when I took my place behind my register Monday morning. "How's Vlaaaaaaad?"

I shrugged coolly at her teasing singsong tone. "Same as he was when I texted you last night, I guess."

"C'mon, Tasha." Gabby flipped her chestnut side bangs and leaned against the back counter. "Tell us about your date. Monty said you didn't get in till almost midnight."

"When did you talk to Monty—er, Montgomery?" Behind her, the long hand on the clock ticked to 6 a.m. Jannell hadn't even unlocked the front door yet.

Note to self: Think twice next time before arriving early to work.

Gabby's amused expression revealed she'd noticed my slip-up. "We were texting when you got in last night. He's got Mascot Media Day today."

"Right." He'd asked for my input on some of his ideas, which I freely gave while he watched me chop vegetables. He'd already spent a weekend in Florida to gather with some of the other mascots for what he playfully dubbed the 'Shenanigans Summit.'

"So? The date?" Gabby prodded. "Monty said you didn't give any details."

Gabby and Monty's close friendship had always annoyed me, especially once they began stunting together all those years ago.

Like we used to be.

Partner-close.

I didn't want to be bitter about it anymore.

Jannell unlocked the door and flipped the sign, and customers began filing in. I turned away from her to close the discussion and stepped up to my assigned register.

Brenna and Brendan Trotter were the first in the door this morning. I waved them over.

"Mornin', Tasha," Brendan said, then addressed Penny and Gabby. "Ladies."

They returned the greeting, and Penny frowned. "You're up early. Morning skate isn't until ten."

"I've got a baby shower brunch at the barn today," Brenna said. "We're heading over to set up so he can help me move the tables before he goes to PT." She and Penny locked eyes.

Now I was frowning. Brenna had never needed anyone to help her before. And Brendan was still recovering from the broken leg he'd sustained in the playoffs.

Penny's eyes widened, as if she'd just received an unexpected telepathic message.

Brendan squeezed Brenna's shoulder and cleared his throat. "My usual, please, Tasha, but decaf. Decaf for Bren, too."

"We're, um, trying to wean off caffeine," Brenna

explained, as her hand splayed over her flat stomach. She quickly dropped her hand, as if the fabric was molten lava.

It wasn't my business to ask, but I'd bet my Crock-Pot the woman was pregnant.

Another Edge baby next summer.

I was happy for her and stretched my lips into a smile. "Montgomery finally got to you about how poisonous coffee is, huh?" I waggled my eyebrows and turned before she could confirm or deny. It was obvious they weren't prepared to announce their news yet.

I selected mugs for each of them from the cubbies that made up our mug wall above the back counter. *My Wife Is Hotter than Coffee* and *My Husband Is Hotter than Coffee* were a new fun set Marie had gifted to her parents for their anniversary. I didn't think Jannell would mind if Bren-squared used them.

Bren-squared. Why did every hockey couple have such cute nicknames? Way better than Coach Monsha.

Not that Monty and I were a couple.

I lightly affixed the printed order stickers to the sides of the mug handles and set them on the counter for Gabby or Jannell to fill, and we all continued with our routine. When I returned from my break after lunch, I was surprised to find Xavier and Vlad chatting up Penny at her register.

"There she is!" Penny gave me a light hip bump. "Our guys are here!"

She was already shipping Vlad and me? I snuck a glance to see how he'd reacted.

Vlad's blinding smile gleamed like the sun reflecting off an unspoiled field of fresh snow.

I smiled back and suddenly felt tongue-tied. It wasn't

because I was smitten or crushing on him, but it wasn't a natural reaction, and I probably should analyze why.

Nah. He was here, he was smitten, and that was all I needed, right?

"Tasha! I am sad. I have just learned your break is over. I was hoping we could sit for a minute?"

I shook my head. "Sorry. Afternoon rush is about to start, and Gabby still needs a break." I signaled to her and nodded my head toward the kitchen door.

As she passed me, she squeezed my shoulder and winked.

Someone needed to tell her winking was creepy, especially from an elder Gen Zer.

Vlad pulled an envelope from the front center pocket of his hoodie. "For you, for later. I am looking forward to Friday night. My first American high school football game!"

I slid it into my apron pocket. "I told you, you don't have to come," I reminded him. "Your presence will make all the guys nervous and the girls giddy. Besides, I can't make it to your preseason game tonight."

"We'll be there Friday, too, Tasha," Xavier said. "Can't miss the first home game for Palmer City High. Some of my camp athletes play for the team. And Penny wants to see your timeout routines and the halftime show."

"I saw them practicing last week," Penny said as she handed Xavier his pregame toffee coffee. "It's going to be awesome!"

"I wish to as well," Vlad interjected.

Now I grinned for real. "My kids are going to knock your socks off," I said.

Vlad looked down. I peeked over the counter to find him wiggling his toes under the band of his team-issued slides. "Spider? Spill? Socks twisted?"

He shook his head. "Knock socks off?"

"It means to impress," Xavier filled in.

"Ah. English is weird."

I laughed. "That it is." I pointed down the counter. "Your order is up." I went back to taking orders and waved goodbye to them when they left.

Gabby returned from her break thirty minutes later. "Have you opened the envelope yet?"

I shook my head no.

"What are you waiting for?" Penny asked.

I shrugged. "Privacy so I can read it alone?"

"Pretend we're not here," Gabby said.

I rolled my eyes.

"C'mon, Tasha," Penny implored. "Aren't you dying to know what's in it?"

"I guess." I pulled it from my pocket. "Fine, I'll read it."

The flap of the envelope was tucked in instead of sealed, so the peach-colored card inside was easy to extract. I lifted the flap to find a note scrawled in loopy script.

My cheeks flamed with fire as I silently read each word. My joy filled his soul? Was he talking about me?

I was pretty sure *joy* wasn't a descriptor that anyone who knew me would use. I was cynical, critical, and sarcastic.

I cleared my throat and slipped the card back in the envelope, then met Penny and Gabby's expectant expressions. "Just a note. He seems to like me."

Penny clapped. "Yay!"

"Was it a poem?" Gabby asked.

I shook my head again. "The man barely knows English." But the note was well-written. Maybe he ran it through an editing program.

"So what are your intentions with Vlad?" Gabby asked. "Dating, marriage, baby in a carriage?"

I shrugged. "Too early to tell, but it'd be nice not to have to work three jobs." I pointed at my sister and cousin in turn. "I'd still work here for funsies, like you two do."

Penny and Gabby exchanged a look.

"What?"

"Tasha, stop," Penny pleaded. "You can't marry a guy you don't know just for his money."

"Why not? You did."

Penny winced. "No, I didn't."

"Okay. For his castle then."

"Stop it, Tasha. We had a soul connection. We'd known each other for years. You don't know anything about this guy. He could be part of a criminal family. And he barely speaks English."

"Even better." I closed my eyes and sighed. "I can grow to love him. Just like you grew to love Xavier."

"I don't like it."

"You don't have to," I retorted, a little more firmly than I intended. "Sorry. But it could be mutually beneficial. I overheard him asking Xavier how long it took to become an American citizen. He doesn't want to go back to the KHL if it doesn't work out for him here."

Penny gasped. "Tasha! He could be courting you for a path to citizenship!" In a very un-Penny-like move, she snatched the envelope from my pocket and pulled out the card, her eyes widening as she read. "This is a love letter."

"Yeah? So?"

"Let me see!" Gabby reached for it, and Penny passed it to her.

I crossed my arms over my chest as they turned and locked concerned eyes on each other. "It's just words," I said.

"Very pretty words." Gabby's eyebrows lifted as she scanned the card. She handed it back to me, and I returned it to the safety of my pocket. "He has the soul of a poet."

"If he even wrote it," I said.

Gabby tapped her chin and turned back to Penny. "Maybe Xavier can verify that?"

Penny nodded. "I'll see if he can find out without being so obvious."

I shook my head. "Please. Let it go."

"If you say so." Penny shrugged.

I spun on my heel and retreated through the kitchen door to read the words again in privacy.

They were pretty words.

But did he mean them? And had he written them for me?

I really *really* hoped so.

CHAPTER 18
Monty

One of my ideas for the team's social media was jump-scaring the players.

Mean? Perhaps. Toronto did it, so the concept wasn't original, but it'd be fun. And if I got slugged, well, the league had good health insurance.

Health insurance got me thinking about Tasha. Tasha led my thoughts to Vlad. And wouldn't you know it?

There he was—walking in the building in his swanky plaid suit in autumn colors, complete with a coordinating fedora and matching plaid band, trying too hard to give David Pastrnak a run for his money this year as the league's fashion favorite.

What a chump.

I motioned to Jared with my fuzzy paw and scooted just inside the hall that intersected Vlad's path to the dressing room.

"Get your phone ready," he said to Mags, our new social media intern.

"Ready!" she called back.

"Now!" Jared hissed.

I launched myself into the hall, directly in front of the six-foot third-line center.

"Aaah!"

Vlad jumped and nearly fell to the ground as he tried to recover his balance.

That was satisfying.

"Got it!" Mags held up her phone.

I high-fived her. "Sweet!"

She laughed. "One down, twenty-two to go!"

Vlad's eyebrows knit together. "Scare everyone?"

Mags nodded. "It was Monty's idea. Great, right?"

I leaned against the wall and raised my voice to be heard through the bear head. "*I* think so."

Vlad nodded. "Fun."

Well, *that* was insincere. Where was the guy's sense of humor?

Down the hall, Xavier and our goalie, Jason Dexter, had just turned the corner and were fast approaching us. "Let's skip these two. If Xavier spills his lucky coffee, we're a goal down. And I don't want to mess with the netminder."

"Smart," Jared agreed. "Even if we *are* playing San Jose. You never know, they could have a lucky night. But why take the chance?"

We greeted them, and then I scooted back into the hall to get ready for my next victim.

"Trotter and Emerson just turned the corner," Jared said. "Ready?"

"Ready," Mags said. I gave a thumbs-up.

"Now!"

This time, I dove to the ground on my side and came to a rest with my head in my hand, elbow bent, like I was a model posing on a beach. Brendan and Trask hooted above me, but I wasn't able to see if they'd jumped in surprise.

"Great one, Monty!" Brendan praised. "You get Dexter yet?"

Jared helped me to my feet. "Not this time. Don't want to mess with the goalie."

"Wise," Trask agreed. "He's so serious. You know how he has all his routines to vibe with before a game. You should definitely get Marsch, though. Payback for all the pranks he plays on us."

Zaki Marsch was a known prankster and, from what I heard, had never been out-pranked, though many players had tried. But he'd retaliated and made them regret it.

I wondered if he'd retaliate on me?

Only one way to find out.

I slipped back into the hallway, and Jared adjusted the costume to make sure the head was secure. Mags decided to skip over all the players who entered before Zaki, just in case he walked in on one of the jumps.

"Here he comes! Right behind ChaCha." Mags tapped me on the shoulder. "Go!"

I waited until Bryce Chambers passed us, then turned with my back to the hall. I squatted with my arms straight out in front of me, and double back-handspringed directly into his path.

"What the—Monty?" Bryce must have turned around. "What are you doing?"

I lifted my arms in a shrug and called out to Mags. "Did we get him?"

"Eh. Not really. He did jump a little, though."

Zaki snorted. "Nice try, guys." He tipped his hat and continued down the hall, flinging a warning over his shoulder. "C'mon ChaCha. You can help me dream up some payback."

Bryce followed him down the hall, turning around to make a slicing motion at his neck. "Y'all are in for it now!" he drawled.

I shrugged and shouted. "Bring it on!"

"No!" Mags laughed. "Maybe we should avoid him completely going forward."

"Yeah, his pranks are legendary," Jared agreed. "I don't want to be in his crosshairs."

"Let him know it was all my idea, then. What's the worst he can do?"

"He put marshmallows in Moreau's wheel wells last year," Jared said. "His brand-new custom Mercedes SL 500 Grand Edition!"

"He posted a picture of Trotter's underwear drawer, open, with ragged tighty-whities he—Zaki—bought at a thrift store," Mags added.

"Okay, so I'll watch my car and not invite him over." They looked nervous. "It'll be fine."

"If you say so," Mags said. "Good luck."

If being the recipient of a Zaki Marsch prank was my penance for making Vlad look ridiculous, so be it.

"Let's do one more of these, take an early dinner break, then head outside to greet fans while it's still light out," Mags said.

"You got it, boss," Jared said.

She giggled, a little too giggly. Was she sweet on him? I looked between the two. He was grinning like she hung the moon.

How sweet.

Twenty minutes later, I retrieved my phone from my

locker and grabbed my lunch bag. The team provided dinner, but Tasha's Crock-Pot braised beef and vegetables was far superior to anything I'd eaten here.

I was pulling it from the microwave when my phone buzzed in my pocket. I set the bowl on the counter and opened my messaging app to find a text from Vlad:

The roses are red and the violets are blue. Your pretty eyes are the ocean and I drown. Dying in your eyes would make me happy man.

You have got to be kidding me.

I thought about how I could rewrite it while I ate. Taking my food to an empty table, I inserted my earbuds to discourage anyone from talking to me.

This would take some work, but I was up to the challenge.

CHAPTER 19

"**Y**ou ready to go?" Monty leaned into the doorframe of my bedroom, arms crossed, sleeves of his FireVolts jacket pushed up on his forearms.

He was handsome, I'd give him that. And that casual doorframe lean would make most women swoon.

Not me, though.

"I need two more minutes," I said. I'd only been home for twenty, and I'd had to email several parents of my high school athletes to address questions about a competition I wanted to take the team to in the spring. It would require massive fundraising, but they were up to the task. And I had ideas for getting sponsorships, thanks to my recent connections to the Edge organization. Jason's wife, Lauren, was a fundraising superstar, and after chatting with her I had a plan and the administration's approval.

Apparently, he didn't take the hint. "You're still here," I said. "Why?"

"Did you eat?"

I shook my head. "I was just going to grab an energy bar. I'll eat when we get home."

He left, and I finished up the email, hit send, and closed my laptop. The peach envelope from Vlad was on a pile of books behind it. I smiled.

"'In a cloudy night sky, 'tis you who light my way. The moon and stars are dulled by your shine, shining and sprinkling light on all that is dark in my world,'" I quoted.

"Aw, that's sweet. And here I was, thinking you hated me."

I jumped in my chair, startled. Monty stood in the doorway again, holding my stainless-steel travel bowl. "You shouldn't sneak up on people!"

"Why not? You can hear the best things when people don't know you're listening." He grinned. "C'mon, you can eat in the car and fill my ears with more sweet nothings."

I shook my head, but I couldn't be mad at him. He was making sure I was fed, and that was nice. "That wasn't meant for your ears. Give me two minutes to change?"

"But I like you the way you are ... Womp womp!"

"Get out!" I shooed him with my hands. His grin widened, and he closed the door as he stepped out of the room.

As I changed into my team leggings and hoodie, it occurred to me that as annoying as Monty was most of the time, he had some endearing qualities. And I had to admit, after three months of rooming together, it was hard to remember sometimes that I was supposed to be eternally mad at him.

"So," Monty said as he turned out of the parking lot. "You writing poetry now?"

I shook my head and twisted my fork into the spaghetti

squash and meatballs with marinara that had been slow-cooking all day. *So good.* He'd even scraped the inside of the squash for me. "I got a letter from an admirer."

"An admirer, huh?" Monty's eyes were fixed on the road. In the distance, the sun was setting behind the mountains.

"Yup."

"And you memorized a line?"

"All of it."

"Must have been good. Care to share more?"

"Mmm." I swallowed the forkful and twisted another. "'Your joy fills my soul and fuels my need to prove to you that I am worthy of your radiance.'"

Monty snorted. "Clearly, this is a man who doesn't know you at all or loves to be verbally abused by someone who thinks your hedgehog cactus self is your version of joy."

I laughed. "Fair."

He stopped at a light and tapped the steering wheel with his thumbs. This was a Monty quirk he'd been doing since he got his license at sixteen.

"What's bugging you?" I asked. "The writing? It's actually pretty sweet."

He shook his head. "I'm not sure I like Vlad."

I sighed. "I'm not sure yet, either. But he sure is trying hard to get my attention." The light turned green, and Monty turned onto Canyon Pass Road. "That's the problem, I think. *Why* is he trying so hard? I mean, I'm a catch, but ..."

Monty laughed. "Just be careful, 'kay? And let me know if he needs a good beating."

I smiled. "I will."

I finished the last bite of my dinner as we pulled into the lot. "Thanks for feeding me."

"Thanks for making amazing food day after day. I'm going

to miss your cooking when I move out." He set the car in park and released his seat belt. "Have you put more thought into the cookbook idea?"

I shook my head. "No, but feel free to copy my recipes. I can sticky-note tab the ones Nana likes."

"That would be great. Thanks. Speaking of Nana, do you mind if we stop by her house after practice? I'd like to check on the reno progress."

"Sure. It's not too far out of the way. Do you think we'll be home by eleven?" Practice ran from seven until nine, and I liked to be in bed shortly after. Five a.m. came quick.

"I'll make sure of it," he promised.

Practice went well. The routine was coming along. We made adjustments, perfected what was working, and ran it over and over. We would be in great shape to perform at the gym-wide showcase in November.

Nana's house wasn't far from the Plex. I'd spent a lot of time here as a kid and teenager. She'd hosted all the team parties, and her doors were always open to Monty's friends. The Victorian mansion cut an impressive silhouette in the night sky, lit up by strategically placed lamps and recessed bulbs along the walkways.

"Beck's still here." I pointed to the Montoya Construction van in the driveway. "That's got to be expensive."

"Worth every penny," Monty said. "I may have added a few projects ..."

"Oh yeah?" We got out of the car. He waited for me at the hood. Instead of him opening the garage to enter the house, I followed him up the newly constructed walk to the front door. "I don't miss the stairs that used to be here," I admitted, "but these switchbacks will be a beast unless Nana has an electric chair. Couldn't she use the elevator in the garage?"

"The garage is full of construction materials," he explained, "and probably will be for months. Anyway, it was mandated. Jury's still out on whether Nana will get an electric chair. She can't be alone yet, and she likes to be pushed. And you know how she is with technology."

I laughed. "There is that." Since I'd known her, she'd always found a way to break or mess up phones, DVD players, smart TVs ...

"Tell me what you think of ... this." Monty opened the front door with a flourish and flicked a switch. The foyer came to life with light from a massive overhead chandelier.

I sucked in a gasp. "Wow," I breathed. "Beck did this?"

"Well, me and my crew." Beck appeared in the archway that led to the formal sitting room. "Hey, Tasha."

"Hey." I turned slowly in a circle, taking in the newly stained woodwork paneling that replaced the old mustard and ivory wainscoting below the chair rail, the matching grand staircase and banister, and the polished marble flooring. "This is ... this is beautiful work, Beck."

"Thank you." I turned in time to see her elbowing Monty. "I told you she'd like it," Beck hissed.

He nodded and caught my gaze. "What's not to like?"

I pointed to the wallpaper that covered the top half of the walls. "It's a bit outdated."

Beck grinned and stuck her hand in her pocket, pulling out a folded piece of paper. Monty held out his hand for it. "You were right. Here's your twenty."

He pocketed the bill. "She's hated this wallpaper since preschool."

"I don't ... hate it. It's just ... a bit hideous. It's like the artist wanted to see what art deco mixed with calico looked like. Pick one or the other. Well, for *this* house, anyway."

"What would you suggest?" Beck asked.

"I don't know," I admitted. "Anything else?" They laughed. "Maybe light peach or an ivory and pastel toile wallpaper. Hang a series of mirrors. It's a dark room, but a lighter color and mirrors could brighten it up, catch the light from the chandelier and the stained glass on the front door." I looked up. "That thing was made for a castle."

"Funny you should say that," Beck said. "It used to hang in Schwannenschloss."

My eyes widened. "Seriously?"

She nodded. "My dad and I did some work there a few years ago, when he was stationed in Munich. Xavier's grandfather gifted it to us, but I knew I'd never use it. Xavier didn't want it. When I saw this foyer, I knew it'd be perfect."

"It is." I looked up at it again. "It's going to be a beast to clean, though."

Beck laughed. "One of the reasons I didn't want it!" She turned to Monty. "Want to see the kitchen?"

Monty nodded, and we followed her through the elegantly decorated rooms to the back of the house, where the kitchen was located.

"We ripped out the wall you requested to create a more open space. The pipes here have already been replaced, so we're working on patching it all up now."

"Looks good," Monty complimented her. "Thanks."

I nodded my affirmation. My nose twitched at the dust that was still in the space, so I kept my mouth closed and pulled up my hoodie to cover the bottom half of my face.

Monty frowned. "What's wrong, Tasha?"

I shook my head and mumbled "Nothing yet" beneath the fabric. "I'll wait for you outside."

Monty stretched his arms out and blocked my exit. "Tell me."

My stomach began to feel queasy. I took a few deep breaths. "Gluten."

"Gluten? Beck, have you cooked here?"

She shook her head. "Nope. But there could be wheat in the drywall or insulation."

"Rip it all out." He lowered his hand and spoke softly to me. "I'll meet you outside."

I nodded and scurried out of the room, bolting for the front door and fresh night air.

Rip it all out? That would cost a fortune and extend the timeline. And it's not like I ever visited here anymore.

Monty and Beck joined me on the wraparound veranda about five minutes later and handed me a bottle of water. "Are you feeling okay?" he asked.

"Yeah." I turned to face them. "You don't have to rip it out. It's not an allergy, just a sensitivity. Minor reaction, promise. Doesn't even require Benadryl. It's just annoying. It shouldn't bother me when it's finished and covered up. And besides, it's not like I ever come here anymore."

"About that," Monty said. "Nana enjoys your visits. I hope you'll come here regularly again when she returns."

I opened my mouth to reply but lost my words. "Thank you," was all I could muster.

"I'm headed out," Beck said. "I'll see you tomorrow at our meeting with your Nana. Bye, Tasha."

We followed her to the driveway. The ride home was quiet, and I used the time to reflect on the history I had with the man sitting in the driver's seat.

I missed our friendship. I missed how easy it used to be between us. I missed our good-natured rivalry that made us both better, iron sharpening iron. And I wish I had the nerve to ask why he ditched me for Gabby.

That betrayal still felt fresh every time I thought about it. And the more time I spent with Monty, the more I replayed that day in my head.

CHAPTER 20
Monty

Mid-October

Opening night for the Edge. By the time warm-ups started, I was a sweaty, exhausted mess. I'd been out on the pavilion for hours, then inside greeting fans and donors. Then back outside for the Kids' Club meet-and-greet. At least there was a chill in the autumn mountain air. I couldn't imagine how mascots in the South got through it. And characters at theme parks?

God bless them.

Jared held Ridgie's head while I shoveled spoonfuls of Tasha's latest experiment into my mouth. That woman could put the most bizarre ingredients together and it not only worked, it was always the best thing to date that she made.

Tonight's dinner was a beef and sweet potato chili. She'd added tomatoes, a bunch of spices, corn, and even a bar of dark chocolate. And somehow, it worked.

Well.

"Fourteen minutes," Jared warned, checking his phone. "You almost done?"

"Yeah." I covered the container and shoved it back into my travel cooler bag. "I'll finish it later."

Jared secured the bear head and followed me through the halls to a bench by the tunnel, where my ice skates were waiting for me. I sat on a chair and pretended to put them on while Mags filmed.

"Got it!" she announced.

Jared slid the skates on my feet and laced them up. I pulled on the paws and he helped me to stand.

"You good?" Mags asked. "The team is coming."

I gave her a thumbs-up, and she handed me a flag with the Edge's logo. We made our way to the end of the tunnel to wait for my cue.

The noise of the crowd was deafening. "Thirty seconds," she shouted.

Behind me, the team was lining up. The goalie always led the team onto the ice, but this team had a tradition where they picked a local youth hockey player to skate a lap with a smaller version of the flag I was holding. Because it was opening night, they'd decided to have me get the crowd going first.

"Ladies and gentlemen, please get on your feet and give a loud welcome to your fa-vo-rite bear, Ridgie!"

"Go!" Jared shouted.

I stepped onto the ice, holding the flagpole in front of me, taking a slow lap around the boards. When I passed the team's family and friends section, I let go with one hand to wave and blow kisses.

The fans ate it up, but I couldn't feel any joy.

Tasha was there with Penny, Gabby, and the other Wags

and their families. I growled when I realized she was wearing Vlad's jersey, number fifteen. And on her face, she'd painted a crescent moon with dash marks around the opening to complete the circle. Which had nothing to do with the Edge and everything to do with a love letter Vlad had given her.

It made sense. We were up to four letters now, and I was just waiting on another grand to hit my bank account before I sent back number five. And he'd taken her out to dinner two of the last four Sundays.

But I didn't like it.

You fill my crescent moon to full.

Gag me. I thought she was too smart to fall for that garbage.

Apparently not.

I handed the flag to Jared and pushed myself through the players waiting for their signal. I heard the crowd quiet as the opening night video played and grow loud again when the kid skated out.

"Ridgie! Wait up!" Jared called, barely audible through the team's intro song, "Livin' on the Edge." "We don't have to rush upstairs yet! And you're still on your skates!"

Right. I wanted to get up to the platform so I could watch Tasha, but I'd break my ankles if I didn't change out my footwear.

Lucky for me, Mags had grabbed my shoes. I sat on the nearest bench and stuck a foot out.

"Diva," Jared muttered. I couldn't see his expression, but he didn't sound mad.

Once my sneakers were on, we rode the elevator up silently. I was sure they were confused by my quick exit, but I didn't owe them an explanation.

The doors parted, and I led the way to the platform. I

waved to the crowd and danced, doing my best to sneak glances down to the ice.

But it was no use. It was too dark, the family section was too far away, and my giant head obstructed any chance of me viewing that section, even if the distance wasn't too far.

After the opening ceremony, Jared, Mags, and I retreated to an unused conference room, where I couldn't get my head off fast enough.

"Bruh, are you all right?" Jared asked. "Breathing okay?"

I thought back to Thursday night, when the drywall or insulation impeded Tasha's breathing. "Yeah. I'm fine. Just needed a break."

"Good," Mags said. "Because the game just started, so we're here for a good three hours. I've got a long wish list of content from my boss."

"We'll get it done," I said. "What's next?"

She scrolled her phone. "Second time-out shenanigans, mini Zamboni ride, T-shirt cannon, pics with our featured veteran and his family …"

We got it all done, and when the final horn sounded, the Edge had won 3-2, with two goals from Xavier—almost unheard of for a defenseman in a first game of the season— and a five-hole goal from Zaki Marsch, right between the goalie's legs. Plastic and stuffed birds flew onto the ice at the buzzer—an homage to last season's pigeon incident—and I had a feeling there would be some bird-related bits in my near future. Thanks to fan demand, and an official vote, there were already talks of adding a second mascot, Percy T. Pigeon. "T" for "the." I hoped they came up with something more creative for its middle name.

It could be worse. At least they weren't dead birds—or

fish. Nashville fans throw catfish; Detroit fans throw octopi … shudder.

I waded into the crowd, taking pictures and posing for fans. It was fun, but my heart wasn't in it. I just wanted to get home and grill Tasha on her relationship with Vlad.

I arrived home just before midnight and wasn't surprised to see Tasha's door closed. I made sure Parfait's food and water dishes were full—they were, bless Tasha's heart—and I set my alarm for 5 a.m.

It came quickly. I dragged myself out of bed and shuffled to the kitchen, reminding myself that after she left, I could go back to bed.

Sometimes, it was good to be me.

But the realization made me feel worse, not better. Tasha *never* slept in, even if she could.

"What are you making?" I asked her.

She looked up from the cutting mat and smiled. "Barbecued pulled pork with carrots and cauliflower. What are you doing up?"

"Looks good," I replied. "It's Tuesday. Going to get in an early workout since we have practice tonight. Only four weeks until the showcase."

"Which we will rock," she said vehemently. "Taylor Brewer sent me a video of the Kalispell Worlds team. Our stunts are far more advanced."

"They always have been," I said, sliding onto a stool at the bar. "Just because they have two former national team members coaching their team, it doesn't mean the squad can actually execute the higher-level stuff." That was only true for *us* and *our* team.

"True," Tasha agreed. "But the team *has* improved tremendously since Taylor and Kane took it over. She can even compete, if she wants to. She demonstrates what she wants from the basket girls."

Taylor was local to Palmer City and a former athlete and coach here at the Plex before she married Brenna's cousin Kingston. He'd been traded to Montana a few years ago, and she now coached at the gym there. "I sent her portions of our routine to critique, and she admitted we were levels above them and most of the other big gyms. They're rooting for us, but we have to beat the Ontario team. They aren't giving any other team a peek at their stunts."

"We already knew that." I shifted in my seat. "Got any connections in Canada?"

She shook her head. "Nope."

"It doesn't matter," I said. "Evan could leave an Olympic gymnast in the dust if he went up against him in a floor routine. Your basket girls can do things in the air no one even dreamed about five years ago. And the FireVolts have the best coaches. How can we lose?"

She grinned. "They do, don't they?"

"One hundred percent," I agreed.

CHAPTER 21
Tasha

The Palmer City Harvest Moon Festival was an event I looked forward to every year. And this year, it lined up with OktoBrewFest, hosted by Brewski's, Brenna's family's sports bar and grill.

On Saturday, Brenna hosted a themed dance in her event barn after the family closed the grounds for the day. Xavier had bought out a full table: he and Penny; Gabby and Noel; Noel's mom, Gemma, and stepdad, Coach Conway of the Voltage; and me and Vlad.

I'd opted to meet Vlad here, on the OktoBrewFest grounds, instead of having him pick me up. It made sense; Monty dropped me off on his way to Nana's Mountainview Manor, where they were having their own version of the Harvest Festival. Xavier had invited him to join us—the tables were capable of seating ten—but Monty declined, citing his anticipation of spending his time with Nana weaving through the pumpkin patch behind the main building.

"There he is!" Penny hissed, pointing toward the entrance within the ropes.

I forced a smile and waved. Vlad was charming, good-looking, and thoughtful. And his love letters were straight swoon and fire.

But there was no chemistry in person.

Zero.

I read on a self-help site that you have to kiss someone to truly test compatibility. So I held out hope for that. Despite four dates now, he hadn't made a move. Xavier said it was because he wanted to be a gentleman and do everything right with me, but it still didn't *seem* right. If he felt as deeply and was as attracted to me as much as his letters claimed, wouldn't he feel compelled to at least *ask* me for a kiss?

Vlad hurried over and laced his fingers through mine, then raised our linked hands up to place a kiss on my knuckles.

I should have swooned, right?

Penny seemed on the verge, with one hand on her growing belly, her smile wider than I'd ever seen it and her eyes all googly and emotional.

"Hi," I said huskily, trying to sound enthusiastic.

"*Privet.* Hello." He squeezed my hand. "Shall we stroll through the corn maze?"

"Sure."

We separated from the group and entered the maze. He towed me down a path that led to a dead end. The moon shone on us. The mood evoked romance. And when he handed me a peach envelope, I prayed his words would flick a switch in my brain that had yet to spark.

Vlad shone his phone's flashlight on my hands as I removed the letter.

Dearest Tasha, it read.

WITH EVERY PIECE OF MY HEART YOU TAKE, IT RESETS AND EXPANDS EVER
LARGER, FUELED BY YOUR BEAUTY, YOUR SMILES, AND YOUR CLEVERNESS.
WAS THERE EVER A WOMAN SO PERFECT? I KNOW NOT. YOU LIGHT UP THE
DAY AND THE DARKNESS WITHIN ME. MY ADMIRATION AND ADORATION GROW
STRONGER EACH DAY, AND MY SOUL LONGS TO TELL YOU WHAT MY WORDS
CANNOT.

I think I stopped breathing.

"Oh Vlad," I said, looking up to meet his gaze. "What beautiful words."

"Beautiful words for a beautiful woman," he said, angling his head toward mine.

Here we go, I thought. *He's going to kiss me.*

Finally.

I lifted on my toes, and our lips met.

It should have been romantic.

It should have lasted longer than a brief touch.

I shouldn't have felt the urge to gag.

There wasn't any good explanation why I ended the kiss, other than ... it felt wrong.

Very wrong.

I couldn't explain. I'd wanted this. For weeks, I'd wanted this.

And now that it'd happened, I realized ... I didn't want this.

I opened my eyes, and our gazes locked. I offered a weak smile and took his hand in mine. I needed time to process our lack of chemistry. "Let's get out of here," I said. Before he could misinterpret my words, I added, "The barn dance starts in twenty minutes."

A confused expression crossed his features, but he recovered quickly and squeezed my hand. "I shall woo you with my finely cultivated dance moves."

Finely cultivated dance moves? His English *had* improved since I met him, but not for the first time, I wondered about the discrepancy between his everyday speaking, his letters, and the phrases he threw out every now and again. Sometimes, it was hard for me to discern how all three versions of him came together.

Brenna had arranged for the hayride drivers to transport festivalgoers from the town park to the corn maze and to the event barn and back. We opted for the short walk along the lantern-lit path. The October chill had replaced the warm sun, and I pulled my cardigan closed with my free hand until we stepped into line to enter the building.

The OktoBrewFest-themed interior was decorated in blue-and-white-checked cloth and other German accents. Autumn photo backdrops for selfies and group pics were stationed around the perimeter. One featured a pair of wooden hedgehogs perched on top of a tall hay bale, which made me think of Monty and his silly comparison of me to a hedgehog cactus.

The barn dance was a blast. My concerns about Vlad melted away as he led me around the dance floor, through traditional folk dances as well as a waltz and even Monty's favorite, the chicken dance. My emotions were all over the place, one moment swoony and the other suspicious. When I excused myself to visit the ladies' room, I took the opportunity to sneak out the side door to catch my breath instead.

I pressed myself to the back of the barn and inhaled the crisp night air into my lungs. My thoughts wandered again to

Monty. Was he home yet? Did Nana have a good time in the pumpkin patch?

I pulled my phone out from the side pocket of the exercise leggings I'd worn under my dirndl. Before I could think twice, I sent off a text.

You make it home okay? I asked.

I didn't have to wait long for his reply. It came through as I stared at the screen. *I'm just getting to my car now. These old ladies are party animals. You having a good time?*

I didn't know how to answer. It was fun, but I was still troubled, and I didn't know why.

Tasha?

I'm here. Just tired.

Want me to pick you up on my way home?

I didn't hesitate to answer. *Yes, please.*

Be there in ten.

I rushed back inside, told Vlad I wasn't feeling well and thanked him for a wonderful time. I kissed him on the cheek, made my excuses to Penny, and hurried out the main door. I didn't stop walking until I reached Brewski's.

I dialed Monty. "I'm almost at Main. I can walk the rest of the way home if you're not close."

"Stay put. I got you," he said softly. "You feeling all right?"

"A little queasy," I croaked. It was true but not for the reasons I was making him think. I felt like a fool running out of there the way I did.

"I see you. I'm going to pull over and get the door for you, okay?"

I nodded. "Thanks." Monty's white truck pulled up to the curb like a legendary steed. He hopped out and ran around to the passenger side to open the door for me.

Unable to look him in the eye, I climbed up into the seat and buckled myself in as he shut the door.

"You're not okay," he observed, easing back onto the road. "What can I do?"

I swallowed the giant rock in my throat—hard—and shook my head. "Nothing," I whispered.

"Pharmacy? Urgent care? Your parents? ER?" His voice rose with each suggestion.

I shook my head vehemently, not wanting him to worry. "It's not a flare-up."

"What then? You look like you're going to be sick."

I drew my knees up to my chest and looked out the passenger-side window. "I feel like I might. But it's not food-related."

"Did Vlad—" He cut himself off. "Do I need to beat his backside back to Russia?"

Despite everything, I couldn't help smiling at the visual. I gave in to the chuckle that bubbled up. Monty kicking Vlad so hard on his rump, sending him sailing into the atmosphere toward Russia, was a funny thing to imagine.

"No. He was ..." I thought carefully. "Perfect?"

"Then what?"

"I don't know."

Monty steered into the lot and pulled up to the entrance. "Go on up. I'll park and meet you inside."

"Okay."

I exited the car and tapped my keycard on the pad next to the door.

He must have found a close spot, because he was beside me at the elevator bank before the car reached the ground level.

"Come 'ere, fraulein." He held his arms open, and I

walked into his beefy embrace, resting my head on his hard chest, just like I'd done after every breakup except that last one.

Was I breaking up with Vlad? Were we even together? I had no idea.

The elevator arrived, and we shuffled into it. Monty held me close while I tried to make sense of the thoughts in my head. When the doors opened on our floor, he walked me to the door, opened it, took my purse off my shoulder, and guided me to the sofa.

"Sit," he commanded.

I sat.

He snapped his fingers, and Parfait came running. "Up on the sofa."

The cat jumped on the cushion next to me, climbed onto my lap, turned in a circle, and began to purr.

I look up at Monty, surprised.

"He's an emotional support cat, remember?"

Unofficially, I wanted to say. Instead, I nodded and watched Monty hang my purse on the pegs by the door and move into the kitchen. He lit my trio of fall-scented candles, filled the teapot with water, set it on the stove, and turned the setting to high. Next, he left the kitchen and sprinted to his room, emerging a moment later with a box of ... hot chocolate?

The teapot whistled. He switched it to another burner. My eyes didn't leave him as he emptied the premade powder into two mugs and poured the boiled water over it. He topped each mug with a splash of oat milk.

Since when did he drink oat milk?

Monty carried the two mugs into the living area and offered one to me. I took it and closed my eyes, letting the steam warm my face and hoping it would bring me some clarity.

When I raised my head, he wore the same expression I'd seen him set on his Nana when he wouldn't let her have a particular sweet treat at the Coffee Loft.

I sipped the hot chocolate and frowned. "This isn't—"

"It's certified gluten-free pumpkin spice hot cocoa."

"You steal it from your nana?" I teased. "I knew you were a closet PSL guy!"

"Nah. It's not sugar-free. I found it online."

"Huh. And you're drinking it?"

"It's not coffee," he reminded me and took a sip. "Think Nana would like it?"

I shook my head no. "Absolutely not. It's terrible." I watched his face fall into a frown, then added, "I'll have to drink all of it. To keep her safe from a major life disappointment."

He laughed, then his face grew serious. "I know a bit about that," he said.

"I know you do." I set my mug down on the table. "Mindy's anniversary is this week."

"Yeah. And as usual, my parents plan to go about the day like it's any other."

"People cope with grief differently," I said quietly. "I'm sure they'll be thinking of her."

"Maybe." He placed his mug on the table next to mine and rested his arm on the back of the sofa. If I leaned backward an inch, my head would be cradled in the crook of his elbow. "Nana's not mobile enough yet for me to take her to Mindy's grave."

"Oh, Monty." I looked up at his face. Water pooled beneath his eyes. I slid one arm between his back and the sofa cushion and wrapped the other around his middle. I gave a light squeeze and rested my head on his chest. "I'm so sorry."

A drop of water landed on the shell of my ear and traveled down to the lobe. I didn't make a move to wipe it away. I just sat there and held him till my eyes grew heavy and I fell asleep.

CHAPTER 22
Monty

Wednesday morning, I stayed in bed until I heard Tasha leave for work. For hours, I'd been awake while the last moments of Mindy's life played on repeat over and over.

She'd been going through treatment again, and I'd heard her doctor advise my parents against taking her home for Mom's big birthday bash. Dad had been adamant they sign off and even promised to hire a nurse. It was only for a few hours. What could go wrong?

Mom insisted it was fine; they could celebrate in the hospital and cancel plans or postpone her fortieth birthday bash. But Dad cut her off, reminding her there was a good chance this would be her last birthday with Mindy. Mom walked away crying, and the next day, we brought Mindy home. A nurse met us at the house and got her situated in a recliner in the expansive living room. After cake, Mindy asked to go lie down. The nurse took her into the first-floor guest room while Mom and Dad said goodbye to the guests.

Rain was in the forecast, so many of the guests opted to

leave early. Me, at eight years old, played a video game on my Nintendo DS on the divan in the corner of the bedroom. At 9 p.m., the nurse left. Mom came in to lie on the bed with Mindy, holding her close and stroking her hair as she slept.

I must have fallen asleep, too, because when I woke up, Mom was screaming at Mindy to wake up and for Dad to call an ambulance. I raced to the other side of the bed, and what I saw made my blood chill.

Mindy's eyes were closed, and she was struggling to breathe. Her IV was beeping, drained of its liquid.

"What's taking so long?" Mom cried. "They should be here!"

Dad got on the phone again and hurried out of the room. I ran after him, outside and into the storm. At the bottom of the hill, flashing lights blinked through the rain. The siren shrilled uphill to meet our ears.

"Stay in the house!" Dad ordered.

But I didn't. I followed him into the storm and down the incline to the bottom of the aspen-lined driveway, where the paramedics were trying to move a fallen tree out of the way just inside the gate.

"Fire rescue is on the way!" one of the men shouted. "Do you have a chain saw?"

Dad shook his head and joined the men trying to move the tree. I pulled at a sturdy branch, and together, the four of us moved the tree, inch by inch, just enough for the ambulance to get around.

The medics jumped inside and raced up the hill. Dad and I trudged back to the house, soaking wet, as they were loading Mindy into the ambulance. Mom climbed in after her, and they took off before we could reach them.

I never got to say goodbye to my sister.

By the time Dad and I got to the hospital, Mindy had slipped into a coma. Three days later, she was gone. And we were all changed forever.

My parents leaned on each other, and I had Nana. By the time I left for prep school, I was practically living with her. She was my rock, my everything.

I visited her pretty regularly, at the gravesite, but on the anniversary of her death, I liked to bring her sunflowers and a new cheer bow, which I hung on a sticky hook that miraculously had lasted through years of weather. She would have been a FireVolt if she'd lived, and I had no doubt she would have made Team USA if she tried out. Lucky for me, there was always a girl on the team who'd accept ten times what her bow was worth after competing so that I'd have a bow to give Mindy. I'd spend the whole day here at her gravesite, chatting about the things I thought a big sister might want to know about.

This year, I'd called Taylor to ask if she could make a special FireVolts bow, like Tasha's, but add "Honorary" in vinyl over the word "Coach."

Today wasn't much different than previous years, except I wouldn't be leaving to pick up Nana and bring her here to sit with me on Mindy's favorite blanket, a fuzzy worn-out supersoft flannel she'd received with a gold medal and championship ring at Summit after her last competition.

"Our Worlds team is going to win. I can feel it. Tasha is by far the most creative choreographer I've ever known. And I'm not just saying that because she used to be my best friend. She's incredibly talented, and I believe she should be on the team, too. She can dance circles around those girls. And I'm sure she could still do the stunt work. But she's refused to try ever since she broke her leg."

Soft footsteps padded on the walk behind me and came to a stop. I didn't turn around, but my heart knew who it was. I wondered if she'd been close enough to hear me talking about her.

"I'm so glad you suggested to Mom and Dad all those years ago that I go to 'baby cheer camp.' Even though I was mad it just was mornings and you got to go all day. But you knew it would be good for me. You *always* knew what would be good for me. And I met Tasha there."

I was ninety-nine percent certain it was Tasha behind me. Anyone else would have shown themselves by now or made a noise to alert me to their presence. All I heard was quiet breathing and an occasional sniff.

"I didn't know until I met her how desperately I needed a best friend. You were awesome, of course, best sister ever, but the five-year gap between us meant I didn't get to see you much. I'll never forget that first day of camp. It was pretty boring until the first water break. This girl with a long ponytail and enormous red bow tapped me on the shoulder and told me I was doing my forward rolls all wrong." I used a high-pitched voice to mimic four-year-old Tasha. "That's *not* how you do a forward roll. Watch me!' And right there, in front of all the other kids by the cubbies, she raised her arms, clicked her feet together, and demonstrated, telling me when and where to tuck my head. She stood up with a flourish and raised her arms in a triumphant *V.* It was pretty amazing."

Above me, Tasha snorted. I took that as encouragement to keep telling my side of the story. "She worked with me until the end of the water break and said, 'That'll have to do, for now. Stick with me and you'll be the best boy here.' So I did. Coach called us back from break and instructed us to pair up.

Tasha scooted over to me, and I took her hand. I wanted to be the best boy so badly."

I closed my eyes, wanting to picture one of my favorite memories.

"We're going to try a basic stunt. Decide which of you will be the base and which will be the flyer."

"I'm the flyer," Tasha informed me.

That settled that. I didn't even know what that meant, but she did. She was so smart.

"Bases, you're going to kneel down and sit back on your heels. Put your hands out in front of you like this … and tuck your head down in front of your knees to create a surface for your flyer. Flyers, you'll stand next to your base and place your inside foot on their bum. Raise your hands into a high V and hold your position. Be very careful not to hurt or stomp on your base."

Some of the kids giggled but not me and Tasha. This was serious business to us. I did as the coach instructed, and Tasha made a few adjustments. "Tuck your head like this. But not all the way because you might have to look up and smile for the audy-dance." Not very gently, she pushed my head into place. I felt her foot on my bum a moment later.

The coach came around to make adjustments but didn't touch either of us. "Great job, you two! No adjusting needed here. Look at me on three with your cheer face … One, two, three!"

I popped my head up with my happy mask—that's what Mindy called it.

"Great job! Now hit your toy soldier positions for me. Awesome! Give your partner a high five!"

"We're the best girl and boy here!" Tasha said gleefully. "Will you be my partner forever?"

"Yeah! We're the best!"

Her eyes narrowed. "To stay the best, you'll have to work hard. Promise?"

"Yeah, I promise." Whatever it took, I wanted to be the best, like my sister.

"Spit on your hand and let's shake on it." Tasha spit on her hand and held it out to me.

I quickly did what she asked and clasped my hand in hers.

"Ew! You two are gross!" a girl said. "Why did you do that, Tasha?"

"Ignore her," Tasha said. "That's my cousin Gabby. She's just jealous 'cause I'm partners with the best boy."

"I'm not jealous!"

"Yes, you are!"

"No, I'm not!"

I stepped back, sure that they were about to fight, but the coach came over and Gabby stalked off before they could be reprimanded.

Tasha turned back to me. "Partners forever?"

"Partners forever," I promised.

A promise I'd broken epically.

I opened my eyes to find Tasha sitting on the blanket next to me. "Aren't you supposed to be at work?" I asked.

She shrugged. "It was slow. Thought I'd come out here and pay respects to the awesomest tumbler I've ever known."

"Hey, I thought I was the awesomest tumbler you've ever known."

She rolled her eyes. "Please. If Mindy were here today, she'd flip circles around you."

"Yeah, she would," I agreed. I turned my gaze from the gravestone to the woman beside me. "Thanks for coming by. It means a lot."

Tasha held my gaze and nodded. "I heard you talking about our first cheer camp. We totally rocked it." She smiled wistfully. It was considerate of her not to mention the part about me breaking my promise. "Remember the one before you went to boarding school in Denver?"

"How could I forget? We won the senior-level partner challenge." It stung to say the word "partner."

"The first of four straight titles." She smiled broadly.

"We totally deserved it. No one else was practicing lifts in the pool until lights out."

"And after." She snickered.

We might have broken a few rules over the years.

I smiled. "Then, after high school, we became coaches, and then it didn't matter if we were in the pool after lights out."

"We were dedicated, for sure."

"We were."

During that third summer of coaching together, between our sophomore and junior year of college, we'd devised new crazy stunts in the pool, and I began to see Tasha in a different light. She'd been struggling with some health issues, and I knew she'd been in a lot of pain. The way she fought through it made me admire her even more.

So much more, it interfered with my concentration.

My greatest fear was dropping her, letting her down literally and figuratively. I didn't think through my decision to partner up with Gabby, how it could hurt Tasha and have lasting effects years later. I figured it was best for the team because, well, because Tasha had become ... distracting.

She'd never asked me why I'd done it, and I was glad, because I'd never wanted to tell her. But sitting here, knowing she'd come here to support me, left work even, it felt like the old us—the old us before I broke our partnership.

I was feeling a growing need to explain, and she'd given me the segue to do it.

"That next summer, camp wasn't the same without you," I said quietly. "That whole year leading up to it, and every year since, hasn't felt the same. The FireVolts weren't the same without you. The national team wasn't the same without you." I turned to face her. "*I* wasn't the same without you. I'm so sorry I requested a new partner and broke us up. I'm sorry your new partner was a hack and dropped you. I'm sorry that drop broke your leg and ended your performance career. I *never* would have let you hit the ground."

She looked away, and I watched her cheeks twitch as she struggled to keep her emotions inside. "I wasn't upset at first. We had a new coach, and new coaches always liked to mix us up, try us out with other partners. But they always put us back together when they could see what we could do. But you stopped coming early. You'd arrive just on time and then rush out, leaving us no time to practice and show them what we could do. Then I found out you *requested* Gabby. That's what stung the most. You knew how competitive the two of us were."

"I was there when you found out, and I'll never forget the expression on your face. I ran into the bathroom to throw up. I knew instantly I'd hurt you and lost my best friend." I hung my head.

"The betrayal was unbearable," she whispered.

When I looked up, she was swiping at her eyes and staring off toward the church. An apology wasn't enough.

I owed her an explanation. "That was never my intention, I promise. You remember that last summer we coached at camp together? We were working on a new kick-out?"

She nodded. "I practiced it every chance I got. I wanted to be the first to master it."

"And I wanted that for you. Instead of the pool, one night we walked down to the lake and swam out to the floating dock so I could toss you higher over the deeper water. The only light was the full moon, and it was enough. We did it over and over and over again."

"We finally got it. We high-fived and decided to do it one more time. You launched me, and then you fell in, too." Tasha turned her head back to me. "We got tangled under the water and came up laughing."

I sucked in my breath. "We steadied each other. And then ..."

"It got quiet. And we just stood there." She tilted her head. "You were looking at me weird. A mix of pride, joy, and something else. What was that?"

I sighed. I'd almost kissed her. And it would have ruined everything. "It was ... something else. And it freaked me out. After that, I became more concerned with you not falling than I was with winning."

Tears welled in her eyes. "Is ..." She swallowed. "Is that why you broke up our partnership?"

I nodded.

"I thought ... all this time, I thought ... I thought ..."

She covered her face with her hands and started to shake. My heart raced. Did she understand what I wasn't saying? Did it repulse her? I wrapped my arms around her and pulled her to me. "What did you think?"

"It's too embarrassing!" She shook her head.

"It can't be more embarrassing than me admitting I ditched you because I was crushing on you. Spill."

Tasha stilled in my arms and sat back. "Promise me you won't laugh."

"I promise."

"I—I was having problems with my stomach that summer. I was on new meds, and I was very gassy. I know on more than one occasion I couldn't hold it in and—"

I *did* want to laugh, and it was hard not to. But I wasn't going to break any more promises to her. I pulled her back to me and tucked her head under my chin. "I noticed, and I didn't care. Not one bit. You were in pain, and I felt helpless."

"You didn't care? Really?" She pushed her hands against my chest. Her tear-streaked cheeks cracked my heart. Her eyes locked on mine and waited for me to answer.

"Really. Why would I? I actually thought it was cool. Made you human. I loved you more for it—Tasha's Standards of Perfectionism are hard to achieve. Piece of cake for me, though, of course."

"Of course," she mumbled. "Um … That's why he dropped me."

"Huh?"

"That's why he dropped me."

I scratched my head and lifted my eyebrows. "I missed something. Why did he drop you?"

"I … startled him?"

I knitted my forehead in mock confusion. "I'm not connecting the dots."

She pushed at me and laughed. "Don't make me say it out loud!"

"What? That you tooted your horn?"

"Oh my gosh!" She slugged me in my bicep and jumped

to her feet, pointing and waving her finger at me. "Don't *ever* say that again!"

"What? That you broke wind? Cut the cheese? Dropped a bomb?"

"Aaaah!" She covered her ears, but she was laughing. "Stop!"

"On one condition."

"Anything."

"Come to the gym with me. Give us a chance to prove we're still the best."

Tasha took a step back and shook her head vehemently. "No way. It's been *years*."

"It has. And it's time you got back up on your horse." I stood up and folded the blanket. "I *promise* I will not let you hit the floor."

"I ... um ... the high school team practice starts at three thirty."

"Plenty of time."

Her gaze swung toward Mindy's gravestone, then back at me. "Okay."

CHAPTER 23
Tasha

W hat had I been thinking?

If it hadn't been Mindy's anniversary, I wouldn't have let him talk me into it. Partner stunting after all these years? I doubt I could even execute a standing back handspring, never mind a flip in the air.

But I'd always felt safe with Monty. And I believed him when he said he wouldn't let me hit the floor.

We were partners for sixteen years. We'd worked through coaches who tried to break us up, significant others who couldn't handle our close friendship and the physical connections the sport required, and pushed ourselves and each other to our limits to be the best in the sport.

He'd failed me when he chose Gabby after our sophomore year of college. He'd broken his promise, and I'd written him off. And then my gassiness startled my new partner to the extent he stepped out of position for my landing and failed to catch me safely. It had been the end of my cheer career.

It was time to forgive Monty, and forgive myself. We were adults now, and if we wanted to repair our friendship—which

I realized I so desperately did—it was going to take some work.

And kindness. And understanding. And grace.

The cemetery behind St. Mary's was about a ten-minute walk from our apartment building, and both of us had opted not to drive there. We jogged home to change into workout clothes, and Monty drove us to the Plex. On the way, he called Nate to see if he was available to spot us during his lunch break.

He was.

This was happening.

Oh my gosh, this was happening!

After warming up—and stretching extensively—we found an open spot by the tumble mats and deferred to Nate to instruct us.

"We'll start easy, basic." My former coaching partner looked past me to Monty, standing behind me. "Hands on her hips. Shoulder sit on my count."

Monty's hands closed over my hips, his thumbs pressing lightly into the dimples on each side of my spine. I closed my fingers around his wrists and exhaled. My heart was flipping at the rate of one of his tumbling passes. "Ready."

Nate counted. "Five, six, seven, eight!"

I prepped as he squatted, taking a small hop. My feet touched the ground for the second time, and then I was airborne, landing comfortably in a seated position on Monty's right shoulder.

"Like riding a bike." Monty held me in place securely. "Ready for something more advanced?"

"Let's see if I can nail the dismount first," I replied warily.

"Count it, Tasha," Nate directed.

"Five, six, seven, eight!"

Monty squatted, and I leapt off him, landing cleanly on my feet with my arms tucked tightly to my side.

"Lookin' good," Nate praised. "How about raising that sit up an arm's length?"

"Um …" I looked at Monty. That would require his hand on my bottom.

"I'm a professional, Tasha." He rolled his eyes. "Your jelly isn't any different from anyone else's."

Nate laughed, and I scrunched my face. I wasn't sure how I felt about that. I stayed in shape and like to think my jelly wasn't very … jelly.

"Whatever." I threw my shoulders back. "Let's do it."

We got into position, and on the way up, I let go of Monty's hands and raised my arms in a high *V* while lifting my right knee up into the liberty position. My bottom came to rest in his palm, and his other hand secured my straight leg.

I was back on the horse. And as cool as I wanted to present myself, I couldn't stop grinning. "Down in five, six, seven, eight!"

Monty bent and boosted me into the air. His hands found my hips again as I landed cleanly on the ground. I lifted my arms to high-five the guys, still wearing my cheesiest smile.

"Felt good, right?" Nate grinned. "Shoulder stand?"

I looked over at Monty. I had no doubt in his basing capabilities; his private clients consisted of everyone from girls on younger teams to college and national team members. But my balance? Would that come back the way I needed it to?

"I got you." There wasn't a hint of anything but determination in his tone.

"Okay." I looked to Nate. "Like riding a bike. I'll count."

Same position as last time. Monty's hands on my hips. My hands on his wrists. "Five, six, seven, eight!"

Hop, jump, soar.

I tightened every muscle in my body on the way up and stared straight ahead of me. Monty held my shoes at his shoulders, then moved his hands to secure them around my calves, locking me in place. It was effortless, steady, and balanced like I was standing on the floor.

Secure.

It was like no time had passed. Monty was still the same partner who synced with me like no other ever could. When I was in his strong, capable hands, I was fearless, fierce, and focused, but more importantly, I felt like I could achieve anything. His touch instantly calmed me. In his grip or in his arms—there was no place I'd ever felt safer.

"Press to full extension!" I called down. "Monty, you count."

"Five, six, seven, eight!"

I held my breath and kept my body tight as I rose higher.

Breathe.

"I got you, Tasha!" Monty didn't have to remind me. I could feel it. From my vantage point, I could see across all four cheer floors and up into the balcony.

I'd missed this. The height, the freedom up here. After all these years, it was still a rush!

Nate called up to me. "Back to shoulders or full dismount?"

"How about a cradle?" I asked.

"Let's do it," Monty said.

I took in a long breath to fill my lungs. "Five, six, seven, eight!"

Down, up, down, catch.

But instead of dumping me out of his arms, Monty held me in position.

"Hey you." He pressed his forehead against mine. "You're amazing, you know that?"

Whew, he was so close I could feel the warmth of his breath mingling with mine. "Save your praise for something more advanced."

Monty tipped me forward and set me on the ground, holding on to my shoulders for a smidge longer than was necessary. He let go and cleared his throat. "How much more time do you have, Nate?"

"Fifteen minutes or so. What's next?"

"Cheese mat," I said determinedly. "I want to see if I can still flip."

Nate and Monty exchanged a look, then they said together, "We can spot you."

I laughed. "Okaaaay … No cheese mat." I looked forlornly at the giant wedge. "Looks like it'll be up to you two to get these legs around and back to the ground."

Monty smirked. "It's not hard. Watch me."

He took a step back, squatted with his arms straight out in front of him, and leapt backward in a textbook-perfect standing back handspring.

"Show-off," I teased.

"I learned from the best," he shot back. The man had the nerve to wink at me.

Oooh, he really knew how to fire me up.

"Whenever you're ready, Tasha," Nate said.

"Let me try a few back walkovers first and see where I'm at." I could still do a backbend; it was part of my stretch routine. But it had been years since I'd pulled my legs over.

I positioned myself between them. "Here goes." I fell

backward, lifting my lead leg into the air. I pulled my core muscles tight as my hands flattened on the ground. Other than a light touch from Nate on my trailing leg, I got over and landed on my feet just fine.

The pride in Monty's eyes caused a warming in my chest I wasn't prepared for. He didn't need to say a word, and he didn't. But I was encouraged, and I suddenly felt invincible.

"One more time," I decided. "Then on to harder things."

Five minutes later, I'd perfected the back walkover, the standing back handspring, and a round-off back handspring.

It felt amazing. And from the look on the guys' faces, I knew it looked amazing, too.

"I've got to get back to the clinic," Nate said. "But we should do this again. You've still got it, Tasha."

"Thanks for coming down here." I turned to Monty. "And thanks for making me do this."

He nodded toward the trampolines. "Next time?"

"Yeah. I think you've revived an old monster."

"*Monsha*," he corrected.

We laughed, and he wrapped an arm around my shoulders as we walked through the gym and to his truck.

We were friends again.

We were *partners* again.

And if Nana's house was ready next week as projected, I was going to miss him as my roommate.

CHAPTER 24

Monty

I dropped Tasha off at home, then drove back to the gym at the Plex to work through all the unwanted thoughts and feelings our little practice session had brought to the surface. The fitness machines were on the ground floor and featured a floor-to-ceiling window wall that rose up several stories and presented a breathtaking view of the mountains.

Up until today, I could pretend I didn't care that she hated me. I could pretend I hated her. Our rivalry was working in the gym. Good Coach Monty praised and inspired; Bad Coach Tasha glared and demanded perfection.

I could pretend she wasn't the most beautiful and desirable woman I knew. I could ignore it when she lounged on the sofa in her tiny athletic shorts and tank top. I might have, on occasion, lowered the temperature on purpose to incite her to cover up so I wouldn't be tempted to stare.

Before this morning, I could pretend I didn't care about hurting her all those years ago. But now that I knew she thought I quit on her because of a health issue? I wanted to prove to her that I not only didn't care about her occasional wind breaking but also that I *did* care about the trials she'd lived through and continued to face with extraordinary strength because her gut was dysfunctional.

In another way, my gut was also dysfunctional. I should have known that choosing Gabby over her would cause Tasha to write me off. They'd been competitive their whole lives. In retrospect, it had to feel like the ultimate slap in the face.

I'd just finished up on a bench press and was restacking the weights with a gym spotter when Nate came in after work. He'd changed into his FireVolts tee and shorts. My expression must have sent a signal I hadn't intended because he lifted his hands up, palms out, like he needed to defend himself. And now I was aware of my eyebrows and chin lifting.

My resting face needed some work. Was it possible to re-train your subconscious expressions?

"I'm not interested in dating Tasha," he said bluntly. "I swear."

I knew he wasn't, but why did he feel the need to state so?

I shrugged. "Neither am I."

Now his eyebrows were reaching new heights. "I was going to text you, but since you're here, I'll just say it."

"Say what?"

"She's fragile. "

I snorted. "If there's one thing she isn't, it's fragile. You saw her on the mat today, right?"

He nodded. "I've seen a lot of other things, too. I was here for your falling-out. I was ten feet away when she fell and broke her leg. I saw your so-called best friend DJ swoop in and try to fill your place in her life, just to prove he could. I was here six months after that, co-coaching with her, doing everything I could to encourage her to get back in the game. Which you did in less than an hour today."

I wasn't following. "Which, again, proves that she's not fragile." I crossed my arms, but my insides were glowing. He'd been trying for *years* to get her back into performing?

"Man, for a smart guy, you sure are dumb sometimes." He sighed loudly in frustration and looked up at the ceiling.

I waited.

Finally, he was done taking whatever dramatic breath he needed and locked his eyes on mine. "She's in love with you. She always has been. And she has no idea, will never admit it, and likely won't ever act on it. But if you hurt her again, it will *destroy* her, even worse than the first time."

I opened my mouth to reply, but it just hung open.

I'd never been so confused in my life.

I managed to find words. "What's your evidence? I need hard proof."

Nate closed his eyes and pinched the skin between his eyes, like I was causing him a headache. "Do you have all night?"

"Yup."

He shook his head. "Just take my word for it. Her pride is everything to her. She's tough on the outside, sure, but she breaks down, just like we all do. And a broken-down Tasha can be taken out by a toddler."

I thought back to her flare-up. How she hadn't wanted me to see her in her weakness. I didn't think an emotionally broken-down Tasha could even be a thing, but what Nate was saying made sense.

Tasha put up big, strong walls on the outside to protect herself on the inside.

Cliché and common, which was why it'd never crossed

my mind. To me, she was invincible and above everyone else. To her family, she was the strength when they needed help. To her athletes, she was the iron coach, incapable of bending and unwilling to compromise, even under intense pressure. And she never got heated or lost her cool.

She was icy. Competitive.

Perfect.

And she was in love with *me?*

Nate was right; she'd never admit it. Because love me or hate me, she needed me in her life.

And I needed her.

"So … What do I do?" I asked him.

He shrugged. "Do you love her?"

"Since I was four," I said simply.

"Then only tell her if you're willing to propose forever. Or you'll lose her again, and this time, for good."

I DROVE by the high school on the way home. The varsity cheerleading squad practiced just inside the fence that separated the outdoor track from the road. The football field was inside the track, and the soccer field just beyond that.

I lowered the passenger-side window as I rolled past like a creeper. Under the lights, Tasha counted out a routine for her athletes, probably for a time-out at this Friday night's game. I glanced at the clock. Almost six o'clock. Practice was running late.

Could Nate be right? Could she have feelings for me that she couldn't—or wouldn't—acknowledge?

And all this time?

Nate's words shocked me like an errant spark from a bonfire, only the bonfire was within me in the form of a new anxiety I didn't know how to counter.

And what of Vlad? I'd concentrated my efforts on helping Tasha fall in love with him, but it wasn't working. Anyone could see they didn't act like a couple who were crazy about each other.

It was too much to believe that she had those feelings for me and that none of her previous relationships had worked out because her heart hadn't been in them.

But—what if it was true?

Back in the apartment, I took a quick shower and was setting the bar with plates and silverware when she walked in. Judging by the aroma, whatever was in the Crock-Pot was something different. I'd eat quickly and then go visit Nana until visiting hours ended.

I'd been by this morning, but I felt the urge to go again. I wasn't sure if I wanted to ask my grandmother about her take on Nate's theory or not, but I did want to just *be* with her. She was a calming presence, the only thing in my life that had always been steady and constant.

I lifted a hand to greet Tasha as she entered, hung up her team jacket, and disappeared into her room, reappearing without her backpack. She smiled at me as she passed me on her way into the kitchen.

"How are you doing?" She lifted the cover of the Crock-Pot and stirred the mixture with a large spoon.

"I'm good. Going to visit Nana after dinner. You?"

"Fine. You should take her some of this." She collected our plates from the bar and set them next to the slow cooker. "If it's any good. I had to modify her recipe."

"What is it?" I asked.

"A gluten-free dairy-free version of mac 'n' cheese with hamburger and peas." I stared at her as she set a plate of the mixture in front of me. "Are you okay?"

I shook my head and covered my face with my hands. Why would Nana give her *that* recipe? I'd told her when I was eight I never wanted to eat this stuff ever again.

"Monty, you're worrying me." She came around the counter and rubbed my back. "What's wrong?"

"P-peas and cheese!" I shook with grief.

"And meat," she added. "Are you laughing or crying?"

I let my hands drop so I could look at the food. Tasha used the end of her sleeve to wipe my tears. "It's Mindy's favorite," I choked out. "I haven't eaten it since she died."

"Oh, Monty." Tasha squeezed her arms around my middle. "Don't eat it, then. I must've misunderstood Nana. We were talking recipes the other day, and she told me this was your favorite. She probably didn't mean for me to make it for you, just add it to my collection."

"No, knowing Nana, this is *exactly* what she intended." I freed my arm from her hug and set it around her back. "Meddling old woman."

Tasha chuckled softly. "Silly Nana Booboo." She looked up at me and quickly looked away, sliding out from under me. "You better get eating so you have enough time to visit. Or do you want me to box it up for you?"

I shook my head. "Nah. I'm actually dying to try it. See if it's as good as Nana's."

"I wouldn't hold out hope. Those substitutions can be disappointing."

I waited until she returned to the bar with her own plate before I tried a bite. It was different but better in some ways. The rice pasta was a little mushy, even though she'd added it just three hours ago. She always added the pasta to whatever the mixture was before she left for her job at the high school.

"It's really good," I praised. "The cheese is a little different, but I think I like it better."

"Oh stop it. You do not." She tapped my bicep playfully.

"I do. And I'll definitely take some to Nana. She's going to love it."

"Now I know you're lying. That woman knows her food is the best of the best."

"And yet, she's never wanted to publish a cookbook of *her* recipes."

I had her on that. She blushed but didn't comment.

ON THE WAY to Nana's, I called Beck for an update.

"Everything is on schedule to be finished sometime next week," she confirmed. "If you can come by Monday for a walk-through, you can let us know if there's anything else you want. Is your Nana ready to move home?"

"She is. She's already planning a party."

Beck laughed. "Glad to hear she hasn't lost her spirit over there."

"Quite the contrary. She's like their queen, ruling over all the social events and game nights. I think she's going to miss it, actually."

"She might. But she doesn't have you or her cat there, so there's that. Oh!" she said excitedly. "I have an idea for the cat. I know he's old and fat, but what would you say to a custom cat tree in the sunroom? I've been itching to make one. I'll only charge you for materials."

I laughed. Parfait was so spoiled. "Send me the info, and I'll run it by Nana."

"You got it!"

I ended the call and pulled into the lot of Mountainview Manor. Halloween was next week, and they'd gone all out with the decor, inside and out. The walkways were lined with floodlights alternating in white, yellow and orange. Candy-corn buntings hung off the roof, and twinkle lights lined the windows. A scarecrow held a sign that said "Candy This Way" and pointed to a series of booths lining the walkway on the side lawn. Kids visiting their grandparents could trick-or-treat with them all next week after dinner.

It was a chilly night, and I hurried inside. "Is Nana in her room?" I asked the receptionist as she read Tasha's ingredients list.

"Nope, she's holding court by the aquarium."

"Thanks." The "aquarium" was no more than a six-by-four-foot fish tank recessed into the wall in one of the common areas.

I heard Nana before I saw her, talking about her favorite subject.

Me, of course.

"And you should see him on skates! In that enormous costume. Graceful like a swan."

I snorted and wondered if her eyesight was going.

"Graceful as a swan, huh? Is he married yet?" An elderly man sat in a recliner near her wheelchair. She called him "Pauli Cracker" because he repeated what people said like a parrot.

Curious as to where this might go, I hid myself behind a column to listen.

"Nope, but he's sweet on someone."

"How can you tell?" Clarice asked.

Nana leaned toward her. "I saw his phone." She sat back into her chair with a smirk. "I was playing solitaire on it while he tinkered with my tablet—you remember the day I accidentally lost all my game apps?"

"I remember," Clarice said. "Go on."

"Well, a message flashed across the screen. It said, 'You are my everything. I wish every day was Sunday so I could see you more' or something like that."

"Ooh! Who was it from?" Clarice demanded.

"Who is it from? You should stay out of his business, Nan," Pauli advised. "Nothing good ever comes out of you meddling."

She ignored him and smiled at Clarice. "I don't know. He didn't have a name attached to the number, and I couldn't find the right screen to read any more of it—or catch the number so I could accidentally call it."

Clarice hooted. "You are too much! Remember when he used to get mad when people called you Nancy? 'Not Nan-cee! Nan-NA!'"

"The boy will be thirty before I blink. He's been lonely for too long."

Pauli snorted. "Too long! Isn't he only twenty-five?"

"Ish. January. And that's not the point," Nana said.

"Not the point. Maybe he wants to be lonely," Pauli said. "Women are expensive."

"Says a millionaire to a millionaire about a millionaire," Clarice pointed to him. "You old miser."

Pauli shrugged. "Miser! Whoever it is, make sure she signs a prenup."

"Sure, sure." Nana waved her hand. "But I really just want to see him happy and settled before I die."

Okay, that was enough. I emerged from behind the column and waved to the group. "Hey, Nana!" I said loud enough for all of them to hear.

"Monty!" Her eyes brightened. "We were just talking about you!"

"Uh-oh," I said, frowning. "Am I in trouble?"

Clarice giggled. "Maybe!"

"Shush," Nana shouted at her. "You too, Pauli. We don't need any of your negativity. Monty, will you wheel me back to my room? Whatever food is in that bag you're carrying, it's demanding to be tasted."

"Yes, ma'am." I handed her the bag and moved behind her chair. "'Night, Clarice. 'Night, Pauli."

I wheeled Nana back to her room and set her up in her recliner with the rolling tray so she could try Tasha's dinner while it was still warm. I sat on the bed and waited for her to comment.

"This is incredible! That girl has got some serious talent turning yucky foods into gourmet delicacies." She pointed her spoon at me. "I might have more than a few bites. Don't rat me out."

I laughed. "Promise." I cleared my throat. "While you eat, I, um, need to come clean about something. I heard you talking about a message you saw on my phone."

She had the decency to look guilty, but I'd bet the cat she didn't feel one ounce of guilt. "And?"

"I don't have a secret girlfriend. I'm helping one of the foreign players polish his love letters to a girl he's interested in."

Nana's eyes widened, and her gaze flicked over my face. But I wasn't lying. She sighed when she realized I was telling the truth.

"That's shady business, Montgomery." She used my full name for emphasis. "It will come back to bite you in the butt. But what do I know? I'm just an old woman."

"Nana, it's fine."

She clucked her tongue. "Speaking of girls—you should ask Tasha to move in with us."

I choked on my saliva. "Wha-*what?*"

Nana chewed her food slowly, taking her time before she answered. "She told me she was moving back with her parents after Christmas because her lease is up and she's got bills. We have plenty of rooms. And I'd enjoy her company. And her cooking. It's better than anything Pru ever made."

"That's a fact," I agreed. Our longtime housekeeper cooked the most basic staples and rarely added seasoning. "But ... that would be weird."

"Why?" Nana snapped. "Aren't you two getting along now? I haven't heard of any roommate issues from you *or* Tasha, and she told me yesterday she thought your friendship was well on its way to being restored." She lifted her spoon and stabbed the air to emphasize her point. "You, sir, have not been the same since the two of you had a falling out; don't try to convince me otherwise. And if you don't ask her to move in with us, *I will.*"

I blew out a long breath. "It's not a good idea, Nana. I— please, think about it first," I pleaded. As much as I'd miss Tasha when I moved out of her apartment, I *wouldn't* miss Vlad—or anyone else—picking her up for dates. Or worse— what if he—or whomever she got serious with—proposed to her on *my* porch or in *my* gazebo or—

"You look ill, Monty," Nana said. "Care to tell me the *real* reason you don't want her moving in?"

I just stared at her.

"Thought so., You don't have a good one, so it's settled. Now put this in the fridge, please, and press the call button. It's been a long, emotional day, and I'm ready for bed. Come give your Nana a hug."

I hugged her fiercely. "I love you, Nana. I wish Mindy was here with us."

"I love you, too, Monty. And you know I wish that, too, with all my heart." She patted my back. "Call me when you get home, okay? I'll wait up."

"I will. Good night, Nana."

"Good night, Monty."

CHAPTER 25
Tasha

Monty Move-out Day.

Now that it was here, I was surprised to realize I was sad about it. Since we were friends again, I was going to feel his absence. Twice a week at practice and the occasional pop-in at the Coffee Loft would hardly make up for all the time we were used to spending together.

The high school football team played on Friday this week, so I had a free Saturday. The Edge weren't playing tonight, so Vlad was taking me out to dinner, since tomorrow night the team was leaving for a road trip. They wouldn't be back until Thanksgiving. I wanted to try one more time with Vlad to see if there could be anything more than friendship between us, but deep in my gut, I already knew the answer.

Monty didn't have a lot of stuff to move out since he'd been able to access his house whenever he needed anything, like winter clothes or books, so he was able to fit everything in his truck. He'd insisted on packing it himself, and I counted seven trips while I prepped my latest Crock-Pot creation.

I hurried to open the door for him for trip number eight. "Don't forget your Halloween wreath." I pointed to the plum, orange, and peach circlet of leaves and mesh hanging on the door.

"Keep it."

"But—"

He shifted the box he was carrying to his hip. "It was made for this door. It's *way* too small for Nana's grand entrance."

Just like Monty. Thoughtful but competitive and one-uppitive. Was that a word? If it was, there was surely a picture of Montgomery Biddington next to it in the dictionary.

"Thanks. I think." I rolled my eyes, then flashed an apologetic smile. "What time are you busting her out? And would you like company?" I purposely didn't offer help. He would insist he didn't need it, like this morning when I tried to roll one of his suitcases to the elevator.

"Five o'clock." He turned and walked out into the hall. "You can come if you want," he tossed over his shoulder as he descended the stairs. "Bring some of that food you're cooking."

It would be ready by four, so I'd bring some for his and Nana's dinner. Nana was throwing her own Welcome Home party tomorrow. She'd been planning it with Brenna for weeks.

Five minutes later, Monty let himself in and padded across the living space to the bar. He dropped a zip-lock bag on the counter. "Building access card and apartment keys."

"Keep them."

"But—"

"You'll be back to steal leftovers."

"Yeah, I will. About that—"

"Don't you dare get mushy on me, Montgomery Bidding-ton, or I'll smack you and give you something to cry about."

"Thanks for letting me stay with you, Tasha." He pock-eted the bag.

"You're welcome. I'd say it was a pleasure, but ..."

"You'd be lying." He grinned, but then his smile waned. *"I'd be lying if I said it wasn't."*

"Aw, look at you being so uncharacteristically nice. I *almost* believe you." I booped him on the nose with my index finger. "Take your cat home and get settled, and I'll meet you at Mountainview at five."

"I'll swing by and pick you up." He waggled his eyebrows. "Just to make sure you don't forget the food. "

I shook my head, and he turned to go, blowing me an exaggerated kiss and waving as he closed the door behind him.

I sent off a text to Vlad, asking him to pick me up at seven instead of six, just in case moving Nana back in took more than three hours.

He texted back right away. *I have reservation for six thirty at Pasta Nacht's. Want me to cancel if no later time?*

I texted him back: *No, keep the 6:30. I'll just need you to pick me up at Monty's Nana's house instead. She's moving home today.*

Good news! We shall celebrate your free of bear home, yes?

I snorted. How could a man who wrote such eloquent letters also write "your free of bear home"?

It did cross my mind that he might be using AI to help him with the letters, but I didn't intend on asking.

The love letters were still coming, even though we hadn't been out together since the Harvest Festival. He'd brought them by the Coffee Loft on game days.

Vlad was a great guy, as far as I could tell, devoted to his sport, his family, and his teammates. He always seemed excited to see me, but I wouldn't say he was *crazy* about me. His kisses were quick pecks, and he was a hand-holder, not a cuddler.

Did I need that, though? Or was it just a luxury for people who didn't have to worry about medical bills or citizenship?

With the food in the slow cooker and nothing else for me to do since Monty had hired someone to clean the apartment, I decided to take a walk down to the Coffee Loft for a pumpkin spice latte. Being here alone was suddenly unnerving.

I took the long route, taking a left out of the front door to Prospect Road, and strolled past the dairy farm and St. Mary's to Main Street, where I turned right. This block was one of my favorite places in town. On my left, the businesses, including the antiques shop and bookstore, backed up to Snowpack Creek, and though it was cold, the creek hadn't yet frozen over. On my right was the church, ice cream shop, and the Coffee Loft, which was perpendicular to the entrance to the back parking lot. Just beyond were the fire department and diner, just before the next intersection at Cross Creek Road.

I pulled open the door and wasn't surprised in the least to see a full queue. I scanned the space for familiar faces. Penny and Xavier were at the table in the front corner, positioned just out of sight of the window, so I hadn't seen them when I walked by.

Their heads were bent together, and from their expressions, I could tell the conversation was serious. Penny had one hand on her abdomen. I hoped the baby was okay. She was recently out of her first trimester and just starting to show. The last couple of weeks, she'd been fighting severe nausea, so I was glad to see her out and about. Not wanting to interrupt, I decided to get my coffee and then check in on them.

"Tasha!" Brenna waved from the end of the counter, holding up her whipped decaf in greeting. She hadn't announced she was pregnant yet, but there'd been a lot of signs—like wearing loose clothing, a new, bigger coat, and allowing Brendan to carry her tote bag. They were too cute together.

"Hey!" I waved back.

She rushed over to me. "Get your coffee and then come sit in the corner with us. Brendan's on his way, and he says he's got some big news!"

I smiled. "Great!"

Betty took my order, and I moved down the counter to take my coffee from Jannell. I thanked her and waded through the people between me and the corner table. Xavier had pulled over extra chairs. I said hello and sat in the empty one between Penny and Brenna. I studied the drinks on the table. I knew their orders by heart. The guys were drinking tall green Matcha Madness shakes, a favorite of theirs since their years playing for the Voltage, and Penny sipped a Lady Grey decaf tea.

The chime over the door tinkled, and Bailey Dexter-Brewer, Jason's sister and the Edge's sports reporter, rushed over to us and sat in the vacant seat next to mine.

"So, what's the news? Any clue? You must know," I said to Bailey.

"Can't say or comment officially until the news goes live publicly," she replied. "But I so want to!"

Brenna grinned widely. "I have an idea, but I made Brendan make a call to see if he could squeeze more details."

"Sweet." I leaned over and whispered in my sister's ear. "Pen, are you feeling okay?"

She nodded. "Just some indigestion. The tea is helping. That's why we came. I wanted to get out of the house. And here we are, in the middle of breaking news." She forced a small smile.

"Here he comes!" Xavier reached to knock on the window.

Brendan was on the phone, but he looked up and smiled, rushing past us and entering the café. He unzipped his jacket and set Brenna's tote bag gently down on her lap as he said goodbye to whoever was on the phone.

"Is it done?" Bailey asked. She scrolled her phone and frowned. "Official?"

Brendan grinned and leaned his head in. "I shouldn't say anything, especially here, but rumors are going to start flying any hour now. And since Bailey's here, I can totally pin it on her."

Bailey snorted and shot Brenna a wink. "I dare you to."

"Don't dare him!" Brenna and Penny shouted in unison at her.

We all laughed. The players had a thing for daring one another and had gotten into some decent scrapes over the years. The best result came in the form of Xavier's pregame good-luck toffee coffee, the result of a triple-dog-dare from Brendan back when they'd both played for the Voltage. He scored that game, and the toffee coffee stuck.

Brenna's head whipped from Brendan to Bailey, who was grinning at her screen. "So it's done?" she squealed. "And it's what I think it is?"

"Not quite," Brendan warned. "From what I understand—
and details are still to be finalized—there's a three-way deal
in the works that will result in the Edge buying out the rest
of Kingston's contract."

"My cousin is coming home!" Brenna shout-whispered.

Penny clapped. "This is awesome!"

"Agreed," Xavier said. "I hate playing against that guy."

We all laughed. I didn't understand how hockey contracts
worked, so I asked. "So who's leaving your team?"

"No one that I can tell," Brendan said. "We have cap
space for the rest of King's contract for this year if we send
our third goalie back to the Volts."

"So who's the other team?" I asked.

"No idea. But whoever it is, they're giving Montana
something real good. Otherwise, they never would have
released Kingston."

"And they get what from you?" I asked.

"Probably a draft pick or future considerations." He
shrugged. "It should all be finalized tonight, and King was
told to meet us in Seattle tomorrow so he can play in the
lineup in Monday's game."

"That's so awesome!" Brenna exclaimed. "I cannot wait
for Monday Night Dinner! I'm going to call Gran and tell her
to plan for us all to stay later to watch the game." She kissed
Brendan on the cheek. "I'll be right back!"

Brendan watched her go, grinning like she was his sun. "I
knew she'd be excited. They've always been close."

"So now all her family is back in Palmer City, right? He
was the last one?" Penny asked.

"Yup," Brendan confirmed. "And the new contract is for
eight years, so it's pretty much permanent as far as hockey
goes."

"So will Taylor take her mindset coaching business fully online, then?" I asked. Taylor not only coached at the Kalispell Plex, but she was also a licensed psychologist specializing in sports mindset coaching and counseling for active and retired athletes—and still made cheer bows on the side.

"I'm not sure, but they'll figure it out," Brendan said. He nodded to Xavier. "You ready to go?"

Xavier nodded and leaned over to kiss Penny goodbye. "Call if *anything* changes. I can afford whatever fine they throw at me to get back to you."

She nodded. "I'm fine, really. Go to practice."

He left frowning, and when he and Brendan exited, Penny sighed. "It's just a little indigestion."

"Following 'just a little morning sickness,'" Brenna air quoted. "I understand why his protective mode kicked in. You had a bad bout that second month."

I turned my eyes on Penny. This was news to me. "Why didn't you call me? I could've helped. Did you keep a food journal?"

She shook her head. "I did, but it didn't reveal anything in particular. And there was nothing to do. Xavier took care of everything, and Lauren checked on me when they were traveling."

"But I'm your sister," I said.

"And you work three jobs and live twenty minutes away. She's next door, Tasha, and she has the same schedule as me. It's practical."

Another reminder I wasn't in their hockey wives club. Penny and Xavier had recently moved into their new home next door to Lauren and Jason. I sat up straighter and tipped my chin. "I've got to go," I said. "I need to figure out what I'm wearing on my date with Vlad tonight."

I didn't know if I was reminding them or myself that I was dating an Edge player.

"We'll see you at the party tomorrow?" Brenna asked.

I nodded. "Wouldn't miss it."

Once I was out the door, I turned right and stopped at the corner to wait for the signal to cross the street. I wasn't ready to return to my empty apartment, so instead I traversed the Creek Walk past Restaurant Row and all the way up to the town park, where I sat on a swinging bench.

The sun was warm, and I took off my jacket and held it in my lap as I rocked back and forth, watching the water rush over the rocks. Elk Creek Falls, just north of us, was the source of the creek water, and it occurred to me that I wasn't far from Nana's house. Behind the town park was the Brewer ranchland, which stretched north to the falls and west to Stagecoach Road.

Monty's great-great-great grandfather had won a chunk of Brewer land in a card game, and he'd sold off all but a patch of prime mountainside property where he built the Victorian mansion Nana still lived in today and Monty would inherit. With profits from the land sales, his oldest son—Monty's great-great-grandfather—traveled to Texas, where he purchased land and began drilling for oil.

He struck liquid gold and returned to Palmer City to try to buy the family's land back. But the proud business owners who'd opened shops along the creek wouldn't sell, so he was limited to what he'd kept. It was a beautiful piece of land, with unobstructed views of the Rockies and a stream fed from the falls that ended in a small lake. And the house? Extraordinary.

They were the richest family I knew, and yet no amount of money could've saved Mindy. And Monty couldn't make his parents love him. When Nana died ... I didn't even want to think about how that might destroy him.

Suddenly feeling the chill, I slid off the swing and pulled my jacket back on for the walk home.

Once inside the apartment, I wandered into Monty's room to see if he left anything. A cursory glance from the doorway revealed everything was in order, except for a stack of papers on the desk, bound by two binder clips.

I squinted at the bundle as I neared it. One third of the way down on the top page read simply, "Tasha's Recipes for Unique Dietary Needs," and he'd scribbled a note with the link to the document.

Heh?

I picked it up and thumbed through the pages. He'd typed up my entire recipe binder! It was all there, from the tried and true slow-cooker staples to the sugar-free desserts I'd Frankensteined for Nana. Plus, all the substitution recommendations and important reminders.

And he'd started each recipe with a quote like "Best mac; hands-down" and "You thought you needed real butter until you tried this," and "Gooier than gourmet."

I snorted. My brownies *were* unusually gooey.

What a thoughtful gesture! I needed to thank him.

I carried the manuscript to the kitchen and set it on the counter so I could text him.

I found the recipes. Thank you! You didn't have to do that. I still don't think anyone would want to buy a book of my hodgepodge creations.

It was nothing. I only have two jobs, so you know, lots of free time.

I laughed. *Yeah, us three-jobsters definitely do not have time to type up a recipe book.*

On the last page is Gia Kubek's email. She said she'd publish it as part of her line of cookbooks if you didn't want to produce it independently.

Oh my gosh, what? In addition to Pasta Nacht's, Astoria Brewer's mother, Gia, known worldwide as Tia Gia, had a multimillion-dollar culinary line of products and foods.

Stop lying. She did not!

No cap, Tasha. Promise. She's expanding out of her Italian niche of products and thinks this would be a great addition.

Oh wow …

You're welcome. See what Gia has to say. I'm sure she's planning to advance you a hefty sum.

I don't know what to say, Monty. Thank you.

You're welcome.

I sank onto the sofa, stunned. How much was an advance? Enough to make a dent in that six-thousand-dollar bill at the top of the stack on my desk?

CHAPTER 26
Monty

I might have still had the key, but it felt more appropriate to knock on the apartment door instead of letting myself in.

"Come in!" Tasha called.

I opened the door. Her back was to me as she packed a grocery tote on the far kitchen counter.

When she turned, I had to blink twice. It took me a minute to process what I was seeing. Tasha's sandy hair fell in sculpted waves over a long white cable-knit sweater dress. The dress covered every inch of her, but it was *snug*. I wanted to toss her my coat and tell her to cover up. And her eyes … She hadn't worn eyeliner or done her lashes like that since she quit cheer.

"Stop staring. You're creeping me out."

Say something. Be rude. Insult her. Banter.

I reached for the right words, words that would both dig at and compliment her, and I came up empty. She'd rendered me speechless.

This did not happen.

Ever.

Where the heck was she going with Vlad that made her decide to get all prom-glam?

"Is it too much?"

"It's a little fancy for moving Nana," I said. "Better stay away from the old guys. You might cause a few heart attacks."

She groaned. "I was aiming for 'fancier than work ... less than performance' face. I probably should have skipped the false eyelashes."

"It's fine," I assured her. "You've got that 'hockey Wag during the playoffs' vibe. Classy but not over the top. Sorry I made you think otherwise."

"Montgomery Biddington," she drawled, her smile widening into a grin, "I *think* you just gave me a genuine compliment."

"Yeah. I'm pretty sure I'm coming down with something. Maybe you should drive separately." I fisted my hand and brought it to my mouth, faking a cough. "Wouldn't want to get Vladdy sick before the big road trip."

Tasha laughed and handed me the bag of food. "Let's check to see if you've got a fever." She reached up to place the back of her hand on my forehead. "Hmm ... a little hot—"

"Thank you."

She snorted. "Hot*headed.*"

"Aw, and here I was thinking you were giving *me* a genuine compliment."

"Maybe another time." She pulled her coat off the hook and slipped it on, pulling her hair free and carefully arranging it in front of her shoulders. "Thank you for typing up my recipes and pitching them to Gia. I don't know how to thank you for that."

"You don't need to," I said softly.

She smiled but didn't reply, so I gestured to the door. Once she was out, I locked it behind us and we headed out.

Nana was signing paperwork in the recliner when we arrived in her room. She looked up from the rolling tray when we entered and pointed her pen at her nurse, Marlene. "My two favorite people are here to break me free! It's been almost half a year, and if I wasn't so happy to get home to my cat, I might cry!"

The nurse was doing her best to hold it together. "You'll come visit, right, Miss Nancy?"

"Of course!" Nana waved at her like she was nuts. "Now that I don't have to live here, I think it's time I stop letting Clarice win at cards." She gave an exaggerated wink, and Marlene laughed.

"Take good care of her," Marlene implored of me. "And if you need anything, just call. The overnight nurse is scheduled to be there at seven."

"Count on it," Monty promised. "C'mon, Nana. Tasha made dinner." The nurse pulled the tray away and brought Nana's wheelchair over. I helped her stand and slowly pivot, then eased her down to the seat.

"Best grandson ever. I'm in good hands, don't you worry, Marlene."

"I won't. But I'll miss you. We all will."

I gestured for Tasha to push Nana so I could roll her bags. I'd been taking things from the room back to the house all week, so when we arrived, Nana's two suitcases filled with her remaining belongings were waiting just inside her door.

"Follow me," Marlene said.

Tasha complied, and I fell in behind them. When Nana turned the corner into the main hall, a cheer erupted. The walls were lined with residents and staff, clapping and shouting well wishes.

One of Nana's nurse assistants stepped forward and handed her a tiara. "For the queen," she said, and curtsied.

"Queen Nancy! Here, here!" Pauli shouted. He elbowed Clarice. "When you leave, they'll bring you a pointy hat!"

Clarice whacked him with a book. "And when you leave, we'll throw a party!"

Nana just smiled and waved like the queen she was until we were through the front door. "I think I might miss this place. Monty, you'll have to bring me here enough so that I remember why I'm glad to be home."

"Anytime, Nana."

Tasha parked the wheelchair by the passenger door and opened it. I loaded the suitcases into the truck and ran over to help Nana inside.

"I can lift you," I offered.

"Let me see if I can do it myself first." She turned her head to Tasha. "One of the things I had to do to get out of there was move from the chair to the commode without falling. Imagine if I fell and Monty had to help when I was bare as a baby from the waist down!"

"Didn't need that visual, Nana!" I called.

Tasha laughed. "You call me if you ever find yourself in that situation and your nurse is MIA. I'll leave wherever I'm at to help you."

Nana patted her hand. "I believe that. Thank you." She gripped the sides of her chair and pushed herself up. I watched as she eyed the running board on the truck "I got this."

Tasha hovered behind Nana with her arms out, ready to react in an instant like she was spotting one of her athletes. I was glad they'd stayed close over the years. I had to admit, if it hadn't been for Nana insisting I take her to the Coffee Loft several times weekly, I probably wouldn't have had the guts to face Tasha after she broke her leg.

Tasha made sure Nana was buckled in as I stowed the wheelchair in the back. When I pulled out of the lot, she twisted around to speak to Tasha in the back seat.

"I'd like you to move in with us."

I glanced in the rearview mirror. To say Tasha was surprised was an understatement.

"I couldn't—"

"Your lease is up at the end of December, right? We have nine bedrooms. You can have a whole hallway if you want. Or the turret room. You always liked hiding out there. I'm a lonely old woman, and I like you. And your food."

Tasha laughed. "I'm happy to cook for you. But I'm planning to move back in with my parents."

"I have a better kitchen."

"You definitely do. But I don't think—"

"Well, *do* think. Because it makes sense. Besides, Parfait misses you terribly, I hear."

"He's only been gone a few hours."

"Montgomery. A little help here, please?"

My eyes met Tasha's in the mirror. "We'd love to have you."

She blew out a breath. "I'll consider it."

"Good," Nana said. "Now tell me about this hot date you've got. Because I know you didn't dress up for me."

I held back a smile as Tasha's cheeks reddened. "She's having dinner with that hockey guy."

"Oooh. Vladimir Ivanov again, huh? He's hot. Tell me everything."

Tasha pressed her lips together to keep from laughing. "He's definitely easy on the eyes. We're still getting to know each other."

Nana questioned Tasha all the way home and while we got her settled. I learned more than I ever needed—or wanted—to know about that guy. I was actually relieved when he arrived to pick her up so I wouldn't have to keep listening to them.

CHAPTER 27

Tasha

H ad I known Nana was going to grill me about Vlad for an hour and a half, I would've driven separately so I could leave. Or maybe I wouldn't have come at all.

I practically ran to Vlad's sports car when he arrived.

"Thanks for picking me up here," I said as I buckled my seat belt.

"No problem." He handed me a peach envelope. "Words I wish I could say out loud."

I smiled and opened the letter as he drove.

My Tasha,
Translating the feelings of my heart into words is tedious, for no words are sufficient to adequately account for your beauty, your selflessness, and the way you encourage others. My feelings live deep in my heart, and it is only here I can confess them, for I fear if I speak them aloud, they would lose value. Can you feel my soul reaching out to you? It cries for your love like a desert flower cries to be watered.

Always yours,
Vladimir

"Oh, Vlad," I breathed. "You have the soul of a poet. How *do* you write such beautiful words in a new language?"

He shrugged. "It is heavily edited. But it is good, no?"

Heavily edited, huh? By AI or a human? I wondered. And to what extent?

I concurred. "It is good." But for the first time, I wondered if he even knew what he was writing. He seemed more excited about impressing me than advancing our relationship.

Astoria greeted us at the host stand at Pasta Nacht's. "You two look amazing. New suit, Vlad? Love the plaid. That rhymes! Special night? Birthday?"

I shook my head and looked up at Vlad. He did look good in plaid. But nothing about him gave me that fluttery feeling inside—unlike his letters, which spoke directly to my heart.

"No birthday," Vlad said. "Just a nice dinner with beautiful hard-working woman who finally has Saturday night off."

I poked him playfully. "Hey, now. You play on a lot of Saturday nights."

Astoria laughed. "I get that! Follow me." She led us to one of the small, private crescent-shaped booths in the back of the restaurant, set the menus down, and held her hands out for our coats. "Coat check number is fifteen." She winked at Vlad.

He grinned, and we slid into the booth from opposite sides, meeting in the middle. "Specials tonight are a filet mignon with traditional German rahm sauce reduction, served with steamed green beans and heirloom potatoes or over rice. Tasha, we can whip up a dairy-free version with plant butter and coconut cream for you if you'd like to try it.

We've also got Maine lobster, served with beer-battered onion rings and coleslaw, and we can also sub ingredients for those. Oh!" She turned to Vlad. "And Keegan's debuting a new seasonal beer that he's featuring here. I haven't tried it because, well—" She patted her baby bump. "But it sure smells good!"

"Baby does not drink the beer, eh?" Vlad asked. "Just kidding!"

Astoria laughed. "Well, we do plan to name her Shandy ..."

"Clever," I said. Astoria and Keegan had fallen in love over crafting the perfect lemon shandy for Brewski's. They'd used her mother's lemonade recipe, which featured lemons from the family's grove in Italy.

"Your server will be over in a few minutes," Astoria promised. "Let me know if you need *anything*."

We thanked her and looked over the menus. I startled when Vlad's phone buzzed in his pocket, sending vibrations through the seat. He reached down to silence it, and I went back to reading the menu.

The server arrived, and Vlad's phone buzzed again as we were ordering.

And again when our drinks arrived.

"I think you should answer it," I said. "I don't mind."

"It is not as important as you," he said.

The phone buzzed again. "I really don't mind. What if it's family news?"

With a sigh, he pulled his phone from his pocket and swiped to check the screen. "Agent," he said. "I am not expecting call."

"Did he leave a text?"

Vlad scrolled his screen. "Da. Yes. He says must speak now. Urgent. I text him back to see how urgent."

His fingers flew over the screen, and then he set the device down on the table. The phone didn't ring anymore, but two short vibrations indicated he'd received a reply.

He pointed to our server walking toward us with our meals. "Eat first. Then I call, okay?"

"Okay."

While we ate, we swapped stories from hockey and cheer camps. He had a twin brother he'd come up with that still played in the KHL. They'd been competitive, and so I told him about how Monty and I sharpened each other growing up.

"Like brother, sister, you are. Work together. Competitive. But always support."

"Yeah," I agreed. "He and his Nana are pretty much family."

I set my knife and fork on my plate to signal I was finished. When I saw Gia Kubek heading toward us, I sat up straighter.

"Tasha! Vlad! So great to see you both. I hope the meal was good?"

"Perfect," I said. Vlad nodded as he chewed his last bite.

"Wonderful. I'm glad I stopped in. I'm prepared to make an offer to publish your cookbook, Tasha. When can we meet?"

"A cookbook!" Vlad nudged me with his shoulder. "Secret project, eh?"

My cheeks reddened. "You could say that."

"My schedule is open next week," Gia said. She placed a business card on the table. "Call me."

"Oh—okay. Thank you."

She smiled. "My pleasure." She pointed to Vlad. "Don't skip dessert. I recommend the New York cheesecake."

Gia left us, and Vlad turned to me. "I leave to take call?"

"You don't have to."

"I will call here. Do not want to miss a minute with you." He was sweet, but the endearment landed flat. My thoughts drifted again to the letters as he dialed his agent.

"Hello, I ... I see. But—it is only November. We are still working on lines ... Then there is nothing to do ..."

Vlad's shoulders sagged. Whatever the news was, it wasn't good.

He ended the call and closed his eyes, pressing them shut tight. Then he set the phone down and tugged at his carefully combed hair.

"What is it?" I asked softly, laying my hand on his shoulder. "Is everything all right?

He shook his head, opening his eyes and dropping his hands into his lap. "Nothing is right. It is nightmare. They have traded me to Miami. I must be on plane at nine in morning."

I gasped. "How—how can they do that?"

Vlad shrugged. "Happens all the time. At least I am still in USA."

"But—didn't they recruit you from the KHL because they wanted you?" I didn't understand any of this.

"Da. Yes. But I am not playing here the way I played in Russia. Chemistry is off. Mixing up is not improvement."

"And they can just trade you away, with less than a day's notice? Where will you live?"

"Yes. There have been rumors this week. I am small piece

in a bigger deal. My agent says we will find out in a few hours what happened."

I frowned. "So, this is goodbye?"

He turned to me and cupped my shoulders, his eyes pleading. "You must come with me."

I shook my head. "I can't go to Miami. My jobs are here. My cheerleaders are depending on me."

"They can hire new coach, no?"

"Vlad." I placed my hands over his and drew them off my shoulders to hold them between us. "I can't go with you. I'm sorry."

"At least say you will come to Miami to see? And we can talk plans for future? Football season is almost over, no? And your Worlds team—you say they can coach themselves. After Christmas, perhaps?"

His earnest plea hurt my heart.

Future. This was what I'd wanted. The whole point of dating a hockey player. A future where I wouldn't have to struggle over money.

But, thanks to Monty, I might have another option now, one where I wouldn't have to be dependent on anyone.

What divine timing.

"No. I'm sorry." I shook my head. "I can't."

His expression cracked my heart further. Vlad was a sweet guy, and one day, he'd find someone who would uproot herself in a heartbeat for him.

Someone that wasn't me.

I KEYED OPEN the door to my apartment and was surprised to find the kitchen light on. I was sure I'd switched it off when I left.

"Oh!" A figure rose up from the sofa, and I jumped so high I nearly hit the ceiling.

"Sorry! So sorry!" Monty apologized. "I texted you I was coming over. I forgot my, um, pillow?"

"You didn't." I narrowed my eyes. "'Fess up. Why are you *really* here?"

He hesitated, sliding his hands into his pockets and lifting his shoulders. "I heard about the trade and thought you might be upset, so I came over once Nana got settled with the night nurse."

"Oh." I hung up my coat and slung my purse strap over the peg next to it. "That was thoughtful of you."

"So? Did Vlad ask you to go with him?"

"To Miami?" I asked.

Monty nodded.

"He did."

"And? Do I need to find a new coaching partner?"

I studied his expression. Tense, like a little boy who wanted to know if he was in trouble. I rushed to reassure him. "I'm not going to Miami, Monty. I wouldn't leave you hanging like that. Especially after you stepped in to help me when Nate quit. And you got me a book deal."

"After the season?"

Monty's tone lacked its trademark self-assurance. I walked over to him and patted his arm.

"No." I sank into the sofa. "Not ever." I pulled a pillow onto my lap. "It's not meant to be."

His shoulders seemed to relax—or maybe I imagined it—

and he lowered himself into the cushion next to mine, folding his arms across his chest. "He's a chump."

"He's not. I'm sad to see him go. But not for the reasons I should be sad." I rubbed my eyes with my fingertips. "It's confusing." My head found his sturdy shoulder, and I sighed. "Shouldn't I be sad? Like breakup-level sad?"

"You're not? You've been dating the guy for months."

"Not really. We've been going ON dates for months. Weeks, really." I thought back over our time together. "Six total, I think? Some group events. Games. Inconsistent texting. We're still getting to know each other. We're not even official."

"He never asked you to be his girlfriend? You wore his jersey to games. That looked pretty official to me."

"Nope. But those letters ... and when he asked me to go to Miami, he implied that he wanted to plan a future with me. He's very sweet and very shy, I think. He told me today it's easier for him to write his feelings than to speak them."

"I don't think he's shy at all," Monty said. "I think he's toying with you. I think he wants a trophy wife he can eventually use to gain citizenship. It's clear he's in no rush to commit."

"That's a terrible thing to say." I glared up at him, surprised by his vitriol. "I'm no trophy wife."

"No kidding. Your resting face is scarier than mine."

"Hey!"

"Kidding." He held up his hands. "But he's still a chump."

"You think you know so much. If you'd read his letters, you'd know how much he cares about me. I think I broke his heart tonight."

"Words. They're meaningless unless they're backed up by actions."

"Oh really?" I huffed. "And what actions do you think would be appropriate? He's a gentleman."

Monty snorted. "Hypothetically?"

I nodded, and he shifted on the sofa, scooching back and turning sideways to face me.

He locked his eyes on mine, and his tone became earnest. "If you were my girl, I'd make sure you knew it. There would be no doubt in your mind. I would look at you like a man in love, and you'd be confident that there was no one else for me but you. Admit it. Be honest—Does he look at you that way?" Monty didn't wait for an answer. "He didn't even walk you to your door tonight. Does he even care about your safety?"

"This building is pretty safe." I felt compelled to defend my not-boyfriend. "Nothing is going to happen to me between the entrance and the apartment."

"Oh really? What about walking in to find a strange man inside sitting on your sofa?"

"You are *definitely* strange," I muttered.

"I'd certainly text you more than once every few days, and I'd call you every day, twice, when I was on the road, just to hear your voice. You think Xavier and Penny or Gabby and Noel go more than eight hours without talking to each other?"

"They're newlyweds. They don't count."

"Ask them. Ask Gabby how often she and Noel texted when they first started dating."

I didn't have to. It was constant.

"So?" I looked down at my hands. "Every couple is different."

"Yeah, but you weren't even a couple. And he kissed you like he was *obligated.*"

My head snapped up. "Ugh! You watched him kiss me?"

"Not on purpose, but I saw him kiss you after the last game, and it was ..." He seemed to fumble for words. "All wrong."

"All wrong?"

"Unequivocally. If you were *my* girl"—his voice turned hoarse, husky and ragged—"I'd kiss you like you're the only source of oxygen in a burning building. Like the air in your lungs was the air I needed to live, and I wouldn't stop until I stole all but your last breath from you. Until our shared breath became our lifelines and our souls were filled." He cleared his throat. "Hypothetically, of course."

"Of course." *I* could hardly breathe right now. Fire flickered through me like a Fourth of July sparkler.

I had to look away.

"Kisses like that aren't real, Monty. Pure fiction," I said. The way he described what kissing should be ... like it was in books and movies.

"I guess you'll never know because you only date chumps."

"Not fair." I pointed at him. "You just have super high standards. I'm realistic."

"You should be less realistic and demand better. You deserve better, Tasha. And you definitely deserve to be kissed right."

Why was he so hung up on how Vlad kissed me? Did it reveal some kind of vibe I wasn't aware of?

"Hypothetically," I said slowly, "and in the pure interest of proving you wrong, *how* would a kiss like that go?"

Monty pulled the pillow from my lap and tugged me up

off the sofa so that we were standing only a few inches from each other. "Hypothetically? First, I'd look into your eyes, tell you how blue they are. My favorite color, a mirror image of my own, like the sky on a clear day."

"Cheesy," I scoffed. "Then what?"

"Permission to touch your face and hair?"

"How romantic." I shrugged. "Go ahead."

Monty cleared his throat and swallowed. He held my gaze as his hand rose slowly until his fingers were threaded through my hair over my ears. "Then I'd run my fingers through your hair from the top of your head to the ends." As he spoke, he did just that.

I was suddenly feeling warm. Way too warm. Had he messed with the thermostat again?

"And tell you how soft and stunning it is and how good it smells and how it's my favorite scent and that I even sneak some of your shampoo sometimes."

"Say what? That's my super expensive gluten-free shampoo! I wondered why it was going so fast!"

"I left two new bottles under the sink in my bathroom for you."

"This isn't very romantic."

"Then I'd step closer. Tell you how beautiful you are, not just on the outside but on the inside, too. That I admire your strength and your intelligence and your ability to do all the things you set your mind to. How you're in the gym practicing tumbling and kickouts and getting your partner-stunting back after all these years, for yourself, not because you have to prove you're better than anyone else. How you care for others and selflessly work day and night to make sure everything and everyone is okay and how unique and amazing of a person that makes you."

"Hypothetically."

"No. That's all true. And any guy who doesn't see it and remark on it and compliment you regularly—out loud, to your face—is a chump."

"Um. Thank you?"

"Then I'd reach for your cheek and hold it in my hand and tip your chin up so that we could look into each other's eyes." His voice dropped lower. He did as he described, and I held my breath.

"Then?" I whispered back. Monty's face was *so close*. His warm breath caressed my nose and cheeks and lingered on my lips.

"Then, I'd drop my gaze from your eyes to your lips and tell you how perfect they were and how much I wanted to feel them against mine. To show you with a kiss what my words claim, that you are the sun and the stars and every source of light in my world." He rubbed his thumb over my cheekbone. "Hypothetically," he whispered.

"Hypothetically," I whispered. "Then?"

"Then, I'd lean in. My other hand would come up and cup your other cheek. I'd hold you in my hands like you're the most precious fragile porcelain. And touch my lips lightly to yours."

Neither of us were moving—or breathing.

"But I wouldn't stop there. I'd trail my lips to your ear, your jaw, the side of your neck." Monty's thumb lightly traced a path as he spoke. "My lips would brand your skin in such a way that you'd have no doubt you were mine. And I'd want you to do the same to me. Sealed with a kiss would take on a whole new meaning."

"Hypothetically?" I searched his eyes. Nothing about this felt hypothetical anymore. Were these *his* feelings?

He didn't answer. Not even a nod. His lack of confirmation was sending my thoughts and heart into a tailspin.

"I've never been kissed like that before," I admitted hoarsely. "What's wrong with me, Monty?"

He snapped back to attention and dropped his hands. "What do you mean? Nothing's wrong with *you.*"

I hung my head and sank back into the sofa. "Why couldn't I ever inspire that kind of passion in any of my relationships? Or make it work with Vlad? He's a great guy, but even I can see that four months of inconsistent dates and communication are never going to sustain a relationship. It went both ways. I *wanted* to fall for him. But it just didn't happen. I'm too … icy? Prickly. Was he so afraid to even *talk* to me that he had to write letters for fear of how I might react to his spoken words?"

Monty plopped down next to me and crossed his arms over his chest. "Chump."

I sighed. "Not a chump." I rushed over to my purse and pulled out the latest letter. "Read this."

I pulled the letter out of the envelope and handed it to him. As he began to read, I closed my eyes, wanting to get the full effect of the beautiful words.

"My feelings live deep in my heart, and it is only here I can confess them, for I fear if I speak them aloud, they would lose value."

He paused, and I snuck a glance over at him.

His eyes flicked to the letter, then to me as he read the remaining sentences:

"Can you *feel* my soul reaching out to you? It cries for your love like a desert flower cries to be watered."

How had he memorized it so quickly? And the way he was reading it … like, he, Monty, meant it.

But that was just because he was a good reader, right? He couldn't possibly feel that way about me. I was love-starved and trying to grab hold of any string of affection that dangled in front of me. He was just being a good friend and looking out for me, like old times.

Right?

"Another thing?" Monty leaned forward, resting his arms on his thighs. "He's got this love letter thing nailed down. How many other women has he written to? He doesn't even use nice paper. I would never write my girl letters on cheap cardstock. Only the finest, most elegant stationery, like what my grandpa used to use to write to Nana."

"He wrote her letters?"

"He did. There's a whole bag full in her closet."

"You were snooping?"

"I was nine and looking for a place to hide. My parents didn't find me for hours."

"I bet. Anything juicy?"

"Nah. Grandpa wasn't very sentimental. Mostly accounts of his time and how much he missed her. Nothing flowery like your letters."

I held the peach card in my hand. It *was* cheap. Part of a multicolor pastel bargain set at Target.

"I should go," he said, popping up from the sofa. "You'll be okay if I leave you?"

"I'm fine. Just another breakup."

"Sort-of breakup," he reminded me. "The chump never made it official, remember?"

"Right. So I shouldn't cry about it." I sighed. "Thanks for coming over to check on me and reminding me I have worth."

"I shouldn't need to remind you, Tasha." He pulled on his

hoodie and picked up his keys from the dish by the door. "But I will, anytime you need to hear it. Hug?"

I walked into his open arms and wrapped mine around his waist. "Thanks."

"Like I said, anytime. Anyone who's intimidated or afraid of your hedgehoggy prickles doesn't deserve your good stuff."

I swatted him and booped him on the nose. "Go home to Nana. I'll see you tomorrow."

He grinned. "See you tomorrow."

CHAPTER 28

Monty

O n Sunday, the skies over Palmer City hung dark and heavy, threatening to storm at a moment's notice. Up in the mountains, it was snowing, but it wouldn't get cold enough here to be anything more than rain. The slow-moving system would hit us right around dinnertime.

Brenna and her event crew had outdone themselves with the decor and theming in Nana's favorite colors—red and blue—and Fyvie from the bakery had brought over a truck-load of diabetic and celiac-friendly desserts from the bakery that looked more tempting than their traditionally made counterparts.

The party was in full swing when Gabby tapped me on the shoulder at the dessert table. "Kitchen. Now."

I raised an eyebrow and held up my gluten-free gooey brownie.

"Bring it with you. This is important, Montgomery."

I winced. She never called me that.

"Am I in trouble?"

"You bet your pom-poms you are."

I rolled my eyes. "Poms are for girls. I had a *megaphone*."

"You're going to have a mega headache if you don't follow me into the kitchen right now."

"Fine, fine."

I hurried after her through the rooms to the kitchen. Brenna's catering staff were all in the dining room, so it was empty.

"Senior year of college. We were taking an online writing class because the day class got dropped and the night class conflicted with Worlds team practice."

"Yeah, so?" I took a bite of the brownie and chewed it slowly.

"We partner-edited." She leaned closer. "Do you remember?"

I shrugged and swallowed the brownie. "Not really." I popped the rest of it into my mouth.

"Well, *I* do. Because your poems were all lovesick odes to some girl you denied existed. You used phrases like 'my feelings live deep in my heart' and 'I fear to speak my heart aloud' and 'my soul reaches out to yours' or something. Phrases that somehow ended up in Tasha's love letters from Vlad."

I sucked in a breath.

Bad idea.

The brownie got stuck in my throat. I coughed it up, and Gabby ran to the fridge to get me a bottle of water.

"One phrase? I could believe it was a coincidence. Two? Still plausible, but I'd give you the benefit of the doubt. Three? Straight up PLAGIARISM. So how did a dude from Russia who speaks minimal English—and can barely read it —get access to your poetry?"

"I don't know what you're talking about," I insisted.

"Then check your Google docs." Her tone softened. "Were you trying to send Tasha messages, Cyrano-style? Or was it truly an act of your subconscious?"

What was she talking about? "Stop reading into it. Vlad asked me for help. I just rewrote what he wanted to say in a way that was intelligible."

"I knew it!" She poked my bicep. "You need to tell that to Tasha. Poor thing is wallowing in guilt about breaking things off with a guy who she thinks is in love with her."

"Guilt? She's not upset that they broke up?"

Gabby shook her head. "I think she knew it was never going to work."

"Then why did she keep trying?" I had to know.

"Have you seen her medical bills?"

I had. One morning when she was at work, I'd gone into her room to borrow her tape to wrap a gift for Nana. Her dispenser was a paperweight, and underneath was a stack of bills. On top was a payment plan stub from the hospital. She hadn't been kidding when she'd told me it would take years to pay it off. After visiting Nana, I went straight to Pasta Nacht's to ask Astoria where I could find her mother.

That was when I began typing up the rest of her recipes in earnest.

The kitchen door opened, and Noel poked his head in. "Hey, Monty. Gab—Coach texted. Our flight is leaving an hour early to beat the worst of the storm. Do you want to go home now or catch a ride with Tasha? She's going to bring Penny home later."

"I'll go now. Be right out." He left, and she turned back to me. "You need to come clean. Don't let Tasha feel any worse than she already does. And"—she poked me again for emphasis—"you may be surprised at her reaction, you big doofus."

I clutched at my heart. "Name-calling? That hurts."

She grinned. "I'll hurt you worse if you don't confess. Don't test me."

Gabby turned on her heel and stalked out of the kitchen. I sighed and followed her so I could thank Noel, Xavier, and Brendan for coming.

It began to rain shortly after, and Tasha and I helped Brenna's crew bring in the tables and chairs that were set up on the veranda. A loud thunderclap made us all jump as lightning crackled over the lake below, treating us to a stunning show of nature's uncontrollable power.

"Have you seen Penny?" Tasha asked once we were back inside. "She's not at her harp. I can't find her."

"Maybe she changed her mind and left?"

Tasha shook her head. "Who would she have left with? I watched her wave goodbye to Xavier, and if she got a ride from someone else, she would have told me."

"And you've searched the house?"

"Well ... just the downstairs. And outside. I don't think she'd go upstairs. She'd be afraid of intruding."

"Probably. But she's pregnant. Maybe she had to go to the bathroom and the downstairs ones were occupied?"

"Maybe. I hadn't thought of that."

"I'll go upstairs and check. You hang out down here in case she comes back."

"Okay."

I jogged up the main stairs to the second floor and opened the first door, a guest room. "Pen?"

No answer. I cut around the bed to the en suite bathroom. Empty.

Back in the hall, I checked the other three rooms before entering my own at the end of the hall. The door to my bathroom was closed, so I knocked. "Pen? Are you in here?"

The toilet flushed, but there was no verbal reply. "Pen? You okay?"

"I—I don't know." Her voice was low, weak.

"I'm going to open the door, okay?"

"'Kay."

I turned the knob and pushed the door open. Penny was kneeling on the floor with her head resting on the closed toilet lid and her hands on her rounded middle. The air was rancid with vomity fumes.

"Is the baby—" Tears burned my eyes. I couldn't finish the sentence.

"She's fine," she said. "I think it was something I ate."

"Can you stand? Do you want to lie down? I have a four-thousand-dollar mattress that will cradle you like a fluffy cloud."

"Can't ... OOOOHmygosh!" She lifted the lid. I sprang into action, gathering her waist-length hair while she heaved.

"I got you," I murmured softly as I reached to flush the toilet. "You Palmer women and your food issues. It's scary."

"I ... n-never had food issues before. S-sorry."

"Penny!" Tasha knelt beside me and hip-checked me out of her way. "What's going on?"

"I ... maybe food poisoning? My indigestion has been so bad. I've eliminated so much from my diet."

"What did you eat today?"

"I had a protein bar before church. Only had eggs and bacon at brunch. I was fine. It was probably the chicken salad I had here? But I thought I was safe because I've had it before. It's Brewski's, right?"

"Yes," I confirmed.

Tasha looked up at me. "Chicken salad could easily be the culprit. The mayo could be bad or the chicken undercooked. And with her stomach already in chaos, it wouldn't take much for it to revolt."

"But no one else is sick." I didn't understand. "Brenna's pregnant, and I saw her eating the chicken salad."

"And she's been eating that stuff her whole life. Her stomach is probably made of steel from all the fried food and junk she's consumed—Penny!—she fainted!"

"I'm fine. Just wanna close m-my eyes," Penny insisted.

"You're not fine, Pen. Monty! Get Nana's nurse."

I ran out of the room and hurried down the stairs to find Nana. Only a few guests remained; most had left when the storm started to pick up, and by this point I'd lost hope my parents would show up. "Where's your nurse?"

Nana snorted. "She's a party pooper, so I sent her off to the sunroom to read in the rain. She's checking on me every twenty minutes though."

"Thanks!" I kissed her on the cheek and ran off toward the back of the house.

I explained Penny's condition, and the nurse followed me upstairs. We reached my room, and I pointed to the open door inside. "She's in there."

I hung back by the door. I wanted to give them space but also stay close enough to see and hear what was happening.

"Penny? I'm Lily. I'm a nurse. Can you open your eyes for me? Good. I'm going to examine you, okay?" The nurse put her stethoscope in her ears and checked Penny's pulse, heartbeat, and breathing.

"Can you lift her shirt for me?" Lily asked Tasha.

I turned away to give them privacy but didn't leave so I could hear everything.

"Is she okay?" Tasha asked. "The baby?"

"The baby's heartbeat is strong, nothing amiss to lead me to believe it's stressed. No cramping or bleeding. But she's weak and dehydrated. I'd suggest taking her to the ER for fluids."

"Okay. Penny, can you stand?"

"Later."

"I got her," I said. "Tasha, go tell Brenna she's in charge. Lily, can you let Nana know what's going on? I'm going to take Penny down the elevator to my truck."

I carefully slid one arm behind Penny's back, the other beneath her knees, lifted her, and carried her out of the room. The elevator had been installed where the back servants' staircase had been, and I'd never been so glad for it. We took it all the way down to the driveway, which was a level below the first floor.

"Just a few more steps, Penny." I kept my voice calm so as not to alarm her.

"'Kay." Her head fell against my chest.

The storm hammered against the roof as I hurried through the breezeway and into the garage.

We got to my truck, I managed to press the fob twice, and the horn honked when the doors unlocked. I stretched my fingers to pull the handle to open the back passenger door but couldn't get a good grip.

"I ... can do it." Penny shifted in my arms.

"You sure?"

"I'm ... pregnant. My arms aren't ... broken." She breathed heavily as she reached out, pulled the handle, and opened the door.

"Good job." I used my shoulder to swing the door open all the way. "Let me get you settled back here."

"L-Look at you, M-Monty. P-Protector vibes look g-good on you."

"Don't tell anyone," I whispered. "You'll ruin my reputation." Penny was stuttering, an old condition that returned every now and again when she was stressed or anxious. Since Xavier wasn't here, it was up to me to make her feel safe and take care of her until we got to the hospital.

She held up her hand in a fist and tapped the nail side of her thumb twice to her lips, the ASL sign for "secret."

"Good." I winked and set her gently on the leather seat, dragged the seat belt across her torso, and clicked it in place.

She slid the lap portion below her belly and closed her eyes. She groaned and rubbed her hand over her belly.

The back door behind the driver's seat flew open. Tasha used the running board to step up, tossed a blanket onto the seat and climbed in. Her phone wedged between her shoulder and ear, she sat down and pulled her own seat belt on.

I pressed the remote start on the fob, and the big V8 engine rumbled to life. On a night like tonight, the extra power might come in handy. I rushed around, yanked open the driver's door, and climbed in behind the wheel. The temperature outside was in the low forties, so I cranked up the heat in the back seat.

"Gotta let you go, Mom. I'll see you there." Tasha ended the call and leaned forward. "I sent you a text with a link to Palmer City General, where Penny's OB has rights. We're going there in case he needs to check on her." She shook open the blanket and laid it over her sister.

My phone automatically connected to my truck's GPS, and I pulled up the text with the location.

"You ready?" I peered at Tasha in the rearview mirror. Her expression was stoic and calm, but her eyes told a different story.

Fear.

"Mrs. Nicks's car was the only one blocking you, and I asked her to move it. So you should be clear."

"Brilliant." I hadn't even thought about that. "Thanks."

I pressed the button on the rearview mirror to open the garage door. It rattled from the heavy wind slamming against it and slowly creaked its way upward. Rain whipped in through the opening, and I caught a glimpse of how extensively the weather conditions had deteriorated.

Tasha twisted to look out the back window. "Oh my gosh. The storm has gotten so much worse. Please drive carefully."

"Count on it." Not a chance in this lifetime I'd let anything happen to either of them.

I backed slowly out of the garage, and the truck was hit by a deluge of water like driving into an automatic car wash, heavy and powerful and blinding. I flipped on the wipers and maneuvered the truck around, careful not to hit Tasha's car. Once I was clear of the remaining guests' vehicles, I cautiously navigated the long, winding driveway down to where it met Stagecoach Road.

Lightning lit up the sky, and thunder rumbled close enough to vibrate the truck. Another bolt hit with an earth-shaking crack in front of us, illuminating the dark sky and the tall pines lining our property.

"Look out!" Tasha shouted and pointed toward the front. "Tree falling!"

I'd begged Nana when I moved in to let me cut down the two trees closest to the driveway. I was concerned they'd fall and block us from getting in or out of the property. But she'd said the odds of what happened the night Mindy died could happen again were slim to none and not to worry so much.

Slim to none wasn't good enough.

But this time, I was prepared.

The tall ponderosa fell as if in slow motion, landing square across the driveway and blocking our path out to the main road.

I slammed the truck into park, headlights aimed at the downed tree, and threw my door open and jumped out of the cab. Wind and rain slapped against me as I ran back to the tailgate. I dropped it down, hoisted myself up, and crawled along the bed to the built-in toolbox. I swiped my arm across my face to wipe away the icy rain, spun the lock dial to the right, then to the left, then right again—Mindy's birthdate—and lifted the lid.

The sharp metal edges of the chain saw blades gleamed up at me. It was made for a night like this. I looped the strap holding the safety glasses over my head, and they hung from my neck. I grabbed the headlamp, stretched the strap around my head, and clicked it on. I hefted the chain saw out of the box and closed the lid. Tasha's wide blue eyes stared out at me through the rear window.

"I'm going to cut it up!" I yelled and pointed at the chainsaw.

"I'll help!" Her voice was muffled, and she spun around.

Before I could protest, she was out of the cab and running through the rain toward the fallen tree.

By the time I reached her, she was straddling the end of the tree and pulling at the branches.

"Cut here first!" Her hair blew around her face as she shouted over the storm.

"You can't be that close!" I shouted into the rain. "I got it! You can help me clear the tree away!"

"Okay!" She hopped off the tree and jogged a safe distance away.

I slid the safety goggles onto my nose and made sure they were secure over my eyes. The headlamp was bright enough to illuminate a wide swath of the tree. I flipped the switch on the chain saw, pulled back the handle guard, and yanked the cord once, twice, and it buzzed to life.

"Pull your sweater up over your face!" I lifted my own shirt to demonstrate, just in case she couldn't hear me.

Neither of us had thought to grab our jackets, and I only had one set of goggles.

Tasha nodded and complied.

I lopped off a few of the smaller branches until I was able to get a clean cut on the fattest part of the tree. I brought the saw down on the exposed trunk, and it chewed through the bark, sending sawdust onto the ground to mix with the rain. As soon as the chain saw made it all the way through, I lifted it away, and yelled, "Clear!"

Tasha lowered her sweater, leaned down, and rolled the piece away. We repeated this process several times, then worked together to pull the cuttings off to the sides of the driveway.

Once the road was clear enough to pass, we hustled back to the truck. Tasha rejoined Penny in the back seat, and I climbed into the bed to secure the equipment in the toolbox. I grabbed two of the towels I kept in there and ran back to the driver's door.

I climbed in and handed one of the towels back to Tasha.

"Here ya go. I'll buy you a new outfit at the gift shop," I promised and dried my hands.

"Thanks." She smiled and dragged the towel over her face.

"Oh my gosh!" Penny said. "You guys were amazing out there."

"We *do* make a pretty good team," I said, towel-drying my face.

"We sure do!" Tasha squeezed her hair with the towel.

"You always have," Penny said, then she moaned a little.

"How are you feeling, Pen?" I asked.

"Tired. And my stomach's kinda crampy."

"We'll be there soon." Tasha tucked the blanket closer around her sister. "I never knew Monty could handle a chainsaw. Did you?" She smirked at me in the rearview mirror. "I'm kinda liking this lumberjack version of him."

I shook my head and smiled. Lumberjack, eh? I'd take it. I *was* a big manly man, after all. My eyes flicked to the rearview mirror again and I took in the vignette of sibling love, a love I had missed for so long.

Penny giggled and let her body lean against her sister. "You're the best sister, Tasha. You're always there for me."

"Aw, it's nothing, Pen. Any person in there would have helped you," she said.

"Yeah, but not the way *you* do. You know me like no one else does. Remember when I needed a job? You vouched for me to the Bevells, knowing full well I wouldn't be able to speak to customers because of my nervous stutter. And you encouraged me to take ASL as my foreign language because I'd have to speak in class with all of the others."

"Really, it was nothing, Pen. Shush, and let me tell you the tale of Lumberjack Monty."

As Tasha chronicled a play-by-play of our tree removal to Penny, my shoulders relaxed, and I let out a long, silent breath.

In a way, this whole incident felt like a redo, a second chance for me. I wasn't able to save my sister, but I *was* able to ensure Penny was no longer in danger.

Nothing would bring Mindy back, but being prepared and able to help a friend in crisis gave me much-needed peace.

I pulled up to the emergency entrance. Mr. and Mrs. Palmer were there waiting for us. Tasha hopped out and ran around to open Penny's door so their dad could help her down from the truck and into a wheelchair.

I pulled away as they whisked her inside, and I navigated to the parking garage. Once I was inside the building, I went straight to the gift shop for new clothes.

"Hey Monty! Got caught in the storm, huh?" The elderly cashier waved me over. I was a frequent customer here and knew all the staff. I usually picked up flowers or toys for the kids I visited.

"Hi, Connie. Nah. Decided to take a dip in the fountain for funsies."

"Oh, you!" She chuckled, and I grinned back. "Let me know if you need any help."

"Will do."

Not much of a selection. Scrubs, athletic gear, tacky touristy threads. I decided on royal blue Denver Edge hoodies and black unisex sweatpants. A two-pack of socks, a pair of boxers and ... I stared at the women's underwear section. There were too many choices, from full-on waist-high coverage to thongs. I had no idea what Tasha wore. I thought back to our stunting. I didn't remember her having a panty line, so that would lead me to think thong, but was

that for practice or every day? And the bras—sports, underwire, no underwire, pushup?

"Women's undies, huh?"

My cheeks heated. "My friend and I got caught in the rain.
She's in the ER with her sister," I explained. "I'm buying us
dry clothes."

"A *friend*, huh?"

"Yes, a *friend*."

"Noted. You got a picture of her?" I nodded. "Let me hold
these, and you find it. I'll see if I can figure out her size,
okay?"

I passed her the bundle of clothing and scrolled until I
found my favorite picture of Tasha. It was from Gabby's
wedding. She'd asked me to take a picture of her standing
outside the barn doors in her bridesmaid dress.

"Ooh, pretty one! Zoom in on her chest."

"What? No. Give me the clothes back, and you do the
zooming."

Connie cackled with laughter. "Testing you. Good news!
You passed!"

I held the bundle while she assessed the picture. "I'd say
she's between a small and a medium. Since you're just
friends, how about a sports bra and boy shorts? Modest
bathing suit kind of coverage."

I released a breath of relief. "Yeah. Good idea."

She plucked a matching set off the wall and added it to
my stack. "Anything else? Shoes?"

I looked down at my soggy sneakers. "Yeah. Whatcha got
in men's thirteen and women's seven?"

"You know her shoe size!" She elbowed me. "Just *friends*,
huh?"

"She was my stunting partner for sixteen years, Connie. I literally held her feet in my hands."

"Uh-huh. You want to be matchy matchy on the shoes, too? Nothing screams *partners* like twinning!"

"Just whatever you have is fine." This was taking way too long.

Ten minutes later, I'd changed into my new clothes and texted Tasha to find out how Penny was doing.

The doctor just left. She's getting fluids. They're going to admit her overnight for observation. Her OB is on the way.

Okay. I'm in the ER waiting room. I got you some dry clothes.

I'll be there in five.

I stuffed my phone in my pocket and walked toward the door that led to the unit.

When Tasha came through the door, I held up the shopping bag with her clothes. Poor thing was damp and shivering.

"Thanks! I'll be right back!"

I stayed put, waiting for her, and when she emerged for the second time, I couldn't help grinning like a clown. "Nice outfit," I teased.

She snorted and pulled on her wet braid. "You realize this isn't a cheer comp, right? We don't have to match."

I shrugged. "Too many choices on the women's wall."

She shook her head. "I'm not complaining. This is warm and soft. Let's go sit."

I followed her to an empty corner, and we placed our bags on the coffee table wedged between perpendicular chairs.

"You were amazing out there," Tasha said. "Thank you."

"Just did what I had to do," I replied. "You were totally the VIP of that operation. You have great instincts, Tasha."

"So do you. We move well together. Five months of being roommates, and we didn't bump into each other once in the kitchen."

"And cleaning up those suds felt like one of your choreographed routines."

She laughed. "Floody bubbles! That was insane."

"And fun."

"Yeah. Once I stopped being annoyed with you."

"Well, no more of that now that I'm finally out of your hair," I said.

Tasha frowned and tugged her knees up to her chest, her new shoes flat on the seat. "Yeah. No more having to listen to your shower concerts. I could hear you through the walls! I do miss the ugly old cat, though." Her lips twitched as she fought a smile.

"Have you given any thought to Nana's invitation?" I asked.

"To move in with you?"

I nodded.

"Every other minute since she asked."

"Really?" I tried not to sound too hopeful.

"Yeah. Who wouldn't want to live there? It's the most gorgeous piece of property I've ever seen. Beautifully decorated. State-of-the-art kitchen. A pool, a lake, a brook, a veranda, a gazebo, turret library, a sunroom, a mud room, a fancy parlor, a study ..."

"You'd be surprised. The last girl I took out talked about building a mansion in the mountains on our first—and only—date. It was a common theme."

"Is that why you stopped dating? Gold-diggers?"

"Pretty much. I'd rather spend time with Nana and the

kids. Once we're sure Penny's okay, I was planning to do a round in the pediatric oncology unit. Want to come with?"

"I'd love to, but you're changing the subject."

"Nah. I'm just done talking about it. So, you moving in or not?"

"Wouldn't it be weird for you?" She rested her chin on her knees and tilted her head.

"Why? You can have the room next to mine, if you want. It'll be like old times. The walls are thicker than at your place, but you could probably still hear me sing. I'll even take requests."

She laughed. "Old times. Like *last week*. Old times!" She was cracking up.

And I loved it.

"I'll even steal your shampoo and hide Cadbury eggs in your room."

"Hide Cadbury eggs? Where? And how did you get them out of season?"

"I have my secret ways."

"That just might be the deciding factor. Those are my *favorite*. You're a good friend, Monty."

"Yeah, I know. I hate that they make you sick, though. I might have to rethink that."

She sighed. "They don't make me sick, per se. They just, um … give my insides a little, ah … *boost* when things are stuck and aren't moving along on their own. Like coffee does."

Her face flamed bright red, and a look of relief crossed her features when her phone rang. She pulled it from her pocket. "It's Mom. Hi … Okay … Is it all right if Monty comes? He's still here … Okay … See you soon." She ended the call. "Mom says Penny's strength is returning by the minute. They're transporting her now, and she should be settled in her room in a half hour or so. You want to go see the kids on the way?"

"Yeah. Let me run our wet stuff to the truck. Meet you at the gift shop?"

She grinned. "See you there."

CHAPTER 29

Tasha

I took Monday off work and called my assistant coach to run the high school cheer practice so that I could sit with Penny all day and reply to Xavier's incessant texting when she was napping. He wanted to fly home, but she insisted he save his "baby daddy requests" for later in the pregnancy. The hospital released her around dinnertime, and I decided to stay with her overnight at their house.

I was late to work on Tuesday, but no one minded. I eased their minds on Penny's recovery, and by the time I'd left, the whole town was updated and praying for my sister.

I ended the high school team practice early and couldn't get to the Plex fast enough. I needed to burn off my stress, so as soon as I was stretched, I headed straight for the tumble mats and trampolines.

Monty was there with Evan, working on the timing of his tumbling passes for our routine. I joined Monty at the edge of the mat to watch Evan take off. His sequence was extraordinary. Monty had choreographed fifteen seconds of

cross-mat tumbling that included eighteen flips, ten twists, and five punchbacks.

"He's going to break your record," I warned Monty. "You sure you don't want to get into the routine to defend it?"

"He's not even close. My Team USA pass was eight seconds longer, and no one's come close since."

"Don't get too cocky, old man. Another year or so, and someone's bound to pass you."

"Are you challenging me?"

I shrugged. "Do you feel challenged?"

"I do, actually." He waved Evan over when he finished his sequence. "Stand with Tasha while I prove I'm still the best."

This was going to be fun to watch.

"What's he doing?" Evan asked.

"Version 3.0 of the pass that won Team USA gold three years in a row."

"No way! He can still do that?"

"We'll see, won't we?"

Monty stalked to the corner of the mat, turned his nose up at us, and took off. He could be annoying, but he wasn't a liar. He *was* the best.

"Twenty-five flips, sixteen twists, eight punchbacks. Perfect form on the layouts. He sets a high bar." How much more could he do? Seeing him tumble like this made me want to challenge him more, push him to his ultimate limits.

Monty didn't just tumble and bounce and twist. He flew. His taut muscles flowed into one elegant move after another until he stuck the landing with the same ease he had when he stepped up to the counter to order a drink at the Coffee Loft.

"We need him on the team. Why doesn't he compete?" Evan asked.

"He's already won all the titles. He likes coaching. And the Ridgie the bear gig isn't optimal for team practices. He's only missed a handful. And he can do *that*."

Monty finished the tumbling pass with a flourish and aimed a smirk at me. He bowed deeply to the audiences on the mats and up in the balcony who'd begun cheering him on when they noticed who it was and what he was doing.

"You don't need him, Evan. This team can win without him showing off." I held my hand up to high-five Monty as he jogged back.

"Still got it!" His hand slapped mine. "You were saying?"

"Great job." I grinned. "Now that you're warmed up, wanna throw some partner stunts? You've inspired me."

He looked up at the clock. "Evan's got three minutes left."

"I yield that time to Coach Tasha," he said. "Want me to spot?"

"Sure," I said. "Go do that pass two more times while I warm up on the tramp."

"Yes, Coach!"

"What do you want to work on today?" Monty asked.

"I was thinking about trying the partner sequence that leads into the pyramid. The Showcase is four days away, and they're all still wobbling in the same spot. I want to feel it, see if I can figure out why it's not coming together smoothly, and figure out a way to modify it without throwing the count off."

"Sounds fun."

I practiced the sequence on the trampoline. Monty and Evan watched me intently the entire time, which encouraged me to be even sharper and land as clean as I could. I didn't want to mess up or fall, especially after Monty had just proven he was still in his top form.

I didn't have any trouble with the flips, twists or kickouts, but I did have an issue during the part I'd referenced. I found myself hesitating a millisecond due to a blind spot.

"I think I figured it out!" I jumped down from the tramp and waved him onto the floor. "Evan, let me know what you think. Monty, you know how this goes, right?"

"I do. I've been working with Evan and Amelia on it. She wobbles in the same spot. Let's do it!"

We got into position, and Monty tossed me up. Due to the blind spot, I wobbled just as the girls had been doing.

When I landed on the mat, I turned to the guys. "What if, instead of a full twist, we switch it out with a half and move the full to the beginning of the sequence. That'll eliminate the blind spot and should make the rest of it flow."

"That should work," Evan said. "Let's see it."

Monty's hands gripped my hips, and I was off. It felt *good* to be back up in the air. I hadn't realized how much I'd missed it until he encouraged me to try it again.

"That looked great, Coach! I think it's going to work." Evan's expression was sheer admiration.

That felt good, too.

Every athlete appreciated a coach who gave their all. This was my all, for now. But I was motivated, and I planned to encourage at least half of our athletes—the ones who were ready—to try out for Team USA.

I couldn't stop smiling, and neither could Monty.

Evan left us with a warning. "If you two keep grinning like that, your Coach Monsha rep will be ruined."

I laughed. "Noted."

When Evan left, I asked Monty if he had dinner plans.

"I figured I'd hit the café in the main building. You?"

"I brought chicken curry stew. There's enough to share if you want some."

"Heck yeah! Thanks."

Over dinner, Monty told me he planned to bring Nana by the Coffee Loft the next day.

"Pumpkin Spice Blah-te season is almost over, and she feels cheated. Even though you or I have brought her one almost daily since it was approved."

"She knows we serve it year-round now, though. Right?"

"Yeah, Penny mentioned that when the management changed. But she likes the fall decor. Christmas stuff is already popping up around town. And Nana does not approve."

"That's true. And the music's been on the radio for weeks." An idea occurred to me. "You still have a friend at the print shop, right?"

"Yeah. Why?"

"If I send a design over, can you call and see if he can make a banner on short notice?" I put my spoon down and held my palms up. "Picture it. Welcome back, Nana Booboo!"

He laughed. "She would love that. I'll bring her crown."

"What time?" I asked. "It's a game day, right?"

"It is. We could come in the morning."

"Hmm. No. Let's time it for just before Xavier comes in for his toffee coffee. More people, a few local hockey celebrities, and Penny will be there. She's not working this week, but she'll be in to make his good-luck coffee. You can still get to the arena on time, right? Or I could bring Nana home before I head to the high school."

"That works. Great idea. She's going to love it."

"Good!" I stirred my stew. "It's a plan."

"Spit and shake on it?"

"Ew, gross, no. What are you, four?"

He waggled his eyebrows. "Only on the inside."

I snort-laughed so deeply it triggered hiccups, which made me laugh harder. That set Monty laughing, and it took a while until we calmed down.

When the hiccups finally stopped, I wiped my eyes and shook my head. "You are too much."

"Yeah, I am. But not for you, I hope?"

I looked up from my curry to find him staring intently at me, absent of his trademark cocky grin—a serious expression like the one from Saturday night, when he was describing how he'd kiss me if I was his girl.

The *zing* was back, firing like shooting stars all through me. For a moment, it even felt like I thought my heart stopped, then it shocked back to life with a grand finale of those zings. I definitely lost track of its beats, but then the pulse in my ears thrummed in earnest, and I realized my heart rate was actually sky-high.

"No," I whispered. "You're not too much for me. You're just right."

CHAPTER 30
Monty

"Look at the Christmas display in the bookstore! Disgraceful! Thanksgiving is a week from tomorrow, and it's like everyone's already moved on from it!"

"Just terrible, Nana," I agreed.

There'd been a rare open parking spot a block up from the Coffee Loft, and I thought it would be nice to take her for a little window-shopping stroll. It was turning out to be quite entertaining—for me.

"And look! Even the antiques store is draping pine over their window. What is wrong with people? I'm going to have to have a talk with Gladys. She should know better. Oh! I know! Can you get Gabby's mom to do an investigative report?"

"She's a weather woman, Nana, not a beat reporter or investigative journalist."

"Hmm. Well, she's got to know *someone* who can film this travesty."

We reached the end of the block at Prospect Road, and I

pressed the button on the traffic pole to cross to the other side.

"And look! St. Mary's already has their nativity out. *Their nativity!* Not just the creche. I can see putting up the structure to stay on schedule, but the start of Advent is still over two weeks away!"

"Maybe everyone is in the Christmas spirit early this year," I offered. "You can't fault them for that. It's the best season." The signal flashed the white walking man, and I pushed Nana across to the other side of Main.

"Oh yes I can! I'm getting old. No season should try to push another season out of the way. Who started this? Do you think it was the bookstore? I heard from Clarice that people start reading Christmas novels in October. October! Before Halloween!"

"I've heard even earlier than that," I stated in my most scandalized conspiratorial tone. "Like July!"

She waved me off. "Yeah, yeah, Christmas in July is a *thing* now. But come August first, put it away until the first Sunday of Advent!"

I stopped in front of the Coffee Loft. "No Christmas here. All pumpkins and leaves and cinnamon sticks and poison coffee."

"Yes, they're the only ones on the block with any sense. All right. End of tangent. Time for some pumpkin spice and dirt cake. Tasha texted me that she made the sugar-free stuff and will have it for me behind the counter. Speaking of Tasha, when are you going to get a girlfriend?"

"That was nice of her. You're the only woman for me, Nana."

"Ha! I'm old, and we're related," she quipped.

"You're a handful, is what you are," I bantered back at

her. I tapped the assistance button next to the old saloon door that hung on the exterior as a tribute to the building's history. The modern door opened slowly and engaged the chimes. I pushed Nana through the doorway and stopped just short of the queue so she could get a full view.

She gazed up at the banner in awe. "They even decorated the spiral stairs railing to the loft in twinkle lights!"

I raised my hand in the air and counted down. "Three, two, one!"

"Welcome back, Nana BooBoo!" The staff and customers cheered, and I pulled out her tiara, which I'd stuffed into my hoodie's center pocket.

"You should put this on," I said.

She grinned and set it on her head. Tasha was the first to approach her with the coveted pumpkin spice latte. We shared a grin as Nana sipped it from a new personalized orange mug that read "Nana's PSL."

"This is perfect," Nana praised. "Did you bring my dirt cake?"

Tasha nodded and pointed to a table that was set with a red tablecloth and blue and white flowers. "Head on over to your VIP table and I'll bring it right out."

"You spoil me. Can't wait till you move in!"

Tasha's lips parted to protest, but I shook my head. She hadn't decided yet, and it wasn't the time to tell Nana that, unless she was prepared to discuss the subject in front of half the town.

I wheeled Nana to the table and sat in the chair across from her. Her eyes were saucerlike as she stared at the heaping portion of sugar-free dirt cake. I sipped on the iced chocolate Tasha set out for me and watched Nana dig in. For once in her life, she seemed speechless.

Not for long, though. When she finished, she set her fork down. "It's good to be back. Thank you for this."

"It was all Tasha's idea," I admitted. "Though I probably would have thought about it if she hadn't."

"Mmmhmm." She patted my hand. "*Sure* you would have." She turned her head toward the register where Tasha was working. "I do love that girl. I wish she didn't have to work so hard."

"Working hard has made her who she is, Nana. You worked hard when you were her age."

"I did. Maybe that's why I relate to her so well. But I never had money worries. Those can choke you. Has she decided about living with us?"

"Not yet, but she's going ahead with the recipe book. She's very excited about it, actually."

"I'm glad. That was nice of you to get that going." She pointed to the entrance. "What's *he* doing here? I thought he got traded?"

I followed her finger to where Vlad had just entered with Xavier, Penny, and Noel. "He did. The Edge is playing Miami tonight."

"Well, there are coffee shops in Denver," she huffed. "Oh look! Brendan brought Kingston!" She clapped and whistled. "Kingston Brewer! You get over here and give Nana Booboo a hug!"

I rolled my eyes. Nana was a big fan of our hometown hero and was crushed when he was traded to Montana a few years ago. Behind the guys, Brenna was arm in arm with Kingston's wife, Taylor.

I waved, and Taylor tugged free of Brenna, wading through the people who had gathered around Kingston to welcome him back to town.

"Monty!" Taylor was little, animated, and bouncy, which had served her well on the cheer floor. We'd been on several teams together over the years. She hugged Nana first, and I stood up to welcome her back.

"Hey, Tay." I released her and tipped my chin toward her husband. "He's stealing Nana's Welcome Back party."

"Sorry. Believe me, I bet he wishes he wasn't! We had no idea this was happening. Thanks for your bow order, by the way." She bit her lip and glanced back over at the crowd, many of which had followed the players in from the street. Xavier was trying to get Penny through so she could make his toffee coffee. "Is it always such a madhouse here on game days?"

"You're welcome. Not usually this mad," I admitted.

Taylor pulled a chair over and sat between me and Nana. "How's your Worlds team coming along?"

I narrowed my eyes. "Are you trying to trick me into spilling our secrets?"

She laughed. "Nope. Kali's team has nothing on the Fire-Volts, especially our tumblers."

"What else is new?" I asked. "You should come to the Showcase Saturday, if you're still in town."

She nodded. "I think I will. I'll be here working remotely with my clients through Thanksgiving, then I'll have to figure out what to do from there. And I can't miss my team's competitions. We'd always hoped for this trade, but the timing was later than we expected. We'd almost given up."

"Seems like perfect timing to me," Nana huffed and leaned toward her. "Have you met that Vlad guy?"

Taylor's brows knitted together. "Yeah. He seems nice. Adorable accent."

Nana rolled her eyes. "He's a hottie, but he wasn't right for our Tasha."

Taylor looked from Vlad to Tasha and then to me. "Huh?"

"I'll explain another time," I said. "Come by the gym tomorrow. You can watch us practice."

"Oh yeah! I'd love to see Nate, too. I'm so proud of him." Taylor and Nate had been partners for almost as long as Tasha and I. "King! Come see Nana before she implodes!"

Kingston was significantly shorter than the other guys, and it was humorous to watch him slip under Brendan's arm and around Noel to get to our table.

"Nana Booboo." He grinned, then kissed her cheek. "It's been too long. You don't look a day older than the last time I saw you."

"Aw, stop it. You're too kind." She raised her eyebrows. "Did you get your Cityside Subs endorsement back?"

He laughed. "Nah. That's all Noel's now. Besides, he looks better on billboards than I do."

"He's not a Palmer City native," she protested. "At least Brewski's can take down that horrid Montana jersey of yours now. They should have kept your Voltage sweater up, if you ask me, no matter how proud they were of you."

He smiled. "You'll be happy to know that Uncle Quinn and Aunt Angie already have an Edge jersey in their possession and are in the process of switching them out."

"Good! And your cats?"

"Luc and Bourque are doing great, a little mad at us about the car ride, but we'll spoil them until they get over it. And I've got my cousin Drew lined up to spoil them when Taylor and I are away."

"Good man! Best cat sitter in town!"

I tuned out of their conversation when I caught a wisp of

peach in my peripheral. Vlad was at the register, handing Tasha what would be his last letter. I'd told him she felt it was a clean break, but he'd insisted on one more, to thank her for being his friend and wishing the cards had been in their favor.

I'd resisted helping him until I realized this would give me the opportunity to also express what *I'd* been feeling. For once, this was a letter I felt good about and wanted to write. If Tasha ever did find out who was behind the words—and I had no plans to tell her—she'd be clear on how I felt about her.

CHAPTER 31

Tasha

The café was insanely busy and crowded. I wasn't sure if I regretted the timing I'd chosen or not. Nana didn't seem to mind one bit that Kingston had stolen her thunder.

When the players left, most of the crowd dispersed with them. Ten minutes after that, it was finally quiet. My shift was almost over, and then I needed to head out to the high school.

I leaned back against the counter and surveyed the café. Penny and Brenna had joined Nana and Monty at her table, and from the way they were looking at and rubbing their bellies, I could deduce what the conversation was about. Monty looked up and caught my gaze and made a funny face. He was probably super uncomfortable.

Out of nowhere, Gabby's hand closed around my wrist. "Kitchen!"

She pulled me toward the door before I could reply. It swung shut behind us. "What?" I asked.

She pointed to the pocket in my apron. "Open it."

"Later."

"Now."

"Why?"

"Because."

I narrowed my eyes. "Not good enough."

Gabby sighed and rolled her eyes. "C'mon, Tasha." Her eyes flicked toward the door. "Just ... I want to hear what he could possibly have to say, and if he made you feel bad, I'll get Noel to check him into the boards tonight."

"With his one kidney?" I asked sarcastically.

"Yes!"

"It's that important you'd risk a future of dialysis for your husband?"

"Just open the letter!"

"Fine." I tore open the flap and pulled it out. "Dearest Tasha." I squinted at the script, reading ahead and not believing what I was seeing. My heart thumped in my chest.

"What is it? What's it say? Why do you look like you've just seen a ghost?"

I peered up at her over the letter. Instead of looking concerned, she wore a satisfied smirk and was practically salivating.

I shook my head and shoved it at her. "Excuse me."

I flew through the door and stalked to Nana's table. "You!" I shouted at Monty, grabbing his wrist much like Gabby had gripped mine. "Kitchen! Now!"

His eyes widened, and I pulled at him as he began to stand. I didn't even bother to excuse my interrupting. I was confused, incensed, confused, elated, *confused* ...

I got him through the door and pointed to the letter in Gabby's hand. "Explain that!"

Gabby's lips twitched. She set the letter on the counter and slipped back into the café.

Monty just stared at the paper. I positioned myself between him and the counter and crossed my arms. "Well?"

He paled, and his expressions twisted and morphed from one to another, like he wasn't sure how to react to being caught. I knew all his faces and recognized panic and torment, then worry. His eyebrows rose with hope, and then he blanched, as if he were in pain or was going to be sick.

I quoted the letter. "I'm 'the sun and the stars and every source of light' in your world. You said those exact words to me Saturday night. Do you think I'm stupid?"

His face scrunched, and he pulled at his hair. "No, Tasha. I think you're very smart."

"Apparently, I'm not smart enough, because I can't figure out why *your* words are in Vlad's letter."

Monty closed his eyes and recited, "I would sacrifice my happiness for yours, even if you never knew."

I gasped. "Has it been you the whole time?"

"Yeah. I'm sorry, Tasha. I was just trying to help the guy … and express how I feel for someone who will never feel the same for me."

"Someone who would never feel the same for you? Who?" I picked up the letter and scanned the words for a clue.

"My heart is heavy with love unclaimed, but I shall be sustained by the memories you gave."

My hand flew to my mouth. "Me?" I whispered.

He covered his face with his hands and nodded.

Monty was in love with me.

Me!

His archenemy. Former partner. Verbal sparring opponent.

I set the letter down again and walked slowly toward him until the toes of our shoes touched. A surge of suppressed feelings rushed through me, and I pulled on his hands, revealing a reddened face and shiny eyes.

"I—I'm sorry, Tasha. I know you're sad about Vlad leaving. I—"

"Shut up," I whispered, pulling his face down to mine. "I'm not." I pressed my lips to his. His arms came around me, and he returned the kiss with fervor, then bent to lift me off my feet. I wrapped my legs around him as he carried me toward the empty counter, setting me on top of it for better leverage for kissing.

For the record, real-life kisses *can* be better than fiction.

When I couldn't breathe, I pulled away and looked up at him shyly. His smile was so big and genuine.

"I love you, Tasha. I always have. That's why I couldn't be your partner. I didn't think I could bear it if my personal feelings put you at risk. But that backfired in the worst way. I hurt you anyway—and worse, at that. I should have apologized a long time ago. I'm sorry. I will *never* hurt you again, I promise."

"You can make up for it by writing me more letters," I decided. "And you have to kiss me like that at least three times every day and make up the deficit when you travel."

"Deal."

"Shake on it?"

Simultaneously, we both spit into our right hands and slapped them together.

Yeah, it was gross. So what? I had a feeling we'd be sharing all kinds of germs in the future.

CHAPTER 32
Monty

R idgie the Bear had the best performance of his life Wednesday night.

It wasn't too hard, since I only had to outdo myself.

But with Tasha watching, wearing the jersey I'd asked the equipment manager to make in haste, with "RIDGIE" across her shoulders over double zeroes, just like mine, I was pumped up more than ever. More than any national, international, or Worlds title I'd achieved.

Somehow, I'd won the heart of the girl I'd loved for over two decades. This bear's feelings were finally out of hibernation.

It seemed like forever until I could get to the family section to greet the kids—and Tasha. She hung back while I goofed around and posed for selfies. Vali was there—she'd been released from the hospital a few weeks ago—and I'd asked Kami if she and Ryleigh would host her and her parents.

Finally, it was Tasha's turn. I blew her a kiss and cast out an invisible fishing line. She laughed when I got Ryleigh and a few of the other kids to help me reel her from her seat to the aisle.

I bent my bear head down, and she kissed me on the nose. A collective "aw" thundered around us as the footage reached the jumbotron during the commercial timeout. My paws flew to my cheeks, and I tilted my head, giving them my best Bashful impression. Tasha wrapped her arms around me, a bear hug for the bear, and then we posed for Mags, who'd snuck away from her usual post by the players' bench.

I had a feeling Bailey was already working on an article about a certain lovestruck mascot for the team's website.

Play resumed, and the crowd forgot about us. I made the ASL sign for "I love you" and pointed to Tasha.

"Oooh, Ridgie's got a girlfriend," Ryleigh sang. "Can I be a flower girl at your wedding? I can provide references."

"Ryleigh!" her mother scolded her, but she was laughing along with the other Wags.

"What? It's true. I've been a flower girl seven times." She tipped her chin up at me. "You know how to get in touch if you decide to go with a *professional.*"

I patted her on the head, then pointed at Tasha and signed for her to call me.

As I turned to leave, the fans erupted. Kingston Brewer had scored his third goal of the game. Hats flew, and I changed course toward Taylor. She high-fived me, and I made a grabby motion with my hands and patted my shoulder. She grinned and scooted in front of me. I squatted, placed my paws on her hips, and boosted her up to sit on my shoulder.

Jared was not pleased.

"Me next!" Ryleigh demanded.

"You gotta be eighteen and sign a waiver," Jared told her.

He totally made that up. There was no rule against me

picking up kids, as far as I knew, but there wasn't much I could do since I couldn't speak, and being purposely defiant in front of the public was frowned upon.

It was a good night. The Edge won 5-3 over the New Orleans Crescents, and a barrage of thousands of stuffed and plastic birds rained down on the ice after the final horn. The players were still celebrating in the dressing room after I showered and changed.

I was surprised to find Tasha waiting for me. "Don't you have to work at the crack of dawn?"

"Hello to you, too." She smirked. "Drive me home?"

"Of course." She snaked her arm around my waist, and I pulled her to me. "I'm glad you came."

"I love watching you work the crowd. Especially the kids. You've really taken this mascot thing to a whole new level."

"Just wait until All-Star Weekend. Those other stuffies better be prepared to be upstaged."

Tasha laughed. "I wouldn't expect anything less."

"I tend to put everything I've got into things that matter to me." We turned the corner. The hall ahead was empty. I let go of her and gestured from my head to my feet. "Are you ready for all of this? All Monty, all the time?"

She crossed her arms and raised her eyebrows. "Hmm. Maybe not *all* the time. Eighty percent? I do have three jobs, you know."

"I'll take every minute you can give me." I dropped my bag to the ground and reached for her. "And every kiss you'll take. Each one is a promise that I'll keep."

"Keep saying things like that, you might work up to one hundred percent." She walked into my arms and pressed her lips to mine.

CHEER SHOWCASE DAY at the Plex.

We'd be the last team to perform, but several of our athletes coached other teams, so Tasha and I hung out behind the curtain that separated the performance mat from the warm-up mats. The risers were packed, and it was standing room only up on the balcony.

Our phones buzzed about thirty minutes in. I checked mine to find a text from Evan: *I'm not going to make it. Fill in for me. My uniform is in my locker. Combo is 02-14-24.*

"Evan?" I asked.

She shook her head. "Nope. I've got one from Amelia. She says she's not going to make it. Everything I need to fill in for her is in Evan's locker?" Her voice rose with each word. "What does she mean, Monty?"

"I don't know. Evan isn't coming either. I think they're setting us up."

"But—why? Why wouldn't they want to perform after all the work they put in?"

I had my ideas, but I'd keep them to myself for now. "We'd better get changed and run through the routine. I'll text the group chat to see who's available to run it with us."

We hurried to the lockers. I grabbed the bag inside, and we raced to the coaches' locker room. I fished out the shirt and pants and gave the bag with the rest to Tasha.

"I can't believe she did this to me! She was just here, coaching her tiny and mini teams! I wondered why she was in warm-ups and not in uniform, but did it occur to me to ask?" She answered her own question. "No! No, it didn't, because *who drops out of the showcase an hour before they're set to perform?* No one!"

"Well, they did." I gently guided her toward a changing stall and nudged her in. "Get dressed so we can go save the show." She entered the stall and slammed the door. I slipped into the one next to hers so I could hear all her mutterings.

"Save the show? They're just darn lucky we made the routine and know the positions well enough to fill in for them! Save the show—ha! *They're* going to need saving the next time I see them!"

I smiled as I listened to her rant on the other side of the wall. Thursday night at practice, Evan and Amelia had stayed after to watch us work out. It felt incredibly freeing to tumble and stunt and goof around with combinations when you weren't under any pressure to perform.

And we *might* have snuck a kiss or two.

The jig was up. Our captains got to witness Coach Monsha at our mushiest.

Tasha was still ranting when I exited my stall to slick my hair into place and pull on my FireVolts Cheerdana.

"It's a good thing my abs still look good! Look at this! Way too much skin!" She pointed to her bare midsection. "Oh, why did I have to choose such a complicated hairstyle? I should have just gone with a simple pony and Cheerdanas! Easy! Simple! And requiring extra hair ties, of which I have *exactly enough*, thanks to Barfy! And have you seen all the colors in this eye shadow palette?" She held it up and waved it in the air. "I hope you still like glitter, because it's gonna be all over you for days."

"Just like old times." I grinned. "Can I help?"

She tapped her chin. "Yeah." She divided her hair into three sections, two at the crown and one at the back. "I don't have any clips. Can you be a human clip and hold the sections I'm not working on?"

"Sure." I stood behind her as she continued to ramble as she braided and twisted her hair, offering supportive and affirmative responses when required. Then I watched her apply her makeup. It took me back in time, and I was determined that we'd pull off our best performance ever.

She might be upset with our captains, but I planned to thank them profusely for this opportunity with my once-again forever partner.

CHAPTER 33
Tasha

"One more time!"

We'd moved through our formal rotations on the warm-up mats, and now we were on deck. The music for the performing team had just begun, so we had just over two and a half minutes to run through our own two-and-a-half-minute routine.

I clapped my hands above my head to signal I wanted their eyes on me. "Listen up, team! Dance full-out, mark the baskets, partner stunts go up. We're doing the pyramid. Make sure you're not in Monty's way for his tumbling passes. Everyone counts out loud. Set!"

The final run-through was a success. I high-fived Monty, who hadn't even broken a sweat. "Nice work, partner."

"Did you expect anything less?"

I swatted him. "Be nice."

"I'm always nice."

I made a face at him.

"Bring it in," he called. "FireVolts on three!" We formed a

crowded circle and pushed all our hands into the middle. "One, two, three—"

"*FireVolts!*"

Our team was directed to line up, and we took our places, two by two, at the curtain.

Go time.

"Don't you dare let me fall," I whispered.

"Never." He kissed my forehead and hugged me tightly.

I still couldn't believe I was doing this. I hadn't performed in front of an audience in years. I was confident Monty wouldn't let me hit the floor, but what if *I* couldn't hit my sequences? Or got stage fright? Or forgot the dance moves?

I didn't have time to finish playing out all my anxious thoughts. The emcee announced our team, and we ran out. In the coaches' spot, just below the stage, were Evan and Amelia.

Those little stinkers!

I didn't have time to gel on that, either. "Set!" I shouted. The mat shook as we sprang into our starting positions.

The music began with a clip from "Everybody Groove," followed by a medley of upbeat hip hop clips. I led the dance group as the first basket tosses launched. Monty and his tumblers did their thing around us, and then we moved into position for our first partner sequence. That was followed by more tumble runs, standing tumbling, and high-level stunting from the basket groups. I met Monty in our spot for the sequence we'd re-configured, then it was into the pyramid, down to the floor, and the big finish. The last section included Monty's fifteen-second tumbling run, the final dance sequence, and our most high-level basket tosses.

The ending pose came too quick. We held for applause, then jumped up and started cheering for ourselves. No falls,

and if this had been scored, we were confident there
wouldn't have been any deductions.

I ran to Monty and jumped into his arms. He caught me
and held me up so I could kiss him, but I didn't stop at his
lips.

Nope.

I left bright red kissy prints all over his cheeks, chin, nose
and forehead.

He carried me off the stage, laughing. Back behind the
curtain, we were greeted by our conspiring team captains.
They'd brought Nate and Taylor with them, probably for
support because they were afraid of how I'd react.

Monty set me down, and I waved my finger in front of
them. "That could have been a disaster of epic proportions.
You sabotaged the whole team!"

Evan and Amelia just grinned at me, then looked at each
other. "Sorry, Coach."

"Let's not be too harsh on them." Monty was grinning,
too. "They gave me a chance to remind everyone I'm still the
best tumbler."

I rolled my eyes. "Extra laps at our next practice, and I am
officially putting you two in charge of the fundraising efforts
for the Florida trip. When we qualify, of course."

"Yes, Coach!"

"Now get out of my sight!" Evan and Amelia rushed
away, and I turned on Nate. "Did you know about this?"

He held up his hands in defense. "I know nothing."

Taylor grinned up at him. "He's not mean enough to be
party to something like this." She patted his arm.

"Hmm." I wasn't convinced.

"You were amazing out there, Tasha." Taylor beamed.
"You and Monty should try out for Team USA. I know they'd

love to have you both back. You've got the skills nailed down."

I shook my head. "I'm good. I much prefer the coaching side of this sport. Besides, I have three—"

"Jobs, we know," Monty finished. "And I'll be busy with the NHL playoffs. If Kingston keeps playing like he played Wednesday night, we've got a good chance to not just get to the final this season but to win it, too."

"Yeah, I hope so! Because ..." Taylor placed a finger over her lips and checked to make sure no one else was listening. "I *really* want a baby-in-the-cup picture!"

"You, too?" I asked, smiling. Straight-up baby fever right now in this town.

She nodded.

"Congratulations!" Monty hugged her.

"Shhh!" I placed a finger over my lips. "They may not want that public yet!"

"Sorry!" Monty apologized.

"It's okay," Taylor assured us. "I don't think anyone heard us. Do you two have plans tonight? Brenna reserved the function room at Brewski's to watch the Edge play Montana. It's a big game for King. He's never played against Alexei Kriz before. It's going to be something."

I looked up at Monty. "We could bring Nana."

He grinned. "She'd love that."

"Great!" Taylor looped her arm through Nate's. "We'll see you there."

Once they were out of earshot, I turned to Monty. "And tomorrow ..."

"Yeah?"

"I was thinking we could start packing up my apartment?"

"Yeah?"

"Yeah." I booped his nose. "But only if the third-floor room between Nana's and the turret library is available."

He scratched at the back of his neck and feigned consideration. "I'll have to check with the boss."

I locked my gaze on his and looped my arms around his neck. "I love that turret room. Best place to think and relax. And I'd like to move in before Christmas. Her place is a magical wonderland in the winter."

"It'll be even more magical with you there." He pressed his forehead to mine and pulled me closer.

"Double the magic," I whispered, pressing the tip of my nose to his. "Monsha forever?"

"Monsha forever," he promised, sweeping me off my feet with a kiss that made my toes tingle and my heart zingle.

Was zingle a word? I didn't care. I was being kissed like a heroine in a love story.

My love story.

And what a tale it was.

Epilogue

MONTY

Six months later

As always, the Worlds team closed out the Plex's annual cheer banquet. Tasha and I would be last at the podium to distribute awards to our athletes. We'd taken first place in every competition we'd entered and beaten every team at Summit, *the* competition in Orlando that featured teams from, well, all over the world.

The emcee called us to the podium, and Tasha and I took turns highlighting each of our athlete's attributes and contributions.

"Amelia." Tasha held up her certificate and trophy as Amelia strode up to the podium. "Your strong leadership, nurturing qualities, and initiative to think outside of the box and challenge others—including your coaches—is unparalleled by anyone I've coached or who's coached me. You've been an integral part of this team's success, to me personally, and to this gym—am I right, Lil' Chargers and Power Ups?"

The tiny and mini teams Amelia co-coached and their

families stood up and cheered as Tasha finished her praise and handed over the award.

My turn. "Last but not least, Evan." I sighed dramatically. "What can I say? He's the best tumbler in competitive cheer. I'd say in the world, but until he can best my twenty-two-second tumbling pass, unfortunately, he's just second best. Maybe next year." I grinned at him as he approached and patted his back. "You're a great leader, inspiring others to push one more time, two more times, however many times it takes to reach the goal. And I'd be remiss if I didn't point out your emotional support of your teammates on and off the mat. It was our honor to coach you this year, and we hope you'll be back."

I handed him his award, and Tasha hip-checked me away from the podium. I rubbed my hip and pretended it hurt, much to the delight of the audience.

"I have one more award." Tasha tipped her chin up and looked down her nose at me. "I think a certain coach deserves recognition, don't you?"

I feigned surprise, but we'd practiced this. I had an award for her, too.

"Mon-ty! Mon-ty!" The crowd chanted and I bowed.

"This guy"—she tossed her thumb at me—"has been a gym rat here since he was four years old. How do I know that, you ask? Well, I was here, too. And on Monty's first day of cheer camp, he was a *disaster*. We preschoolers who'd been lucky enough to have his big sister Melinda as our tiny cheer assistant coach expected so much more from him. He couldn't even do a forward roll!"

I will not cry. I will not cry. I'd cried when she'd rehearsed it. Got it all out.

So I thought.

"Well, I marched up to him at our first water break and told him just how bad he was and proceeded to demonstrate the correct form. He just needed the right teacher. Whatever I told him to do, he did. For sixteen years!" She laughed. "He may be a little cocky, a touch of snobby, and a bit self-centered at times." She looked over to me, and I bent my arms up in a shrug for the audience. "But when you need anything, anything at all, he'll be there. He takes exceptional care of his Nana." We both waved to her. She dabbed her eyes and waved back. "He's besties with dozens of kids going through treatments for childhood cancer and other conditions, and he's proven here at the gym that he can sub in for anyone, anytime."

Here was where I was supposed to wave elbow-elbow-wrist-wrist, royalty style, but instead I was losing my cool. Between her words about me and the speech I had planned for her, my emotions had a mind of their own.

"This award not only exemplifies his attributes but also his willingness to model and demonstrate them, like when he pulled in Ryleigh Spencer to fill in at a qualifying competition. Monty, Ryleigh, you made dreams come true that day for the Circuit Breakers. They hit zero, took first place, and received a gold bid to Nationals, where they took first place." She paused for applause. I leapt off the stage and ran out to Ryleigh. She put down her Lofty-size pink and blue Magic Charm shake real quick and I almost shuddered at how much sugar was in that thing. I pushed the thought aside and boosted her onto my shoulder so she could bask in the praise.

"To Coach Monty, I present the award for Best Clutch Performance." I set Ryleigh down and strode back up to the stage to rejoin Tasha at the podium. She handed me the certificate, and I leaned down to kiss her.

Then I hip-checked her away from the podium.

Gently, of course. We'd rehearsed it.

"As Coach Tasha mentioned, we met on the cheer mat the summer before prekindergarten. Even then, she was a smart know-it-all and could back up her bragging by outperforming anyone who challenged her. Best forward roll? Tasha. Best walkover? Tasha. But she wasn't just the best, she was the first. For every new skill, she was the first to ring the bell, and she'd prance in front of the team to demonstrate. And she was the first—and only—girl to steal my heart."

"Awwwwwwwwww." All the athletes and their families chorused.

"It took me over two decades to tell her so, but it's the truth. I remind her every day with fancy words and love letters. I even taught myself cursive. Right, babe?"

Tasha sighed and rolled her eyes, but she was smiling. She nodded in affirmation as the audience collectively swooned at the admission of my romantic gestures.

I grinned and continued. "What she didn't tell you about the day we met was that we partnered up for a stunt. She pushed and poked and prodded me until my form was perfect, and of course, we were the best. The only pair the coach didn't have to adjust. So I asked her to be my partner forever."

"Awwwwwwwwww."

"We spit on our hands and shook on it. Today, I'm honored to present her with the Best Partner award." I handed her the certificate and a bouquet of peach carnations I'd stowed under the podium. Poking out of the bouquet was a small stuffed hedgehog. "There's no one better. And if she'll have me, I'd like to renew that promise of 'partners forever,' right here, right now, with you all here to witness it."

I hip-checked her one more time to push her farther from the podium, but instead of holding her hand and raising it into the air as we'd planned, I dropped to one knee.

"Tasha, will you marry me and seal us as Monsha forever?"

As I expected, gasps of *aw*, high-pitched squeals, whistles, and other such cheers became the soundtrack to my proposal.

Tasha's mouth dropped open in surprise, but she was quick to nod in the affirmative.

But instead of saying yes, a look of confusion marred her face. "Penny?"

"Huh?"

She pointed, and I turned to look behind me. Penny was standing in the wings with Xavier. She was wearing a long, flowy dress in FireVolts colors and was clutching her belly. I'd invited them, but Xavier declined, texting that Penny wasn't feeling well. But here they were.

"Say yes, Tasha!" Penny called. "My water broke! I gotta goooooo!"

"What—oh! Yes!"

I slid the ring on her finger and stood up to kiss her and spin her around.

Standing ovation, as expected. To the tune of "Mon-sha! Mon-sha!"

I set her down, and we spoke at the same time. "Hospital?"

"Yes! Wait! Nana first. And there's something I need to pick up at home," I added as we hurried off the stage.

We reached the parking lot in record time, and I stopped the wheelchair short when I caught sight of my truck.

"Montgomery!" Nana exclaimed. "Your vehicle is oozing birdseed!"

Each of the four windows were open to allow the birdseed to trickle out and down the side of the doors. The bed was filled to overflowing with the substance, and little puddles were forming on the ground alongside it.

Tasha was laughing, and I shot her a disapproving glare. She jingled her keys. "Good thing we drove separately."

"Freaking Zaki Marsch," I muttered. "Change of plans, Nana."

We followed Tasha to her car, and I drove us home, dreaming up schemes to get back at the clown who mildly inconvenienced us for the sake of payback.

He had no idea who he was messing with.

Game on.

"I'm going to be an aunty!" Tasha sang from the back seat. She held up her left hand so I could see her diamond in the mirror. "And a wife! Best day ever!"

"And an author," Nana said, pointing at the box sitting on the front stoop. "I believe your books have arrived."

I pulled into the garage and set up Nana's wheelchair as my fiancée helped her out of the car. She'd lost weight eating Tasha's food and was walking much better, but she tired out quickly.

"Get Nana settled, and I'll bring your books in," I suggested.

"Will do. Thanks." She lifted her chin for a kiss.

If she was expecting a quick peck, she was engaged to the wrong guy. I swept her into my arms, held her tight, and dipped her low.

"Get a room, you two!" Nana teased. "Whew! I need a fan after watching that. Good thing you didn't pull that move on stage, Monty."

I twisted Tasha up and squeezed her to my side. "I planned to, but someone had to get all water breaky on us."

Tasha, wearing a smile and a deep pink blush from our kiss, shook her head as she pushed Nana into the elevator. We rode it up, and when the doors opened, I hurried toward the front of the house and out the front door.

The yellow box was heavy and bore the Tia Gia logo. I carried it inside and placed it on the coffee table by Nana's recliner.

Tasha stared at it.

Nana pointed to her sewing basket. "Monty. Scissors."

I retrieved the scissors and cut the tape along the creases. And snuck in a soft forehead kiss before I stepped away.

Tasha continued to stare at the box.

"C'mon, Tasha. Open the box before your niece turns one!" Nana encouraged, as only Nana could.

"You do it, Monty," Tasha said. "You're the one who made it happen."

"It's all your content, Tasha." I picked up my phone. "Let's do an unboxing video."

"Okay. Give me a sec." She closed her eyes and took a deep breath. "Ready."

"Three, two, one … go!"

With care, Tasha opened the flaps and pulled out a copy of her book. As she turned it over in her hands, her smile grew. Pure joy.

She held the cover up and locked her eyes on my phone like a deer in headlights.

It wasn't your typical unboxing video, but she could voice over it later or set it to music.

"This is amazing." She handed the book to Nana. "Have one."

Nana received it graciously and hugged it to her chest. "I'll read it cover to cover and let you know if I find any typos," she pledged seriously.

Tasha laughed. "Thanks." She turned to me. "Can we go now?"

"Grab a book for Penny, and I'll be right back." I hustled to my room and returned with a pink "Welcome Baby" gift bag.

"Aw! You got a gift for my sister's baby!" Tasha clapped. "Uncle Monty rocks."

I liked the sound of that.

"What did you get her?" Nana asked.

"I think you'll both approve." I reached into the bag and pulled out the peach onesie with a pumpkin on it. Inside the pumpkin were the words *Pumpkin Spice Spice Baby*.

Tasha snorted, and Nana hooted deep from her gut until they were both roaring. I just stood there grinning like the fool I was.

A fool in love.

I still stood by my claim that coffee was poison, but I knew how to compromise.

That laugh and smile on Tasha's face?

I'd do anything for that.

Maybe even try that vile brown liquid.

But that was for another day.

Thank you for reading Pumpkin Spice Spice Baby!

Want to read a bonus epilogue of Tasha & Monty's wedding day?

Follow the link below to join your favorite frenemies the night before their wedding, read love letters to and for each other, celebrate at their wedding reception, and watch them lead their family and friends through a new line dance they created together! Plus four more fun recipes!

Find it at tinyurl.com/PSSBBonus

When you download the bonus scene, you'll also be subscribed to my newsletter. Your welcome email will contain a password to the Freebies tab at KerryEvelyn.com. Inside, you'll find all the Palmer City world extras, including bonus epilogues, recipes, team rosters, coloring pages, *Sparks on the Ice,* and more!

XOXO!

Love, Kerry

Recipes

NANA'S PUMPKIN SPICE LATTE

Ingredients:

- 1/2 cup brewed coffee
- 2 cups 2% milk
- 2 tablespoon pumpkin puree
- 1 tablespoon sugar
- 1 tablespoon vanilla extract
- 1 teaspoon pumpkin pie spice for coffee, split
- Whipped cream
- 2 cinnamon sticks

Instructions:

1. Add milk, pumpkin puree, and sugar to a saucepan over medium heat. Slowly heat the milk until hot. Do not boil.

2. Remove from heat and whisk in coffee, vanilla extract, sugar, and pumpkin pie spice.
3. Top with a dollop of whipped cream and dust with pumpkin pie spice.
4. Garnish with 2 cinnamon sticks.

TASHA'S PUMPKIN SPICE COFFEE

Ingredients:

- 8 ounces brewed dark roast coffee
- 1 teaspoon vanilla extract
- 1 tablespoon sugar
- 3 1/2 teaspoon ground cinnamon
- 3/4 teaspoon ground ginger
- 3/4 teaspoon nutmeg
- 1/2 teaspoon ground allspice
- 1/2 teaspoon ground clove
- 1 cinnamon sticks

Instructions:

1. Add vanilla extract, sugar, and spices to coffee.
2. Stir well.
3. Garnish with cinnamon stick.

MONTY'S KEY LIME PROTEIN SHAKE

Ingredients:

- 2 cups ice
- 1 scoop vanilla protein powder
- 3/4 cup unsweetened almond milk
- 1/2 cup freshly squeezed lime juice
- 1 tablespoon lime zest
- Pinch of salt
- 1 crushed graham cracker
- 1 slice lime

Instructions:

1. Combine ice, protein powder, almond milk, lime juice, lime zest, and salt.
2. Blend until smooth.
3. Top with graham cracker crumbs and garnish with lime.

TASHA'S RECOVERY SOUP

Ingredients:

- 1 tablespoon extra-virgin olive oil
- 2 stalks celery, diced
- 2 large carrots, sliced into 1/4-inch disks
- 1/2 cup kale, thinly chopped
- 1 large zucchini, chopped
- 8 cups chicken bone broth
- 2 chicken breasts
- 1 teaspoon ground turmeric
- 1/2 teaspoon ground black pepper,
- 1 teaspoon ground ginger
- 1 ½ teaspoons dried thyme
- 1 tablespoon fresh parsley, chopped
- 1 tablespoon fresh cilantro, chopped
- 1 pinch sea salt
- 1 splash lemon juice
- 1 tablespoon zest of orange
- 12 ounces gluten-free egg noodles

Instructions:

1. Add all ingredients except the egg noodles to the Crockpot and heat on high for 30 minutes.
2. Reduce heat to medium and cook for 2-4 hours.
3. Add noodles 30-60 minutes prior to serving.

TABBI'S DIRT CAKE

Ingredients:

- 2 large (or 3 small) boxes Jell-O vanilla pudding
- 3 cups of milk
- 2 8-ounce boxes cream cheese, softened at room temperature
- 16 ounces Cool Whip
- 1 package of Family-Size Double Stuffed Oreo cookies
- 1 package gummy worms

Instructions:

1. Remove cream cheese from refrigerator and set on counter for 30-60 minutes until softened.

2. In a food processor, crush up half the Oreos and layer onto the bottom of a cake pan.

3. Mix the pudding and milk, adding one package of cream cheese and half the Cool Whip until smooth.

4. Add in the remaining package of cream cheese and Cool Whip.

5. Layer mixture onto the Oreos in the pan.

6. Crush the remaining Oreos and sprinkle over top of cake.

7. Garnish with gummy worms and serve chilled.

The Coffee Loft Series

Welcome to *The Coffee Loft*,
a place where romance is always brewing.

Grab your favorite table over in the corner and be prepared to be swept off your feet! This multi-author collection features some of your favorite sweet romance authors that you already know and love, as well as a few new names you'll be rushing to check out.

From cold brews to cappuccinos and frothy frappes, there's something on the menu for every romantic comedy reader. Fake dates, meddling matchmakers, friends-to-lovers, and so much more; each stand-alone story is the right blend of sweet, guaranteed to warm your heart.

Happily-ever-afters coming right up!

J.P. Sterling *No More Mr. Chai Guy*
Amy Stephens *Love Me Tender, Love Me Brew*

Ellie Hall *Don't You Forget About Tea*
Kerry Evelyn *Pumpkin Spice Spice Baby*
Susanne Ash *Beanful Wishes*
Tia Marlee *You Mocha Me Crazy*
TJ Amberson *A Double Shot of Love*
Mel Walker *Grounds for Romance*
Tracy Broemmer *Soy Into You*
Meg Easton *Spiced Chais and Secret Spies*
D.E. Malone *A Café Au Lait Kind of Love*
Kimberley Montpetit *Snow Is Falling, Cocoa Is Calling*
H.M. Shander *It's a Brewtiful Day*
Bella Greene *Espresso Your Love*
Coffee Loft Fall Collection

https://books.bookfunnel.com/thecoffeeloftseries
fallcollection

And don't miss the Season One collection!

Amy Stephens *Love at First Sip*
J.P. Sterling *Pardon My French Press*
Tia Marlee *Bean Wishing for a Latte Love*
Kimberly Krey *Java Hearts & Cupid Darts*
Kimberley Montpetit *Wake Me Up Before You Cocoa*
Jenna Brandt *By Any Beans Necessary*
Ginny Sterling *May the Froth Be with You*
Carly Greer *Frappe to Know You*
Katie O'Connor *Cappuccino Mugs and Fire Fighter Hugs*
H.M. Shander *Living La Vida Mocha*
Audrey Carnes *Caffeine Kisses and Winter Wishes*
Kerry Evelyn *That Thing You Brew*

Kaci Lane *Brewin' Up Love*
R.S. Jonesee *Love You a Latte*

Coffee Loft Season One
https://books.bookfunnel.com/thecoffeeloftseries

His life was perfect—until she showed up.
A little competition, a dash of mischief, and a smidge of something
sweet won't be the only things brewing this holiday season.

Keegan Brewer's life is perfectly fine. He's content with his perfected daily routine: early mornings dreaming up new craft beers for his family's restaurant, afternoons managing Brewski's from behind the scenes, and evenings syncing Christmas songs to the LED light display on and around his tiny caboose home on his grandparents' ranchland. Sure, it irks him that his favorite retired hockey player is opening a rival restaurant across the street, and he'll defend his family's business no matter what it takes. One thing he knows for sure is that he wants nothing to do with the bombshell blonde who wants his brewery secrets to make her dad's restaurant a success.

Daughter of a hockey legend, heiress to a billion-dollar sports equipment and fashion empire, and Olympic champion in her own right, Astoria Kubek practically grew up at Brewski's. A lifetime ago, she and the Brewer kids were friends, on and off the ice, playing peewee hockey and pranking the pros. She's been tasked with creating a signature brew to put their new family restaurant on the map. And she wants Keegan's help.

It'll take everything she's got to get the grumpy brewer's attention, never mind his assistance. But the man won't even look at her. Astoria is used to winning, but winning Keegan over becomes more than a job—especially when she discovers the power of his dimples and his adoration of her crazy foster kitten. Making him smile is her new mission, even if her messy life gives him hives. She'll do whatever it takes to bring him true Christmas joy—including unleashing her adorable kitty as a secret weapon. Together, can they craft a perfect beer and gift each other with the most special Christmas gift of all?

One Margarita is a sweet enemies-to-more grumpy-sunshine workplace romance with heartwarming characters, small-town shenanigans, and the Fluffiest Furball in the West.

Excerpt from ONE MARGARITA

KEEGAN

I closed my eyes to concentrate on the hum of the air-conditioning vent above my desk. This would be a busier than usual holiday at Brewski's, our family's sports bar and grill, and I wasn't sure I was ready for it.

The restaurant was ready. It was the peopling I'd have to do that I wasn't looking forward to.

"Bro! Keegan! Hey! You coming? The bride-to-be just pulled up." My brother Drew, who lived for peopling, poked his head into the doorway to my office, set behind the kitchen. His brows knitted in confusion. "Why are you hiding in here anyway? It's a beautiful day."

I glared at him. It *was* a beautiful day, but I was getting a headache. Red, White, and Brews was a big enough event in itself, without the impromptu wedding our sister Brenna had planned. The bride didn't even know about it. But knowing Brenna, she'd thought it through down to every minute detail. No doubt it would go off without a hitch.

Ha. *Hitch.* I smirked at my own humor.

"Well?" Drew crossed his arms and narrowed his eyes.

I pushed back in my chair and pulled at my hair. "I don't feel much like celebrating. I'll come out for the wedding, but then I've got work to do."

Drew blinked at me. "It's the Fourth of July. Independence Day. A holiday. A federal day off. No work allowed."

"Really? You know we're the owners, right? And the staff? We don't get holidays." I stood up and met my younger brother's gaze. "Except Christmas."

Drew laughed. I didn't care. There was a reason I'd

painted my house red and trimmed it in green. I loved Christmas. It was the only time of the year some people were nice to each other.

Only one hundred and seventy-three days to go.

Not that I was counting or anything.

I followed Drew down the hall, across the kitchen and through the swinging door, emerging next to the bar area. Running my hand along the edge of the polished wood, I took in the buzzing restaurant. Brewski's was so-called for two reasons: because of our last name and for the fact that when Dad opened the place, he'd had grand visions of brewing his own label of craft beers and having a whole tap set of our own brews. Over the years, he'd pared it down to three plus a seasonal, but I'd caught the bug one summer when I was home from college.

Since then, I'd been the one experimenting, and we'd added three more regular flavors. It was the eighth and final flavor that eluded us. Recently, several guests had enjoyed my peanut butter recipe, but I didn't feel it was quite right. And with so many people allergic to peanuts these days—a few inquired about their safety in the restaurant due to possible cross-contamination—I was reluctant to add it to the menu permanently.

The lemon shandy had also been a bust. Without the support of a well-known popular lemonade brand, customers found it easy to pass it over, despite enjoying the samples.

And the eight-layer stout ... I shuddered. Colossal failure that never even made it out of my own kitchen. Months of my life, wasted.

Next week was the local brewer exposition in Colorado Springs that could be the first step to putting us on the map for our craft brewing part of the business. I planned to take both the peanut butter and the shandy for feedback. I'd been weighing the merits of adjusting one of the brews or attempting a new product altogether. At the very least, we could bottle the two, even if we didn't serve them on tap in the restaurant. I could test it out on patrons at our annual OktoBrewFest if everything went well.

Drew waved to the hostess as we exited the front door and emerged into the bright sunlight. We headed straight for the side lawn, where the annual outdoor celebration was taking place. Drew strode past his usual spot behind the pop-up cash bar toward a small gathering of friends, and I looked for a quiet spot off to the side somewhere.

There. In the far corner, my cousin Liam was deep in conversation with Brenna's friend Becky. Beck, she liked to be called now. As I approached, their heads snapped apart and they both turned to look at me.

I regarded them warily. "Am I interrupting?"

"No," they answered together.

Beck glanced up at Liam, then turned a grin on me. "We were just, um, catching up. Er … discussing the project we're starting for you tomorrow. Right, Willy? Er—Liam?"

My cousin's face turned a dark shade of red at her usage of the long-retired nickname. No one had called him that since he was a kid.

"Right," he said.

"Mmmhmm." I wasn't buying it. They were acting too familiar, too comfortable with each other. And for someone who lived in Rhode Island, Liam had sure been spending a lot of time in Colorado these last six months. Something was up between these two, and I wondered when they'd have the guts go public with it. I would bet the restaurant they were in a secret relationship.

Relationships were weird.

Take my brother. Drew went on meaningless dates here and there while he pined for the girl who wouldn't give him the time of day—except as a friend—since they were in high school. When Ellabee joined the military, she wrote him a letter every week. They were inseparable when she was home on leave, but it was strictly platonic. Broke his poor heart into pieces every time she left again. And lately, the letters had tapered off.

Yeah. I didn't want any of that.

Then there was my sister. Brenna had finally figured out what Brendan Trotter meant to her after a year of keeping him in the friend zone. The poor sap was just like my brother. A high school crush that stuck for years and years.

I didn't have time to pine for anyone. Brenna joked I didn't have a romantic bone in my body. Maybe I would, if the right person came along. Anyone less than someone worthy to bring to my grandparents' house for Monday Night Dinner was a colossal waste of time. Gran's rule was royally inspired: no admittance unless there was an intention to become a permanent part of the family.

If and until that happened, I was content to work the business and make Brewski's as successful as it could be.

And just in time, too. The land across the street had just been bought up by a new German-Italian fusion restaurant. The obnoxiously big sign by the road boasted that Pasta Nacht's had authentic food and beverages. That meant beer. I had to make sure Brewski's wouldn't suffer from the direct competition.

My gaze drifted to the "Congrats Jason" sign above where Drew was now standing with Brendan. They pulled at the bottom corners, and the sign unfolded to include "and

Lauren!" I cracked a half smile as gasps of surprise filled the air around us. Lauren thought they were celebrating Jason's new contract with Denver's professional hockey team, the Edge, but he and their friends had secretly set up an engagement party instead.

Or a wedding, if Lauren was up for it. Her entire family was visiting from Vermont, and Jason's family was in town from Atlanta. When Jason conspired with Brenna to turn Red, White, and Brews into a surprise engagement party, she also asked if he really wanted to wait until Labor Day for their wedding or spend his off-season summer months in marital bliss.

It was a no-brainer for the besotted goalie, and apparently Lauren as well, as she was now hurrying after Brenna into the restaurant. My sister had tied up the function room—again—with wedding-related stuff. On a holiday, no less. We could've rented out the space. She'd contracted Liam, an architect, to draw up the plans and Beck's company to build a separate structure for a bridal changing room and salon, but it wouldn't be ready until December at the earliest.

Phase two of the nuptial plans was at the gazebo behind Brenna's wedding barn at the back of the restaurant's property. After checking in with my shift manager that all was well, I followed family and friends across the back lawn to the barn and stood off to the side. Brenna, along with Jason's sister Bailey, had spent the morning draping the gazebo in tulle and securing flowers into the folds. On each side of the white runner, several dozen chairs were set up. They filled quickly with their family, friends, and Jason's teammates and their families.

"You should sit down, son," my father suggested softly as he passed me on his way to the gazebo. My dad had recently become certified as a Justice of the Peace and had officiated the double wedding of my cousins Jackson and Kingston a few weeks ago. Brenna joked at this past Monday's family dinner about how convenient it was to have an officiant on the premises for pop-up weddings. Apparently, she hadn't been kidding.

Drew sat off to the side on a barstool with his ukulele. Another surprise. My brother was a man of many interests and talents. Whether mixing up new cocktail recipes or making balloon animals, he was always surprising us with something new and sometimes weird.

As far as I knew, Drew only knew one song. Sure enough, "Somewhere Over the Rainbow" began as Jason, along with Lauren's brother Brady, stepped into place to the right of Dad.

Out of the corner of my eye, I spotted a large man in a lavender suit crossing the lawn. I squinted at the familiar form. It was Denver Edge legend Roman Kubek, "Kooby-Doo" as he was fondly called by former teammates and fans. We Brewer kids called him Uncle Kooby and his wife Tia Gia.

The retired six-foot-six center had been my favorite player and became the face of the Western Conference when I was growing up. Before being called up to the Edge, he'd spent a lot of time at Brewski's when he played for the Voltage, the Edge's minor league affiliate. All seven of us Brewer kids had even played peewee hockey with his girls. The family moved to Denver, but he still stopped by occasionally to catch up with my dad.

Since he moved his family away, the talented Czech forward with Hollywood looks and a comedic and charming personality had built himself a worldwide billion-dollar sports equipment and athletic apparel company that rivaled the most well-known US brands.

Rumors had been swirling all summer that he wanted to purchase the team and had bought a chunk of land in Elk Creek Falls for a family compound. But what was he doing *here?* Did Jason know him? That had to be the connection.

The man suddenly stopped, checked his phone, and pivoted on his heel to turn back toward the restaurant. A wide grin spread across his face as a stunning woman with long blond hair, oversize designer sunglasses, a huge tote bag, and a coordinating lavender sundress approached him. Roman offered his arm, and she slid hers into the crook of his elbow, looking up—way up—with an expression of pure adoration.

Eyes widening, I took in the vignette like a train wreck, unable to look away. *Unbelievable.* The woman was at least half Roman's age. And it wasn't his wife. Gia DeLuca Kubek was a native New Yorker from a big Italian family and a self-made celebrity herself, supplying restaurants and grocery stores with her pasta sauces and spices. And as far as I knew, she'd never been blond.

I forced myself to look away, disappointed. One, that a superstar like Kubek would be so blatant with his infidelity, and two, that someone so beautiful and self-assured as this woman would go after a married man twice her age.

That's why you don't meet your idols.

I shouldn't be surprised. It was a story as old as time. Roman had a lot to offer, if you wanted material things. And he'd aged well, not looking anywhere near the fifty years I knew him to be. But he'd always been so family-centered, even in his younger days. Pictures and videos of him and Gia teaching their little girls to skate had gone what we would now call "viral" before they decided to keep their family and children private. I guessed time, fame, and money could change anyone.

So why did it bother me? Wasn't my problem. She was a pretty face, a knockout. So what? I knew a lot of beautiful women.

And I wasn't interested in any of them. Hadn't been since ... Well, no sense in dredging *that* memory up.

As I watched the ceremony, the memory fought itself to the surface. The pang of sadness was an improvement from the gut-wrenching pain.

I'd been close to having that fairytale ending once. At least I'd thought I was close, until the relationship—if you could even call it that, but my inexperienced stupid heart had no reason to think otherwise—blew up in my face. I'd been young and smitten and was glad I'd kept it a secret from my family and friends. I couldn't have gotten through it if the fallout had been public.

She'd insisted on a secret relationship, for reasons that made sense at the time. I could never have suspected or imagined the real reason.

Not until it was too late.

As Jason and Lauren kissed to seal their commitment, I truly wished them the best. I'd wanted that, too, when I'd been young and sentimental. Now I was focused on my career and taking the Brewski's Brews label international. Nothing would get in the way of my goal.

Especially not a woman.

My gaze wandered back to the blonde in the lavender dress, leaning her head on Roman's forearm, which was wrapped around her shoulders. Why wasn't anyone else staring at them? Surely, everyone here had to know she wasn't his wife. Why were they so easily complacent?

I supposed a wedding probably wasn't the best place to tell a man how stupid he was. But with social media, a picture or video was sure to leak, and he'd be caught.

If a family man like Roman—who brought his wife and kids to Brewski's when he played for the Voltage and showed up at peewee games and practices to help coach and support them—could move on from a woman like Tia Gia, who could trust love?

Maybe Kubek didn't care. Maybe he and his wife had an arrangement. Maybe they were separated. I didn't pay much attention to celebrity news or gossip, or even sports anymore, for that matter. Or maybe the blonde was "just a friend."

I shouldn't care. Why *was* this bugging me so much?

Instead of following the crowd into the barn for the reception, I turned back toward the restaurant. I still had to make a packing list and finalize plans for my booth at the brewer exposition. If I was going to get the attention of an international distributor, both my beer and my branding had to stand out.

Liam had helped me design my booth, and tomorrow, Beck and her dad would help me build it—a series of smaller pieces that would hook together to create the experience I'd dreamed up and could be used multiple times if I had the opportunity to promote the Brewski's brand elsewhere.

With everything at stake, including a good chunk of this year's profits, I should have no trouble focusing on the tasks at hand.

So why did my thoughts keep going back to the blonde?

ASTORIA

Keegan Brewer was glaring at me. *Glaring.* His slitted eyes oozed vitriol, and his lips were pressed tight. When I caught him, he jerked his chin back toward the altar.

The grumpy brown-eyed stare might have been cute, if it hadn't been directed towards me. We used to be buds.

Sure, that was back when we were kids, and we'd lost touch, but I'd expected to be greeted like an old friend. Unless ... Unless he thought I had something to do with a particular breakup?

Hmm. Maybe. Now that I thought of it, he'd always been the grudge-holding type. He stuck by his family and friends and expected others to do the same.

Well, I'd just have to set him straight. Loyalties aside, I knew right from wrong.

"Mrow."

"Just a few more minutes," I whispered into my cat-carrier tote. The little kitty I was fostering was getting restless. I couldn't blame her. She'd been cooped up in the bag going on two hours.

The ceremony ended, and as soon as Jason and Lauren reached the end of the aisle, Keegan bolted back toward the restaurant. I was torn between wanting to follow him there or join the crowd filing into the barn for the reception. The kitty's even more persistent meowing made the decision for me.

"Ready?" My dad offered his arm, and I slipped my hand into its crook. A self-proclaimed fashionista, he looked especially dapper today in his lavender suit, which complemented my dress.

"Yes, but ... save me a seat? Kitty here needs a potty

break." We stopped just shy of a group of Denver Edge players and retirees gathering outside the barn. "I'll be back soon."

"Will do." He kissed the top of my head, and I gave him a one-armed hug.

I turned around, looking for a spot where the kitten could frolic away from the crowd. The open field between the barn and restaurant would do.

Thanking myself for wearing western boots and not heels, I trudged across the field. Brewski's was hopping today. I wasn't surprised Keegan had decided to skip the reception and go back to work.

Only ... I squinted toward the back of the building where the employees parked. Yep, that was him getting into a black SUV. He pulled out and turned toward the dirt road that led deeper into the Brewer property. Was he going home?

One way to find out. I hurried to my car. If he wasn't attending the reception, I wouldn't get my opportunity to ask him for help on my new project, the whole reason I'd decided to move back to Palmer City.

Well, technically, the new family home was in Elk Creek Falls, on the Palmer City border. Land in this town was carefully guarded and held on to by the Brewers and Palmers.

Reaching my car, I whispered an apology to the kitten and promised extra play time as I set the bag carefully on the passenger seat and put the car in gear. A few minutes later, Keegan's grandparents' farmhouse came into view, and beyond that ... a caboose?

Sure enough, his SUV was parked next to an old red train car. Trimmed in green, it reminded me of a Christmas train set I'd loved as a kid.

I pulled up next to his vehicle, plucked the tote off the

seat, and exited my car. As soon as I was a safe distance away from the cars—kittens had a knack for climbing up inside engines, I'd been told—I set the bag on the ground. "First things first," I said, unzipping the side compartment and pulling down the door flap.

The sweet little thing poked her head out. Nose twitching, she placed one paw, then another in front of her until she was in the grass.

"That's a good girl!" I praised, setting myself on the ground a safe distance away from the spot she'd chosen to water the field. I glanced up at the door to the caboose, expecting Keegan to come out and ask me what I was doing here. But the tiny home remained eerily silent.

No worries. Once the little fluffball was done, I'd knock on his door.

She really needed a name. Free of her confines, she ran and played like it was her job. She reminded me a bit of myself. *Graceful on the ice, a mess in real life.* The stinging words I'd overheard my mother tell my grandmother when I made the Olympic team replayed in my head for the gazillionth time. *"You know our Astoria. So many open tabs. It's a wonder she doesn't crash."*

She was right though. And I did crash, occasionally, when life outpaced my coping skills. I had a million things going in my brain at once and often forgot what I was doing mid-task—or thought. It was different on the ice. I was hyperfocused and hyperfixated on one goal—scoring one.

But as all athletic careers do, mine ended, and real life came knocking. Turned out I was no good at keeping my grown-up life organized. Dad, bless his heart, decided to bring me in on his restaurant project and give me a task that he thought might become a new hobby and insert me into the Palmer City community, which I'd always loved and talked incessantly about during my years away. Brewing beer intrigued me. But so far, I was no good at it. And my fancy, state-of the-art equipment wasn't helping.

My mom had gifted me a copy of her therapist friend's book *Focus Over Fog* last week, just before she left with my sisters for the Hamptons. Dr. Mary Keelhannaugh sure knew her stuff. It was like she was in my head. I was still on the first chapter, but it mostly held my interest, affirming my habits, cognitive wiring, strengths, challenges, and superpowers. I really should read more of it. Maybe she had a solution for unpacking in an organized fashion.

Of course, it probably didn't help that the way I'd pack up my stuff was anything *but* organized.

"Hey, where are you going?" Kitty was off and running, chasing a butterfly toward the caboose. I stood and hurried after her but was too late. She squeezed through the latticework and disappeared into the underbelly of the caboose before I could grab her.

"You silly girl!" Spotting a latch off to one side, I disengaged it and pulled open a section of the lattice. If its purpose was to keep out small critters, it wasn't very effective.

"Lumos," I said to my phone, and the flashlight turned on. I loved that feature. The beam of light lit up the dusty earth under the caboose.

The little troublemaker had found a support beam to climb. "Oh no!" Her little tail disappeared into the abyss.

I backed out and ran to the steps. "Keegan!" Knocking loud, I pleaded for his help. "Keegan! There's a kitten stuck up under your house!"

No answer, no movement. Maybe he wasn't home? He could have gone to his grandparents' house.

Hmm. Well.

I'd just have to add a new item to my resume. I could totally do this myself. I didn't earn an Olympic gold medal by not being a problem solver.

Astoria Kubek, Cat Rescuer.

It had a ring to it.

I returned to the lattice gate and poked my head in. No sign of Kitty Knievel. I'd have to army-crawl to get under there.

My dress might end up worse for wear, but what else was there to do?

Not bring a cat to a wedding, maybe?

Well, there was that. But my guest cottage at my parents' new property wasn't in any shape to host a kitty by herself yet. Poor baby would be cooped up in the bathroom until I could get my place together. The vet had assured me the space was large enough, so there was that. Plus, I hadn't wanted to leave her. She'd already been left to fend for herself once when I'd found her by the air pumps at a rest stop, shivering and alone.

Maybe a treat would entice her out? I reached for the tote and poured a few into my hands.

"Here, kitty! You want a treat?"

Nothing.

I took a deep breath and got into position, belly down. It was a good thing I always packed a spare outfit, because this dress was now up close and personal to some of the Rockies' finest dirt.

"Mrow!"

She was above my head. Gingerly, I turned onto my back

and pushed my sunglasses onto my head. I'd totally forgotten I was wearing them. Settled, I squinted into the dim light and lifted the treat-filled hand upward. "Right here! Good kitty! Come get a treat!"

I blinked into the darkness as my eyes adjusted. Where had my phone gotten to? I was always misplacing that thing. Good thing I now had a handy-dandy tracker for it on my key ring.

Dr. Mary was so smart. I had trackers for a lot of things now, thanks to her. It had been the first piece of advice in her book. Clip one of the little gadgets to your keys and its partner to something you don't want to lose. Press one to make the other sing, or track them with an app. That one suggestion had probably saved me hours of time just in the last few days. Except when I misplaced both my phone and my keys and had to track down my tablet to access the app, which wasn't installed on it yet. So I had to download it, but I couldn't remember my password, so I had to reset it, but eventually, I got in and tracked my stuff.

A typical day in the life of Astoria Kubek.

Now, where was that kitty? *There!* Her little sandpaper tongue grazed my palm, and I made a swipe for her while she was chewing.

But she was too fast. The little puff grabbed the treats and was off again.

I groaned. Loudly. Maybe she'd think I was hurt and come to help?

"Uh, what are you doing under my house?" The deep, masculine baritone threw me off guard.

Keegan Brewer had grown up to have a very nice voice. The kind of voice you listened to at night to relax while you were trying to clear your mind to go to sleep.

"Hello?"

Right. I should answer him. But how to explain my predicament?

"Ma'am, are you hurt?" The inflection in his inquest was sweet and almost enough to distract from being called ma'am. So polite.

I hated being called ma'am.

My mother was a ma'am. My grandmother was a ma'am. Teachers and coaches were ma'ams. Dr. Mary Keelhannaugh was a ma'am.

Not me. I wasn't old enough for that title yet.

"Ma'am, do you need help?"

As a matter of fact ... but now probably wasn't the best time to discuss his helping me in the brew room. Or whatever such a place was called.

That request would have to wait. The cat was the priority.

"Hey, what the—there's a cat in my window!"

I had to laugh. "My kitten crawled up into the caboose!" I yelled as loud as I could.

"How did it—never mind. Are you okay? Should I help you or the cat first?"

How chivalrous to ask. And how very unlike his rudeness earlier.

"The cat! I'm good!"

"On it!"

Gingerly, I slowly extracted myself from underneath the train car and inspected my dress. Just dusty, thank goodness. I'd have to ask him how the back of my dress looked. That would be awkward.

I trudged through the grass to the stairs at the end of the caboose and jogged up to the platform. Better not open the door in case the cat decided to run out. I peeked into the uncovered window. Inside, Keegan was bent over a small sink, at eye level with Kitty Knievel and scratching her chin. She climbed up onto his arm and nuzzled into his shoulder.

Awwww.

I lifted up onto my toes for a better view—and immediately wished I hadn't. The floor was littered with papers. Across from the sink, more papers lay scattered on the small table. No doubt Keegan had left them in a neat, tidy pile and the mess was the work of my dear little cat.

Keegan had always hated things out of place. He had routines and specific ways to do things. I admired that when we were kids. Mostly. It got annoying at times, like when games would go into overtime and he knew he wouldn't be home in time to start his rigid bedtime ritual, or a tournament would pop up on a day he had plans to do something else.

Flexible he wasn't. Neat, he was.

I knocked on the door and stepped back. I'd wait for him out here.

"Found it!" he called from inside. "It got a name?"

"Not yet! She's a foster."

"If she was mine, I'd call her Purr-Snickety."

"If she were your cat, that would make total sense!" I laughed. I'd never met any kid as fussy as Keegan Brewer had been.

A moment later, the metal door swung open, and he appeared, smiling down at the kitty in his arms. As his chin lifted, he froze. Our gaze met for a fleeting second before his mouth turned into a frown and his eyes narrowed.

Huh? It was the same look he'd given me at the wedding. All previous signs of friendliness melted away, leaving a grumpy but mostly adorable expression.

It was a skill to be cute when you were mad. At least, that's what my grandpa told me. Apparently, I had a talent for it, too.

"Here's your cat." He held the small ball of wiggly fur out in front of him, and I scrambled to grab her.

Once she was safely in my arms, he abruptly turned away and slammed the door. A shade dropped in behind the window, and the unmistakable *clang* of a lock clicked into place.

What in the world?

Keep reading at Amazon!

Books by Kerry Evelyn

Crane's Cove

Love on the Edge

Love on the Rocks

Love on the Beach

Love on the Fly

Love on the Heart

Love on the Brain

Crane's Cove Chronicles

Cat's Paw Cove

Moon Mist Manor Book 1: Christmas at Moon Mist Manor

Moon Mist Manor Book 2: Love Overrules the Lawyer

Moon Mist Manor Book 3 The Beachcomber's Buccaneer Bounty

Palmer City Voltage

Love on the Ice: A Sweet Small-Town Second Chance Hockey Romance Novelette

Cruising on Ice: A Sweet Small-Town Friends-to Lovers Hockey Romance

Christmas on Ice: A Sweet Small-Town Holiday Hockey Romance

Sparks on the Ice: A Sweet Small-Town Christmas Auction Short Story (Subscriber Bonus)

Melting the Ice: A Sweet Small-Town Late to Love Hockey Romance

Celebration on Ice: A Small-Town Sweet Second Chance Hockey Romance

Crushing on Ice: A Sweet Small-Town Fake Dating Hockey Romance

Goodnight Kiss

Make it Sweet

Barn Song

Nobody But You

Acknowledgments

I need to start with my Bookstagrammers friends for this one! Your creative and public support and love for *That Think You Brew* and the Coffee Loft series as a whole made me want to return to write a sequel. I'm so glad I did! These two books haven't just brought words to be read, they've brought friendships and connections—all over the world! I am so blessed! And to Alora, thank you for making my characters come to life in ways that surpass my imagination! Kim, Cindy, Rachel, Jane, Amanda K., Lissa, Heather H., Brittney H., Hannah S., Allegra, Anna Louise, Debbie, Stacey, Amanda P., Lori, Robyn, Shayna, Megan, Terri, Hilary. Ruth, McKenna, Lilly, Amanda B., Holly, Tami, Stephanie, Aubrey Ann, Renee, Alicia, Ali, Abby, Amy, Joan, Moni, Jackie, Denise, Koren, Jodi, Esther, Audrey, Jenny, Marie, Tracy, Kaity, Laura, Erralee, Koren, Laura, Kelli, Katie, Lu, Mindy, M, Dina, Darla, Haley, Heather K., Lisa, Randi, Hilma, Lantana, LittleOne, and the Brew Crew! (And anyone I missed! So sorry! I searched all my tags, but IG and FB aren't always reliable!)

A little story for ya! Tasha has been around since *Sparks on the Ice*. I needed an antagonist in that story, and a competitive cousin seemed like a good idea. I'm close in age with one of my cousins, and the drive to try to outdo one another seemed to come naturally when we were young. I'm older by three months, and the first grandkid on that side of the family. It was just us for a few years, and I remember having so much fun playing with him and also battling for our grandparents' attention. As we grew older and our grandpa paid out more money for A's than B's on our report card, I had to have the most A's. We went to different high schools, but that didn't stop the competition. (At some point I think it became one-sided, with me trying to do the one-upping.) I was the homecoming queen, and he was voted Mr. Dartmouth. We set the bar pretty high for the rest of the grandkids, ha ha! Anyway, I must thank him for those years. And though he will probably never read this book, the spirit of him and our rivalry is here. That spirit and the drive to be the best returned to me as I wrote Tasha, Gabby, and even Monty's characters.

To J.P. Sterling and Amy Stephens, thank you for creating such a fun series, and for all the work you've done and time you've put into it to make it the hit that it is. The butterfly effect of your ideas and care have impacted and entertained thousands upon thousands of readers looking for a fun escape into lighthearted worlds. No words can thank you enough!

To the Coffee Loft Fall Collection featured authors, thank you for being so wonderful to work with! Tia Marlee, H.M. Shander, TJ Amberson, Meg Easton, Ellie Hall, D.E. Malone, Kimberley Montpetit, Mel Walker, Tracy Broemmer, Bella Greene, and Susanne Ash—we are having a blast and I'm so grateful!

To Beck & Dot, thank you for another superfun, most perfect cover for my frenemies!

To my beta readers, thank you for moving things around in your personal lives to make time to read my messages, emails, and stories. In reverse ABC order this time! Valerie,

Tabbi, Shanna, Monica, Jane, Gail, and Andrea, I love our friendships so much! Your encouragement, insight, and ability to catch my vision and help enhance it is such a God-given thing. I thank him for you all every day! The beverages, the recipes, the kids, the pigeon! And the typos and missing words you catch—you are straight up rock stars! I love that your footprints are all over these pages! And another big thank you to my JP and HM for reading an early version of the story and for your friendships. I've loved getting to know you and being on this mugnificent ride with you!

An extra big thank you to Jane, for sharing the best hockey reels with me, especially a certain one with a pigeon on the loose! You inspired me to dream up my own version of the event, and then you named the bird. He came to life in my head and just *had* to be in my story. It was so much fun to write that scene and watch it all blow up into something so much bigger than a lost bird. I laughed so hard while I was writing! I needed that! The Edge's beloved Percy T. Bird is quickly becoming the fictional version of Victor E. Rat, and I am here for it!

MY TONYA!!! THANK YOU FOR ALL THE THINGS! SHOUTING FROM THE ROOFTOPS SO YOU CAN HEAR ME ALL THE WAY IN TEXAS!

So much thanks to my writer besties!! TMACKS, STAR and SSCG, I'm a better writer and a better person for all the years I've spent with you all. Saturdays are writing days, and we've been through a lot together. I get verklempt every time I think about where we started and how far we've come. Thank you for being on this journey with me, and for letting me stick around when I get annoying!

Korin!! Thank you for all the secret things you do for me that people think I do all by myself, thus making me look good, and also muchas gracias for the shenanigans! Or should I say … Bananagans? Ha ha! MWAH!

To my experts who helped fine-tune the little big things! Jen Renz, for her insight into celiac and reactions; Pat Higgins for helping me understand how youth hockey works; Mike Valcy for being my NHL guy on the inside, and Andrew Kuligowski for making sure all my hockey details are correct and make sense. My readers thank you all, too!

To the Crane's Cove Crew, I LOVE hanging out with you every day! Thanks for making the group a fun, safe place for book lovers. Jannell, thanks again for loaning yourself and your family to own and manage my fictional café!

Tammy, I always feel so bad when I message you an estimation of when the book will be done, and it's never the day I predict, and you STILL return the proofed copy to me within twenty-four hours, usually at the expense of sleep and Chaos cuddles. I appreciate it SO MUCH and I want to promise next time I'll be on time, but you've been in the biz long enough to know that's just wishful thinking. Ha! XOXO!!!

Chris, thanks for always finding time for me and all my projects, big and small. I couldn't do this without you, and I know how much of your own projects you put aside when I message you needed a cover, logo, ad, poster, 76k edited when I estimated 40k … You are THE BEST!

To my mom, Judy, I don't know how to thank you for all the encouragement and being the best fan ever. I love you so much!

To my family: Anthony, Kailyn, and Nicholas, someday this writing thing will make money and we will travel the world. It may only be across town at SeaWorld, but I see a day where this can fund season passes. Ha ha! I love y'all so much!

And to God, thank you for blessing me with all the voices in my head, and their stories. I am but Your vessel, spreading love, humor, inspiration, and a bit of education at Your will. I am honored to be tasked with such a blessed calling.

About the Author

Kerry Evelyn's sweet romance novels feature small towns and unforgettable characters pursuing heartwarming happily-ever-afters. This international award-winning *NSYNC fanatic is fueled on faith, Dunkin' iced coffee, and a love for people, including her amazing family. Kerry loves (in ever-changing order) books, boybands, cats, hockey, sweet drinks, taking selfies, traveling, and the madness of getting the stories in her head onto the page. Find out more and sign up for her newsletter at KerryEvelyn.com/links.

Website: KerryEvelyn.com
Reader Group: Facebook.com/groups/CranesCoveCrew
Email: Kerry@KerryEvelyn.com
Spotify: tinyurl.com/KerryEvelynSpotify

facebook.com/KerryEvelynAuthor
instagram.com/KerryEvelynBooks
tiktok.com/@KerryEvelynAuthor
pinterest.com/KerryEvelynBooks
amazon.com/Kerry-Evelyn/e/B077LWTYXJ
goodreads.com/kerryevelynauthor
bookbub.com/authors/kerry-evelyn

www.ingramcontent.com/pod-product-compliance
Lightning Source LLC
Chambersburg PA
CBHW020403260626
47156CB00007B/2209